Chris Sel...
C000279719

Daniel Evan Weiss is the auth
Have No King, The Swine's W
His nonfiction includes *The (*
American. He lives in New Y

**Also by Daniel Evan Weiss and published
by Serpent's Tail**

The Roaches Have No King
The Swine's Wedding

Hell on Wheels

Daniel Evan Weiss

Library of Congress Catalog Card Number: 97–81176

A complete catalogue record for this book can be
obtained from the British Library on request

The right of Daniel Evan Weiss to be identified as the
author of this work has been asserted by him in
accordance with the Copyright, Designs and Patents
Act 1988

Copyright © by Daniel Evan Weiss 1991

First published in this edition in 1998 by Serpent's Tail,
4 Blackstock Mews, London N4

website: www.serpentstail.com

Printed in Great Britain by Mackays of Chatham plc,
Chatham, Kent

10 9 8 7 6 5 4 3 2 1

For Judy

The longer Lucy's away the more exciting it gets. Not right here. Things here stay pretty much the same. It's Lucy. The longer I wait for her the wilder my imagination gets. What will she be like this time? What are they doing to her out there?

Sometimes it gets out of hand. Late the other night I heard a sound outside and I thought it was her shuffling up to the door. Walking with her arms and legs straight out, like the Mummy. For a minute I even thought she was all wrapped up in bandages. Which is weird, since I've never even seen her with a Bandaid. I'm the guy with the bandages.

I don't know why I do this. Most of the time Lucy is a very normal person. She's got a great walk. Lots of hip action. So she's been away for a while. Big deal.

I think the problem is that I never got very good at waiting. In the old days I was too busy to wait for anyone. I was always on the move. Working, drinking beer with my buddies, introducing myself to the ladies. Stuff like that.

Now I wait. I don't mean that's all I do, or that I wait for many people. I only wait for Lucy. But I do it a lot.

The last time she made me wait for her I knew she'd do it again. And I know after she comes back and everything seems normal for a while she's going to do it again. No matter what I do. Even if I yell at her and jump around like a maniac. I'm not complaining, since I know what she's going to do. I decide to put up with it. It's my choice.

Sometimes it bothers me, though. I can't help it.

Maybe it's not really the waiting that's bothering me.

She's not holding me up or anything. It's not like I'd be out and about if she was back. My day is the same with her and without her. Except for eating.

Maybe what's bothering me is that the longer she's away the more I think about waiting for her. I sit around sometimes, looking at the front door. Like that's going to make her walk in. I see the light coming through the blinds into the dust, just the same as it always does. Probably not the same dust. The old stuff is in somebody's socks now. But it makes me think that nothing changes. I sit here waiting for Lucy. And nothing changes.

It reminds me of racing on a track. You get up to the starting line. The gun goes off. You go like crazy, around and around in circles, until you're ready to drop. You try to be the first one to break the tape. Even if you do, where do you end up? Right where you started.

If I ever race again, this is what I'm going to do. After the gun I'm just going to stay right there at the starting line. Let the other guys go around the track like mad. I'll wait until they put up the tape. Then I'll pop through it. No sweat. What difference does it make how many times you go around before you break it. At the end it's the same.

That's what I'm thinking about Lucy. I was sitting here waiting for her at the beginning of this story. I'm sitting here waiting for her at the end. In between I was running around like crazy. Next time I'm going to be smarter. I'm just going to sit here the whole time and watch the dust settle.

With Lucy the tape went up before and it's going to go up again. Right in the same spot. Here.

One

I've really got no beef with Lucy. It's been a long time since I waited for her. But I remember the last time as clear as day, after all this time. I was in my apartment, as usual. I was running out of food, as usual. I went into the kitchen and reached into the back of the cabinet. There was nothing but a few cans left. I had a burp. Tuna and tomato soup. I looked at the cans. Tuna and tomato soup. I couldn't stand it any more.

Every day I thought Lucy was going to show up with some food. That's what she said. But she didn't show up at all.

I had to go out. That's why I remember that day so well. Going out is a big deal for me.

I went to the closet and put myself together. I looked at myself in the mirror. I decided to wear my trench coat. I figured that would draw me less attention. I couldn't help thinking that everybody saw everything about me that I saw.

I wheeled outside. The sun was real bright. It stung. I hadn't been in the sun in weeks. Some kids were playing whiffle ball in the front yard of the house next door. I waved to a girl. I didn't really know her. I saw her out here now and then. She held the ball and just stared at me. Welcome to the outside, Marty. It wasn't her. Everyone felt that way. She was just a little more direct about it.

I was winded inside of two blocks. I did exercises every day, but somehow that didn't help when I wheeled. Different muscles, I guess. And my tailbone started to ache. I was thinking maybe I should get a new set of shocks for my chair.

A few blocks later my hands started to sting. Blisters. I didn't get out enough. I was getting soft.

This was the problem with Lucy. Sometimes she babied me. Sometimes she starved me.

I remember almost getting pissed off at her again. Pain did that to me. But there was another way to look at it: why should she put up with me at all? I couldn't answer that.

It was a long way to the store. I was thinking of going back for my gloves. Maybe my donut cushion too. But I always hate going back. If I was back inside I wouldn't come out again. I'd sit and wait for Lucy, even though I didn't know where the hell she was. I could get pretty slim that way.

I don't drive a car any more. I can't reach the pedals. If I drove I wouldn't have shopped in Harry's Superette. I would have driven to a big supermarket with wide aisles. There isn't any in my neighborhood. There's a 7–11, if you go the other way. It has nice aisles. But you can't shop there unless you live on Ding Dongs.

There was nothing fancy about Harry's. No electric eye. I had to push open the damn door and go in sideways. Push with one hand, wheel with the other. Then the odor hit me. Like the stuff on the shelves just came off a steamboat returning from the jungle. I could handle that. I like ripe smells. The part I had trouble with was the floor. The aisles were too narrow for me to turn around. And there were deep ruts in the linoleum. The shopping carts dug them.

I headed for the bread section. A loaf of Wonder and I knew I could make it through the day. Suddenly my chair pulled out of control, like somebody was pushing me from behind. I looked. My wheel was running in a rut. I smacked into a display. Bags of Cheetos and Cheez Doodles came pouring down on me.

I backed up. My back wheel crunched. I tried pushing myself out of the rut going forward. The front wheel crunched. I tried to put the bags in my lap back up on the display. I couldn't reach it. There was no room on the shelves. A good thing I have a sense of humor about myself.

'Mr Champion! Is that you?' It was Amal, the owner. He was over at the register. He couldn't see me but he acted like I crashed into displays every time I came. That was insulting.

I pretended I didn't hear him. I grabbed a loaf of bread, some milk, a couple of Chunkies, and other stuff. I put them in the bag behind the seat of the chair.

I made the turn on to the last aisle. There was a kid in my way. A boy, three or four years old. He was standing with his hands behind his back.

I smiled. I said hello. He didn't say anything.

I motioned to him to back up. He didn't. I asked if I could get by. He just stood there, staring at my legs.

I started wheeling toward him. His eyes were huge. He was scared.

I reached out to him. I was going to pat his head, I think. Before I could, he pulled a shoe out from behind his back and put it in my hand. Stuffing was coming out the top. I looked down. It was my shoe. Stuffing was coming out of the bottom of my right leg. I didn't feel the shoe tear off, or hear it. It must have been loose when I left my place. I probably lost it in the pile of Cheez Doodles.

'Thank you,' I said. 'Thank you. Bye-bye.' I picked a bottle of vanilla extract off the shelf and handed it to him. It was the best I could offer. It was a bad aisle.

I shoved the end of the leg into the shoe. They wouldn't stay together. The fabric was torn. This never happened before. I didn't know what to do with the shoe. It wouldn't stay on the footrest of the chair. If I put it in the bag Amal would check it out at the register. He would love that.

I stuffed it inside my coat. I hated to close the coat. My shirt was already sticking to me.

11

I wheeled to the register. The boy was with Amal. The boy put a hand over his mouth.

'Don't be afraid, Ibrahim,' he said, or something like that. I have a hard time with Amal's accent. 'Mr Champion will not hurt you.'

Amal took the goods from the back of the chair and rang them up on the register. His hand was made of pink plastic and steel. The plastic was supposed to match his skin. It wasn't close. Amal looks like an extra from *Lawrence of Arabia.* I think he should paint the hand a hairy color. I almost told him so once.

Amal says he lost his hand fighting Zionists. Once I heard somebody in the store say he lost it in a garbage disposal. Anyway, Amal loves to clatter the hook against the register keys. He loves to use it to pluck bills from the customers' hands. He pretends to make mistakes just so he can tear up the tape and start over. I don't think this does anything for business. He should use the hand that matches. Even when he isn't using it Amal keeps the plastic hand up on the check-out counter. He scratches with it. He scratches a lot. He wears short-sleeved shirts all year long. I don't understand this. Not that a fake hand is something to be ashamed of. But I don't see that it's something to show off either.

But what do I know. I don't even know why Amal's store is named Harry's Superette. Generally I don't like to ask questions. I don't like to give people an excuse to start blabbing at me.

Amal doesn't feel that way. 'You see this, Mr Champion?' he said. He tapped the side of the cash register. A flyer was taped to it. I knew the style of the lettering. The Olympian Games. The hysteria was beginning again. It felt like it just ended.

'You will defend?' said Amal.

'I retired.'

'What retired!' He snorted. I could feel his breath on my arm. 'When I was your age I work twelve hours a day and dance all night.'

Stuffing from my leg was sifting on to the dirty linoleum. It looked like a very small snowstorm. I was trying to decide whether to remind Amal that at my age he had legs.

'There's a new generation of handicapped to carry on,' I said.

'You must defend. If not for you for all the rest. You are a champion. You have a responsibility.'

I won the 1,000-meter wheelchair race the year before. To Amal that made me the shining light for America's youth. Even though I'm middle-aged.

I said, 'I won the race for me, Amal. I didn't sign on to be a hero.'

'That's why you're a hero. You won. All people want to beat the others.'

'But everyone can't beat everyone. There have to be losers.'

'I don't think about them,' he said. He loaded the bag of groceries into the pouch on the chair.

I thought about the losers. How can you be in a wheelchair race and not think about losers.

'When you win the race you show that we can win.' He waved his hook in my face. 'We can win too.'

We. Him and me. People missing parts.

There was only one other guy in the race. He lost. How come he wasn't showing Amal that we can lose too?

This was the hell of it. In a way I was like Amal, missing legs and everything. But I didn't feel like I had anything to do with him. The guy who just jogged by the door listening to his Walkman. That was me.

I said, 'I'll tell you what, Amal. I'll defend if you join the games too.'

'But I have never used a chair.' He held up his hook. 'It could get caught in the spokes.'

'Not in my race. In the discus.'

'The discus?'

'You have to throw it with your hook. You're pretty handy with that thing.'

13

'It could come right off!' he said. 'You are a madman!'

Amal felt he could say anything to me because I was in the group. Lots of people thought that. Complete strangers. In the store or on the street: 'What happened to you?' But they were wrong. I was just a guy buying groceries. I had a right to be left alone. I wheeled out of the store.

Amal wouldn't say anything to Lucy if she was shopping. No, he would. It would be about him and her and a Mediterranean holiday. Showing her his quaint old village. The wheelchair stays home.

I felt better outside. I thought about the Olympian Games. It wasn't that I couldn't race again. I didn't want to. I didn't practice. Lots of guys did. They lifted weights and got huge. I didn't need to be huge. I had timing. Over 1,000 meters nobody in the county could take me.

I stopped the chair. Then I gave myself the starter's gun. I came out of the blocks like a bat out of hell. I was tearing up the sidewalk; my hair whipping back, the wind burning my eyes. It was like tennis court days. Full out, tracking down a drop. God, I loved speed.

I flew toward the end of the block. From the corner of my eye I saw someone walking out from behind the last store. I jammed my palms on to the rails of the wheels. I started to skid and swerve. The metal was cold, then it burned. The blisters were tearing open. I grabbed the arms of the chair. I almost flew out of my seat. The chair stopped with two feet to spare. My coat came open. The shoe rolled down my legs and fell to the ground.

I grabbed for it. A man who could move so fast shouldn't let this happen. But the person I just missed bent down and got it first. I could only see the legs. Great legs. It was a woman.

She brought the shoe to the bottom of my leg. There was still stuffing coming out. I was afraid she was going to try to put it back on. I touched her shoulder to stop her. My face was burning. Being crippled can be humiliating.

A smell rose to my nose. Then I understood why she was down there. I understood the whole thing.

'Esther,' I said.

She looked up at me and smiled. Before I knew her by her legs or her hair I knew her smell.

'And you must be Cinderella,' she said. She handed me the shoe. I tucked it back in and closed my coat.

I looked at her. I had waited a long time for this. But I couldn't get the torn leg out of my mind. It was like the Wicked Witch of the East after the house falls on her. When her legs roll up and disappear. Even when I had legs I thought that was creepy.

'In a hurry?' she said. 'Off to the ball?'

Now I noticed the stroller behind her. A baby was staring at me.

'Yours?' I said.

'Rented.'

'How old is . . . he? she?'

'Jerold. He's two.'

'Oh, yes, someone told me.' I was trying to get the leg out of my mind. This was Esther. This one I spent a long time waiting for and she never showed. She was too busy. She was making this baby. It pissed me off.

I could have asked the usual mother questions, but I didn't care about her baby. I cared about something, a lot. I didn't know how to start.

'You look good,' she said.

'I've been dieting. I lost some height.' She smiled at that line. Everybody did.

'Around the face.' She ran her finger along my cheek. 'You look more determined. Stronger.'

'I am stronger,' whatever the hell that meant.

'I hear you see a lot of Lucy. How's it going?'

'Fine,' I said. 'Real good.'

She smiled, like she was setting me up with that one.

15

But she wasn't getting away with anything. Not this time.

'How's married life?' I said. 'How's . . .' I remembered his name. I didn't want to hear it coming out of my mouth. I didn't want her to think I ever thought about him.

She smiled again. 'Sanford. He's fine. I'm very happy.' There was a big rock on her finger. Her clothes were just right. I believed her.

'Are you working?' I said.

'This little man is my work.' She picked him out of the stroller and held him in front of me. He closed his hand on my nose. His fingers were all wet. I tried to hold him off without getting tough with him. 'What about your law career?'

'If the time comes to practice again, that's what I'll do. Now is not the time.'

After all the shit I heard about her career. 'So what brings you here?' I said.

'I like this neighborhood. It's colorful. I want Jerold to see life all over, not just the view from the mansion.'

'The mansion?'

'It's not a mansion. That's what we call it. Wishful thinking, really. It's just a twelve room Colonial.'

I pulled Jerold's finger from my nostril. 'So, how do you like it in the slums, Jerold? Your mom used to hang out here with her old boyfriend.'

'Don't start in front of the b-o-y.'

The b-o-y started to cry and kick. His mom put him back into the stroller and strapped him in. She checked her coat for scuff marks. He kicked the hell out of the stroller.

'He knows how to spell already?' I said.

'I'm not sure. He's sharp.' She lit a cigarette. 'Do you live around here?'

'Two blocks from the corner. That red brick garden apartment. The one with the ramp.'

'Yes, I saw it. The ramp looks like fun.'

'Fun? Yes, it's lots of fun. It's like riding the flumes at the amusement park. You should try it sometime.'

She nodded.

I said, 'It was designed by an architect from New York.'

She tilted her head. Probably thinking: now he goes around talking about wheelchair ramps. That's right. The new me.

'You didn't used to smoke,' I said.

'Cigarettes calm me.' She squinted when she inhaled. There were lines around her eyes. They showed through her makeup. In every other way she looked as young as she used to. Too bad.

'You don't seem calm,' I said.

'You don't either.'

'I'm calm. What's wrong with telling the b-o-y that you used to know me.'

He started to kick again. He knew how to spell that word.

Esther said, 'He's just a little fellow. I don't want to confuse him.'

'You never minded confusing me.' That just fired out. Like a hiccup.

She looked surprised. She laughed. 'In that case, I'll have to unconfuse you.'

What? I looked at her. She blew smoke forcefully into the air. 'You've lost weight, Marty. It doesn't suit you.'

'You just said I look stronger.'

'You're too thin. Isn't she taking care of you?'

'She takes great care of me. As if you care.'

'Is she home now?'

'Why do you ask?'

'I'm just wondering why you're out here doing your own food shopping. Why isn't she doing it for you?'

'I felt like getting out. A little exercise.'

She shook her head, blowing smoke out both sides

17

of her mouth. Then she took my hand and turned it over. It was all torn up. 'She hasn't changed. Still unreliable.'

'She's changed,' I said. 'We've all changed. Look at you.' I felt the leather of her boot with my hand. It was expensive, like velvet. I got a little blood on it. It was an accident, but I liked leaving my mark.

She used to be kind of scruffy. A hippie with cash.

'And look at you,' she said.

'Yeah. Look at me.'

She pulled a scrap from her purse and scribbled on it. 'If you need something you call me.' She put it in my hand.

'You mean like Amway products?'

'I won't let you go without necessities. Well, put it in your pocket. I don't want my unlisted number blowing around this neighborhood.'

I put the number away. 'I thought you liked this neighborhood.'

She snuffed her cigarette with the toe of her boot. 'We have to run. Jerold has a play-date. I would take you home, but I can't push both of you at the same time.'

'I think I can manage. So long, Jerold.' He heard his name and started waving.

But as they started to leave I knew I couldn't leave it at that. Not after all this time. I took her arm. 'Don't you have something to say to me?'

She looked me right in the eyes. 'Yes, I do. And soon I'll say it.'

For some reason that was enough. Like I really believed she was going to say something that would mean something to me.

I watched them go. She had great legs. Great style. He looked like a prince. In a year or two he would outgrow his wheels and start running. Become a great little athlete.

My athlete days were over. I would always need my

wheels. Too bad I couldn't take over being her kid.

I turned toward home. Things rushed at me from the back of my head. I was confused.

Suddenly I felt a knife of pain. My right calf was twisting. Knotting. Like it would snap right off. I was sweaty again. Puffing. I squeezed the handles of my chair so hard they creaked. It didn't help. I sat up as long as I could. I didn't want Esther to see me and come back.

I couldn't help myself. I bent over and grabbed the calf. All I got was a handful of stuffed pantyhose. I no longer had a right calf. All I had left was terrible pain. My eyes filled with tears. I pounded the end of what was left of my leg. My stump. Anything to try to dull those nerves. No-one on the sidewalk stopped to help me. No-one came close. I probably looked insane.

Finally the pain eased. Time was the only thing that helped. I had no idea how long. Minutes. Hours. I sat back, exhausted.

I hadn't had an attack like this in six months. Phantom pain, they call it. Like hell. I've been flattened by 250-pound linebackers. I fell off a dirt bike at thirty m.p.h. That was real pain. But real pain was nothing compared to phantom pain.

I always felt phantom pain came for a reason. Like my body was trying to tell me something. You wouldn't do that to yourself for nothing.

I listened to my body. It was telling me something weird. But I obeyed. On the way home I went two blocks out of my way, to the flower shop. Lucy loves peonies.

Two

I closed the door to my apartment. When I took off my coat the shoe plopped out, like a loud turd. I loosened my pants and dropped my legs to the floor.

I made these legs by filling a pair of pantyhose with stuffing from an old chair. I did that almost three years ago, when I lost my legs. After a while the stuffing got really hard. The knee parts were locked in the sitting position. The good part was that the top part, around my stumps, was real firm.

I looked at the legs lying on the floor. Now it was hard to believe that I wore them against my flesh. They looked like two snakes coming out of my trousers. One's head in a shoe. The other one wounded, bleeding stuffing.

I wore the legs to make me look more normal. Today they made me look like a freak. If a guy's fly is open that's all you see. If a guy is leaking stuffing from his leg you want to be someplace else.

Unfortunately I needed the legs. I went out without them a few times in the beginning. People turned away. Pretended I wasn't there. When I wore the legs they could speak to me. In a forced, twisted way. But they could speak.

I tossed the legs and the shoe over to the work area. I stuck out my stumps. My knobby bayonets. The sweat was drying. They tingled. I could feel each pore. I used to like cooling off after playing a match. It never felt like this. Maybe these shriveled bones are more sensitive than my thighs were. Finer instruments. That's what they tell you at the Center for Remarkable People.

I went to park the chair. I had two parking spots against the wall. They were marked on the floor. I painted them right after I got home from the hospital. The handicapped symbol was in each one, in case anyone could forget I was handicapped. Also I didn't want anybody to park there, I guess. I must have been thinking about the guys who flew down the hospital corridors and did whatever they wanted. The veterans especially. Those guys were animals.

My first chair was always parked in one spot. I never used it any more. The big wheels were missing. The axle was resting on two piles of cinder blocks.

The back of the seat was painted with a big black locomotive. The only one I ever painted. It looked like it was coming right out at you. Some people said it was macho. Like I thought I was a locomotive, with my wheels. No way. Maybe on a good day I thought I was as macho as a handcar.

Underneath the train I painted the chair's name. 'Hell on Wheels'. When I came in I always looked over there. It kept me honest. Reminded me what it was all about.

Now I parallel parked in the other space. I didn't have to. I like the feeling. I used to love to drive.

I took the bag of groceries and walked to the kitchen. Not exactly walked. I pushed off my stumps. When I started to fall forward I put out my free hand to catch myself. Then I slid my stumps and the groceries up toward my hand. I hated moving like this. I spent more energy than a weight lifter and walked slower than Jerold.

I put the groceries away. Now I could ape-walk. I put my hands forward and shot my body through. Sometimes I turned my hands over, knuckles to the floor. I felt like Mighty Joe Young. My knuckles are always black now. I can never get them clean.

Best of all I like to travel by air. My apartment has ropes coming from the ceiling. Nine in the main room, six in the bedroom, three in the bathroom, three in the kitchen. Hemp ropes going all the way to the floor. I had them installed when I moved in. I can swing from one to the next without touching the floor. From one end of the apartment to the other.

I love the way the ropes flex my muscles. Before the accident I was in pretty good shape. I could get around a tennis court or a baseball diamond and do anything I needed to. I didn't go to the gym to push pieces of iron. I always thought that was pretty dumb. I figured: leave the iron in peace. It never bothered me any. Now I'm in great shape. Sometimes I get a glimpse of myself in the mirror as I swing by. Perfect arms and shoulders. Not huge. But in perfect proportion. Every move runs fingers up to my shoulders. As clear as the fingers on my hands. My veins are like ropes. Sometimes I wonder how good an athlete I would have been if I was this strong back then. It's a bad thing to think about.

When I fly I feel I belong here. In my own territory. Sometimes I fly when other people are here. I won't ape-walk. When I ape-walk I still feel like an imposter. Like I'm still evolving. When I fly I'm the real thing.

Flying doesn't take care of all my muscles. When you lose your legs some muscles don't get used. In the buttocks, the back, the abdomen. If you let them get too weak the spine bends. You can't sit up. Your life is over. It looks bad too.

I flew over to the weight table. I strapped weights to my stumps and went through my routines. I make myself do them every day. It was hard to concentrate that day because I was so tired. I made myself think about my aching tail bone and the awful things that could happen to it if I didn't work out. I've seen it at the hospital.

I puffed and sweated. Iron clanged. Sets of ten. I counted out loud. I sounded like the gym at the CRP.

22

There guys turn themselves into oxen. What I do is something else.

When I finished I swung across three ropes to the work area. I have two benches bolted together in the corner. Two pegboards full of tools for metal- and wood-working. Living in a chair you need to adapt things all the time. And invent things. Gizmos. I make almost everything I need.

I sat down and put on my hard hat. For atmosphere.

I took a look at the shoe. It was intact. The pants were torn. A strip of cloth was still sewn to the shoe. The pantyhose was torn too.

I'm no expert on cloth. But I had to fix this set of legs. I only have two sets altogether.

The easiest part would be sewing the sock. It fit over the pantyhose. I lost some stuffing. I had to replace it or one leg would be a little shorter than the other. Then I thought: What am I worrying? That people will think I'm deformed?

As I sewed the door opened. Lucy came striding in. A tall, lanky blonde. She has great legs, and she was showing them today. A mane of long wavy blonde hair. She was smiling. She was gorgeous. She was wearing a summer suit, even though it was cold out. Her cheeks were rosy.

She kissed me. 'Say, that's a mighty big tool you got there.'

'This?' I held out the needle.

'This.' She ran her hand over the stuffed sock. I was holding it between my legs.

At least she came back in a good mood.

She tossed her attaché on a chair. She bent down and hugged me. Her hair fell into my face. I loved it. 'It's so good to see you, Shorty.'

'Where have you been?'

'I've been so busy. Quarterly reports were due. I had clients in town. It's been crazy.'

23

'Why didn't you call me?' I'd given up trying to get her by phone. It was hopeless.

'I'm here almost every day, baby. I didn't think you'd mind.'

'It's been four days, Lucy.'

'Four days? You must be kidding.' She pulled out her Filofax. 'What's today?'

'Wednesday.'

'The 19th?'

'The 12th.' I saw the front of the newspaper at Harry's. Otherwise I wouldn't have known.

She flipped pages back and forth. 'By golly, you're right. Four days. Did you miss me?'

'I depend on you for food. Remember?' I wasn't being a demanding asshole about this. It was her idea, right from the start.

She patted my stomach. 'You look like you ate all right.'

'I went out.'

'That's good. I worry when you sit here all the time.'

'It's not good. I went out for food! My goddamn shoe tore off at Harry's. Some kid picked it up.'

'Why are you yelling? Obviously he gave it back to you.'

I stuck the needle into the leg. I snapped off the light over the bench. From the stool I swung to the couch. 'It's not good when I go out. You don't know what it's like to get gawked at.'

'Don't I?'

'You feel like a moving accident. "Expect five minute rubbernecking delays along Sheridan Avenue. Marty is going to the mailbox."'

'You shouldn't let yourself think about it that way.'

I can't stand people talking to me about attitude. Especially not whole people. Coming from anyone else this would be the end of the conversation.

But Lucy is different. I looked at her standing behind

24

the chair. She was in motion. She shifted her weight from high heel to high heel, moving her trim hips, tilting her big model's shoulders, bobbing her head. Very slightly. Like she was wearing a Walkman. She wasn't.

There was no point trying to explain my feelings. I couldn't get through. She wasn't available that way today.

I couldn't be mad. I was happy to see her. I accepted her this way. She accepted me this way. Unlike me she had a choice.

She turned sideways and pushed out her butt. A very nice tight butt. Went with the legs. 'I get a look every now and then,' she said. I bet she did. 'I can handle it.'

Enough of this. 'There's something on the kitchen counter for you.'

She went and came back nuzzling a little bottle. 'Paprika. How sweet.'

'The flowers.'

'Flowers?' She returned to the kitchen. 'Peonies! My favorite! And look at all this food. There's a whole loaf of Wonderbread. I knew I didn't leave you dry.'

She came back with the flowers in a vase. She was sniffing them. 'This was so sweet of you.'

I grabbed her. I pulled her head down until we touched noses. 'You left me for four days. I went out in my wheelchair and bought the food in the kitchen. Do you understand?'

She smiled madly. She put down the flowers and started to straighten up. I locked my hands around the back of her neck. She was one of those fragile-looking women with amazing strength. In this mood she was superhuman. She carried boxes around when I first moved in. Heavy ones I had trouble with, and I'm a strong guy. I never saw anything like it.

I couldn't stop her. I was too light and there was nothing to grab. She lifted me off the couch. I didn't trust her when she was in this state.

She took hold of my stumps. She had complete control of me. I felt like a decoration. An ornament on her hood. A cripple pendant.

She started to walk. I was going backwards. It made me dizzy. We went through the doorway. She ducked her head and let go with her hands. I landed on the bed.

She was laughing. I drew myself into a ball. She reached for me. I fastened the top button of my shirt. She slapped my hands away and pulled it open. She made quick work of my clothes. I stopped fighting her.

She knelt at the end of the bed and pulled off my shorts. Then she stopped. She had that special look in her eyes. For the first time since she came in I knew she was looking at me. At me, Marty. I knew it because of the way she made me feel. Naked. More naked than anyone ever made me feel. Even more than the pimply medical students at the hospital. I tried to hide my stumps under the sheet. She put down her hands to stop me.

She leaned forward. I backed away. She reached out and stroked my chest. She had a soft touch. She said, 'Look at this body. You have no idea how much you turn me on, lover boy.' Her voice was warm wax.

I didn't know what to say. Compliments used to seem natural to me years ago. No more. I wondered why she was talking this way. I wondered every time.

She didn't wait for an answer. She reached for my stumps. I didn't know how she could do it. Shrunken and purple, crossed with scars. I'm used to the life, but I'll never get used to the stumps.

Lucy didn't have a problem with them. She never had. Not since the day I brought them home.

She closed her hands around them and squeezed. I jumped. She had the touch.

'You know what I think when I see you?' she said.

'You think: God, watch what I'm doing with this guy. And remember it when I die.'

'You don't believe in God, do you?'

'God exists. I'm sure of it. I hate him so bad that it's not possible he doesn't exist.'

Lucy kissed my forehead. 'When I see you I think of Gulliver, staked to the beach with hundreds of little ropes. The waves break over you day and night, month after month. The little people leave you there because they're too frightened to let you up.' She made the sound of the waves. Her hands became breakers on my stumps. 'Slowly the waves erode you. Still the little people leave you there. Know why? Because no matter your size, you're still a giant.'

I snorted. I never read Gulliver. But I saw the old cartoon movie. I tried to see myself as a giant on the sand. Instead I kept seeing myself as Gabby.

'You're my captive now,' she said. She took hold of my cock. It was as big as it gets. She had the goods on me. 'You're so massive I can only wonder how they managed to hold you down.'

It bothered me how she could get me so easy. Especially after disappearing for four days. But it was ridiculous to feel this way. Before the accident I never did. Hard was hard. Nothing else mattered.

I said, 'I'll bet your friends are real entertained hearing about the cripple's cock.'

She laughed. 'Do you think I'd advertise you, with a cock damned near as long as your leg? Do you think I'm that dumb?'

'Anybody can have one. Just cut off your legs.'

She put her finger across my lips. 'I don't care how you got it, lover. Just that you did.'

She kissed me. She had me.

'What am I going to do with you?' I said.

She leaped across the room and opened the bottom dresser drawer. The loinskin. She held it up to me and said, 'Tarzan me.'

She had it made for me last Valentine's Day. I had to give it to her, she knew how to make the most of an amputation.

27

She was thrilled by the loinskin. But I was exhausted. 'The trip to the store took it out of me.'

She batted her eyes. I couldn't resist. Or maybe it was the hand on my cock.

I slipped into the rough loinskin. It was made of coyote. Maybe it was roadkill. Like me.

I reached up for the rope beside the bed. My balls slipped out. Lucy squealed and turned away. She hiked up her skirt. She was bare underneath. She must have come in that way. What a woman.

She knelt on the bed, facing away. She stuck her ass up. Welcome home. I told her to take everything off, which she seemed to do with one tug. I pulled myself up the rope and got behind her. I aimed. I couldn't hit the damn thing. I was swinging just a little. She was tight. There was no room for error.

I was going to ask her to place me. But it wasn't right. Tarzan never needed help with anything. I let go with one hand and grabbed her behind. Then I slid into her.

'My animal,' she whispered. She threw her head back. Her wild mane slapped her shoulder blades and slid off. It was perfect.

She never looked back at me. It would have ruined everything. Her fantasy was about a wildman lover swinging into her on a long vine. Risking death from fierce jungle animals. She told me this once when she was drunk.

I swung hard into her. Soon she was covered with sweat. When I pulled back there was a smack. She braced herself with her arms. Her head was down. Her hair spread over the sheets like some huge golden jungle flower.

Sweat was rolling down my sides and dripping to the bed like rain. I was working hard. I loved it. I loved the whole thing. But I got too energetic. I slipped out.

I tried to let go of the rope with one hand. But I

needed to hold on with both. I was wearing out. My cock was aching out in the cold air.

I felt a firm, warm hand. 'Jane help,' Lucy said. She had a new husky voice. I liked it. She slid me back in.

I held on to the rope. 'Jane getting there,' she said. Now she wasn't taking chances. She grabbed my stumps like rickshaw poles. She was the driver.

'Jane close . . . Jane closer . . . Jane closest . . .' She was talking through her teeth. Her hands tightened on my stumps and swung me hard. She had me doing the twist. 'Jane here!'

I knew what she wanted. But I couldn't do it. Even a guy on a rope in a coyote loincloth gets embarrassed.

Jane raked her nails along the bottom of my stumps. The tender part, where the biggest scars are. 'Now!'

The pain raced through my buttocks and up my spine. My chest got prickly. My face turned hot. I let out a jungle scream. Just like Johnny Weismuller.

'Yes,' said Jane. She shook. She tucked my stumps under her arms and locked them against her sides. Her face thudded to the bed. She bent a pillow around her face.

Her ass settled on to her heels. To stay in place I came two hands down the rope. She kept twitching for a long time. Maybe she'd remember this one. Maybe next time she wouldn't wait four days.

The gouges in my stumps from her fingernails burned. I was furious.

I pulled my stumps free. I gave her a few hard thrusts. I heard little whimpers from the pillow. Another voice. This one I knew. The little pink behind. Of course! Cheetah!

I swung over her and let go of the rope. I fell on to her back. Planting my stumps into the mattress I plowed her across the bed. She crawled ahead of me, shrieking like a chimp. When I came I fell on top of her.

I fell asleep. Her fingers woke me up. I looked at the clock. 'Give me a few minutes,' I said.

'I can't. You inspire me.'

'Sometimes I'm amazed you didn't pull down my pants right there in the road.'

'What?'

'On Brooklyn Heights Road.'

She looked blank.

'When you found me. Remember? The accident?'

'Of course I remember. Don't glare at me as if I should go around thinking about it all the time.'

She shook her head and swallowed me up. I couldn't resist her. Soon she was on top of me. Head back, eyes closed. Her hair whipped around like those revolving brushes in a carwash. She moved her hips so fast I thought our pubic hair was going to catch fire. She started saying, 'Ooh baby.' I knew when she came because she growled too. But she never stopped talking. She never stopped moving. I looked at her face. I wondered where she was and what it was like there.

I held back because I loved watching her. I wanted to outlast her. To drain her. Fat chance. She quickly came five more times. But she never broke her rhythm.

I couldn't wait. When I came she didn't pay any attention. I made loud groans. I was faking. Like a woman.

She didn't open her eyes. She didn't slow down any. Her bone kept pounding into me. As I got soft it felt like a grindstone.

'Lucy, damn it!' I yelled. I pushed her off by the points of her hips.

She looked like I just woke her up. She smiled and fell on me. She sighed in my ear, 'I love you.' Finally she was still.

She only told me she loved me after sex. This bothered me a little. Like a woman. I never thought about it before the accident. What did I expect to be loved for? Being a cripple? I should have blessed my stars that she loved me for this.

'Let me ask you something,' I said. 'And I'm not fishing for compliments.'

'Uh oh.'

'Do you think I've changed. You know, my looks?'

'You're looking even more virile than usual, if that's possible.'

'In general. You know what I mean. Over time.'

'I don't know what you mean.' She was up on an elbow.

I didn't know how to put it.

She gave me a close look. 'Is this another "Are you glad you saved me?" question?'

'I ran into Esther at the store today.'

Lucy smiled. 'She got a charge card at Harry's, did she?'

'She said I look stronger. More determined.'

'To me you've always looked strong and determined, and sexy, and lots of other things. Perhaps I've been too close to you.'

I took the hint and shut up. Soon I fell asleep. I woke up hours later. Lucy was not in the bed. A sheet of light was coming from the living room. Music was playing.

I ape-walked to the crack beside the door. The music was my 'Best of the 60s' tape. Lucy was in the living room, dressed in only a pair of my boxer shorts. She was doing some old dance steps. I couldn't remember their names. She flailed her arms, bobbed her head, wiggled her butt, spun around. Her hair was flying. During slow numbers she hugged herself. She spent a lot of time in a squat, looking at herself in the wall mirror. It was set at my height. That took determination. And strong thighs. She never stopped singing. She was way out of tune.

Lucy was in high season. It would last awhile. Then it would end. I had to let her enjoy it while she could. Even though to me her high season was a pain in the ass.

I didn't interfere. She might go really wild and

31

disappear for a long time. I hoped she didn't. That's all I could do. Hope.

I woke up again when the sun came up. It was early. She was gone. I wasn't surprised. The tape was still playing. It was set on auto-reverse. My shorts were on the floor. The front door wasn't closed all the way.

Three

Next morning there was a tap on the door. It was Mr Casey, my neighbor. A nice old guy. He picks up my mail every day. Not that I ever get much.

He came in. I never lock the door. I don't have much worth taking. And there isn't a whole lot more they could do to me.

Mr Casey was holding his glasses in his hand. He was squeezing the bridge of his nose with the other hand.

'Headache?' I said.

'Afraid so.'

Mr Casey had a headache every time he came into the apartment. That way he didn't ever have to look at me through his glasses. He wasn't into stumps.

'Anything interesting?' I said about the mail.

'Let's see.' He slipped on his glasses, but only for a second. 'A letter from the Joshua Indian School. Looks like they're raising money for a football stadium. Bet you a dime to a dollar there's a picture of Jim Thorpe inside. Then there's a reminder from the electric company. And something from the Center for Remarkable People.'

'That'll keep me busy. Thanks. I hope your head feels better.' I said that every day.

When he left I swung over and got the letters. I looked at the one from the Center for Remarkable People. The CRP. I was on their mailing list. Probably another irresistible invitation. A square dance for amputees. Or a spelling bee for retards. The CRP is a good place. Don't get me wrong. But I wonder how they come up with some of these ideas.

I opened it. It wasn't a xerox. It was a letter to me.

33

It was official. There was a seal at the top of the page that I could feel with my fingers.

I read it. I couldn't believe it. I read it again. I couldn't believe this was happening. A dream come true.

Somebody was commissioning a sculpture through the CRP. From me. They wanted me to make it. Not only that, it was going to be cast in bronze. Me. A bronze. I always wanted to make a bronze.

I should explain. Usually a regular guy like me doesn't want anything to do with sculpture. For most of my life this was true. When I was a kid I did anything to get out of art class. I kept taking shop class instead. That's how I learned how to make things.

I remember teaching tennis at a resort up in the foothills. People set up easels in the field behind the courts. They used to stand there, or sit there, hour after hour. Dabbing and smearing their paint. Making copies of things they saw every day. Things they could get ten times better with a Polaroid. One day I hit a couple of balls toward them. They didn't pay any attention. I didn't think they could see things that were moving.

These people could have come on to the court and played. I would have taught them. They weren't old, or crippled. They could have made themselves feel alive. Instead they painted.

At dinner one night I asked one of the guys about making all this art stuff. He went on and on like he lived for it. It didn't make any sense to me.

After my accident the doctors and the nurses kept trying to make me go to the arts and crafts room. I wouldn't do it. I didn't want to make lanyards. I told them to bring me a six-pack. I could make a necktie out of the plastic holder.

A month of sitting still and I was going crazy. I said OK. Wheel me in. Give me some pipecleaners. I'll make little trees. Or whatever they say.

34

There was a lot going on in arts and crafts. The people were into it. I decided to give it a try. First was painting. I was no good. Everything I tried turned to slop. I made things brown. I don't like brown.

I decided to try lanyards. That I thought I could do. My teacher wouldn't let me. Angela. Nice legs. She said I was giving up. Life was going to be hard enough now. I had to try new things and see them through. I couldn't develop an attitude.

She could see I had talent, she said. How? From my hands, she said. I said a mechanic has good hands. Or a casino dealer. She said my problem was concentration. It was important to pick something I cared about.

I asked her to pose for me.

She laughed. It was a nice laugh. But I never had a woman laugh at me about something like that before. She took me back to my room. No-one ever wheeled me home from a date, either. She was forcing me to see how things were going to be.

I liked her. I kept coming around to arts and crafts. Anyway it was better than going to the physical therapy room. Less yelling.

I looked at the other crafts. Everything you could think of. I could see trying them. But first I had to find a subject I really cared about.

One day I was doodling on some paper. I wasn't paying attention to what I was doing. I was thinking about my accident. The little I could remember. When I looked, I saw that I actually drew something. For the first time. It was tigers, one on each sheet. I was sure of it.

The image stayed in my mind. The mighty tiger.

People kept spilling paint with their new prostheses. Bumping the table with their wheelchairs. Now I hardly noticed. The tiger. This was something I could get interested in. Even though I had no idea why.

I told Angela. She started talking about light and

shade, perspective, and all that. I told her to cut the chatter and set up an easel. I wanted to work away from the table. I started with charcoal. She watched. That made me nervous. I got better as the day went on. By the next day I was making better stuff than anybody else. But I didn't show anybody.

Angela gave me oil paint, acrylics, then watercolor. I didn't have the smoothest technique. I wasn't interested in technique. I found a way to create just what I wanted.

Then I tried sculpture. Clay, plaster, wood. My years of shopwork came in handy. I was used to making things in 3-D.

Angela was amazed. She asked if I was sure I never studied art. She never saw anybody pick it up so quickly.

'I hate art,' I said.

'What do you call all these drawings, paintings, and sculpture?'

'These are tigers. That's what I care about.' Until I said that I didn't know I cared about them.

Angel said, 'Why? What is it about tigers?'

'They're powerful. Graceful. Independent. Like me.'

She laughed. She laughed at all the wrong times. 'Why don't you try another subject? The room is starting to look like a tiger hatchery.'

I wanted to make her happy, so I tried. Portraits. Still lifes. They came out like brown slop. I just didn't care about them.

But the tiger was inside me. My sense of it was so strong that I always knew what would work and what wouldn't. No matter what medium. No matter how abstract. I could have made a tiger out of popsicle sticks.

I went to a hospital shrink twice a week. His job was to convince me it was all right to be a cripple. He said the same things over and over. Dr Feelgood stuff. I nodded. He had no idea what it was like being a cripple.

One day I asked him about the tigers. What did this mean? He got real excited. A new topic.

He tugged on his beard for a minute. Then he came up with this: 'My guess is that the tiger is you. You're a man of a certain stripe. In psychology we look for the truth behind the expression. You're strong and sexual. It's important that handicapped people don't neglect their sexuality. It happens much too often.

'The tiger is an idealized form of you before your accident. This is how you remember yourself. Notice you don't make drawings of tennis players. By rendering yourself as a tiger you are separating the past you from the present you. Now you are a man. Then you were an animal. In this sense I think the tiger is very healthy for you. It is your attempt to move ahead with your life. You can recreate your past on canvas or in clay. But you know these are monuments. They are inanimate. You have outgrown the tiger and become someone new.'

That's when I knew it was time to get out of the hospital.

I moved into the place I live in now. It was too far to use the facilities at the hospital. I started going to the Center for Remarkable People. It was closer. I used their art room. It was a pretty good setup. Lots of expensive supplies. Federal money.

I worked there a week. Then I noticed extra tigers around the room. Ones I didn't make. Other people were doing them too. I didn't care what other people did. But the tigers were mine.

I set up an area in my apartment so I could work there. It wasn't huge, but it was big enough. The light wasn't bad. And nobody was going to copy what I did.

I'm still hooked up with the CRP. I go over there every now and then. Twice a year they have art fairs. The cripples and the retards make things and people

37

get all dressed up and buy them for ten times what they're worth. It makes them feel good. I send over all my tigers. They sell out every time. The money hasn't been bad.

Now someone was going to pay me up front for a sculpture I hadn't even made yet. A lot of money. More money than all the other tigers put together.

The letter said, '. . . a sculpture in celebration of the wild beauty of nature.' A bronze for an outside garden. It didn't say what it was supposed to be. I knew it was a tiger. I couldn't make anything else.

The patron didn't give his name. This was strange. Usually they like to call the newspapers and brag about their generosity. Pose for pictures next to the guys in their wheelchairs.

The only person I had to deal with would give me half the money in advance. And pay for my supplies, 'within reason'.

His name was in the last paragraph. The accountant of the CRP. Sanford Shoreham. Esther's husband.

Good old Sanford. But even if he gave me grief I wasn't going to let him ruin it for me. This opportunity was too great. I figured a Porsche that gets splattered by a pigeon is still a Porsche.

A bronze. I couldn't get over it. They look like a piece of nature. They last forever.

'How are you going to make bronze in here?' said Lucy. 'You better check with the fire department.' She showed up two days later, with groceries.

'I don't make the bronze. I make the sculpture out of clay. Then it goes to a foundry. They make the bronze.'

'How do they do that?'

'They make a mold of the statue. Then they use the mold to make a wax copy of the statue. The wax is packed with some stuff. Then they melt the wax out. That leaves a cavity. They pour bronze into the cavity. It makes a bronze copy of the original sculpture. It's called the lost-wax method.' Angela taught me this.

'I always thought the lost-wax method was a secret the Romans used, but we don't know it because it was lost.'

'I guess they found it.'

Lucy made dinner. She was geared up. 'Would you say that plain dental floss is lost wax . . . ? Would you say that after the war, when women left the army, it was lost WACs?'

'No, I wouldn't say that.'

After dinner she asked to see the letter. 'I'm really proud of you,' she said. 'You have a wonderful talent, and you deserve to be recognized.'

'They're going to pay me before they see it.'

'Sanford Shoreham. Does that worry you?'

'Why should it? He got what he wanted. I got what I want.'

I don't know if either of us bought it.

Four

How should I pose my garden tiger? Most of my tigers were on the attack. That's how I thought of them. Leaping from the high grass, jaws open, claws out. Or with flesh hanging from the corners of their mouth. Blood running over their fur.

That didn't seem right for a garden. A garden should have a cool tiger. Laid back. Not that it wouldn't be fierce. But you'd have to see that in the pose. In the eyes. You'd have to look twice.

I never tried to make anything laid back before. I decided I better draw some sketches. Usually I didn't bother. Soon I had it. A cat sitting. Calm. Not very big. The power in the proportion, not the size. The head turned back. The ears and eyes locked. The tiger just heard something. The violence is a moment away.

People would walk through this garden. They wouldn't hang out too long.

I ordered supplies by phone. They arrived the next day.

I sawed up the wood and nailed the pieces together in the rough form of the tiger. The skeleton. I tacked in chicken wire to make ribs. That way I wouldn't have to put the clay on too thick. More chicken wire for the head. Two little pieces for the ears.

This was the armature. It looked like a chicken coop after a tornado. Too bad I was just a hayseed cripple. If I lived in New York City I could have sold it like this.

I could already see the finished tiger. It was going to

look so alive that people would say they saw its breath in the winter.

It needed a name. Sidney. That was good. I don't know why.

I opened the first bag of clay and dug out a handful. I love the first scoop in a fresh bag. Smooth as pudding. Stinking like the woods. I slapped the first flesh on Sidney's flank.

A knock on the door. Mail time. I wondered if Sidney would make Mr Casey put on his glasses.

The door didn't open right away. There was bumping and scraping. It wasn't him. I sat down and pulled a blanket over my lap. The door cracked open, then closed, then flew open. It was Jerold, in his stroller. Then Esther, his mother.

She closed the door and stood in the hall. 'Brrr!' she said.

'What are you doing here?' I said.

'Jerold and I agreed that you seemed lonely the other day.'

'I never get lonely.'

'Then why did you tell me where you live?'

'You asked.'

She unbuttoned Jerold's coat, then her own. She let out that smell that was all hers. She looked at the room. 'It's lovely, Marty. Who was your decorator, a gym teacher?'

'I was.'

She pulled on a rope. 'Don't you think you overdid the hemp motif?'

'That's how I get around.'

'You can't walk at all?'

'I have no fucking goddamn legs! How am I supposed to walk?' I was yelling . . . I never yell at people. I don't believe in it.

Esther clamped her hands over Jerold's ears. She said, 'I'm sorry. I didn't know exactly how bad it was. That's one of the reasons I'm here.'

41

'I'm sorry,' I said. I wasn't really. It was confusing having her in my home. Why didn't I kick her the hell out?

My calf began to twist. My 'phantom' pain. Twice this year. Twice around her.

I didn't want to reach for my stump in front of her. I looked away. Pretended she wasn't here. I thought it might help.

She said, 'Can I look around?'

I concentrated on Sidney. I thought about what I would do to him as soon as these intruders left. My calf slowly loosened up.

I looked back at Jerold. He was still in his stroller. He was pulling on a rope, sending little waves up to the ceiling.

Esther appeared in the bedroom doorway, hand on hip. Nice hips. 'So, what do you do, swing from rope to rope without coming down? Is that why the floor is so dirty, because you don't use it?'

'You get used to having no legs. You get used to dirt.'

'Doesn't that woman ever clean?'

'I do the cleaning. This is my apartment.' Actually Lucy did most of the cleaning. When she remembered to come by.

Esther walked around. She shook her head and made weird sounds with her tongue. 'I just don't like it. The ropes. The wheelchair. The dirt. You're better than this.'

'Really? What do you think I should do?'

'What about prostheses? At least with them you could get around by yourself.'

This was too much. 'Who the hell do you think you are? Who the hell do you think you are walking in here after three years and telling me how to live?'

'Well, you asked me.'

This was the thing about Esther. Before the accident we were tight. More than tight. I thought she was the real McCoy for me. That is, whenever I was loaded enough to think about things that way. We were together for years.

But when I woke up after the accident she was gone. That was three years ago. I never saw her or heard from her. Not until the other day, outside Harry's.

Lucy took over my life. I didn't ask her to. She just did it. I knew her longer than I knew Esther. We went out before I met Esther. And every now and then after I did. On the sly.

My friends never said a word to me about the switch. That's how weird they thought it was. Or maybe they were trying to tell me Lucy was a better pick.

Lucy's a good woman. She takes good care of me. Sure, sometimes she turns into different people who look just like her but act very strange. And she disappears from time to time. But when you're short like me you don't pick. You eat what's on your plate.

With Lucy around I stopped thinking about Esther after too long. I'd been content all this time. Until Esther came in my door. Actually, until I got that first whiff of her.

'Don't give me that baleful stare. I'm not facing you across the net. You asked. And I might add that asking me was not always your forte. There was one thing in particular I recall you never asked me,' she said. 'Let's not forget that.'

Oh, yes. The question all women live to hear. Let's not forget that. As if that had anything to do with anything now.

Jerold cried for his mom. He was frustrated with the rope. It wouldn't come down. Esther patted him. It didn't work. His voice made me think of shards of glass. He pounded the stroller bar with his fists. He was a loud person.

She picked him up. He liked that. He yanked her hair.

'So really, what about the legs?' she said to me.

43

What about the legs? Who else would ever say this to me?

I said, 'When the monkeys fell out of the trees they had four legs. Then they stood up and used their hands. They evolved, right? To two legs. I went from two legs to none. More evolution. I'm at the top of the goddamn tree.' I'd heard this from Bruno at the CRP. He looked like he got caught in a wood chipper. He was good at shutting people up. He had to be.

'I'm serious, Marty.'

'I am what I am, Esther. I'm not going to stagger around on plastic sticks. People have to jump to keep out of your way. It's pathetic.'

She looked at me. Her face changed. 'I remember the first time I saw you on the tennis court. I spilled my iced tea into my lap I was so mesmerized. You moved like a cat. You were beautiful.'

'God!' I cried. I hopped into the chair and raced to the bedroom.

I was trembling. I didn't want her to see.

Why was she pushing me back into that hell? She had nothing against me. I let her escape after the car crash. I didn't go after her. She was living the good life with her accountant husband and her kid. Why show up here?

Why. That was always the question with her. I wouldn't be able to figure it out if I sat here until Jerold's senior prom. In a lot of ways she was a mystery to me. Always was.

I cooled off. Then I returned to the living room. Jerold was standing there by himself.

I called for Esther. There was no answer. Then I saw a note on the table: 'You misunderstood. You're still beautiful. Running errands. Back soon. Have fun.'

She was up to something. Maybe she was trying to show me I couldn't take care of a kid. So we never could have made it together. So it was OK that she split on me.

It wasn't OK. It was disgusting.

But Jerold was here. It wasn't his fault.

I heard a crash. He was clearing things from my work table.

I opened my arms. 'Come here, Jerold, you cute little motherfucker.'

He could just reach the table top. He pulled down whatever he got his hands on. My Yellowstone mug shattered on the floor. I got it when I was ten years old.

I wheeled toward him. He shrieked and ran to the end table. He squeezed between the table and the wall. I wheeled around the side of the table. He backed out of my reach. He was laughing. Drool was running down his lapel. It was great fun.

When I wheeled around the other side I knew he would move away. I couldn't get him. I waited in the middle of the room. I didn't go for his feints. I needed a clear shot at him.

He got cocky. I knew he would. He broke across the room, arms out to the sides and churning. I swooped down on him. As I was about to grab him, he looked back. He gurgled and went down. I missed him and rolled past. I spun and came back. But I couldn't get enough of him to pick him up. He knew this. He crawled to safety behind the chair. I wheeled along with him, trying to get him. He laughed. My fingers were tickling him.

This was enough grief from the Shoreham family. I got out of the wheelchair. I pulled myself up on a rope and swung through the room. Jerold's eyes grew huge. He ducked behind the arm of the chair. I landed on the seat and dropped to the floor. I grabbed him around the waist. He let out a weak cry. His body was rigid.

'I'm not going to hurt you, old man,' I said. 'Take it easy.'

I let him go. He pressed back against the wall. He wailed softly. He was even too scared to call for his mom.

His first airborne attack. A scary experience. There was more than that. I followed his eyes. The ends of my cut-off pants were loose. I didn't fasten them. I wasn't expecting company.

Jerold was facing his first naked stumps.

I slapped one to show him it sounded like flesh, even if it didn't quite look like it. I ape-walked a little circle. They worked too.

I pointed to his leg and said, 'Leg.' I pointed to my stump and said, 'Stump.' I repeated both a couple of times. We weren't getting anywhere.

I grabbed his leg. He fell on to his back and tried to kick loose. I tickled the back of his thighs. I lay down beside him and tickled my stump. I laughed. He looked at me like I was crazy. I didn't stop. Finally he gave in and started laughing with me.

I ape-walked across the room. I took hold of his stroller. 'Stroller,' I said. I hopped into the wheelchair and said the same thing.

He bent over and put his hands on the floor. He was trying to ape-walk. On the first step he went down on his face.

I picked him up. If his mother could see him now. I stood beside him and assumed the position. His legs were too long. Or his arms were too short. He fell again.

He rose on hands and knees. He reached out a pudgy finger and touched my stump. He looked up at my face and smiled.

'Stump,' I said.

'Tum!' He put his leg on the floor beside mine.

'Listen. You – leg.' I pointed. 'Me – stump.'

The distinction didn't interest him. 'Tum, tum, tum,' he said. He started whipping his head back and forth, slapping both of us. Then he stopped. He made a serious face. 'Oo.' He pulled at his laces.

'Shoe?' I said. He smiled.

I think he noticed that his legs ended in shoes and

mine didn't. This was the big difference between us. If only his mother had seen me this way.

I pulled off one of his shoes and stuck it on the end of my stump. His face lit up. 'Oo!' He clapped. I think that did it. We were friends.

We played the rest of the afternoon. We had no more trouble.

Esther burst in the door. 'Sorry I took so long. I was afraid the pharmacy was going to close. Did you have fun?'

I was in the wheelchair. Jerold was trying to push me from behind. I was wearing both his shoes.

'What is this?' she said. She swept Jerold up with one arm. She reached for the shoes. But she didn't take them. She straightened up. 'Is this some kind of sick joke?'

'Ask Jerold. He put them on me. No. He put one of them on me.'

Jerold reached for me with both arms. 'Tum, tum!'

'Tum?' she asked.

'Tummy. I think he's hungry.'

'We'll go eat.'

I offered her the shoes. She ignored me.

'What's the matter with you?' I said. 'Afraid I'm going to infect him with stump disease?'

'I thought I could trust you with my child.'

'Why?'

She thought about that. Then she said, 'I thought you'd understand what it feels like to be at the mercy of others.'

'You mean of people like you?'

She strapped Jerold into his stroller. He was in his socks. She stood over me. Her lips were pursed. 'I've heard that amputations can have unfortuante psychological consequences.'

'Where did you hear that? Ann Landers?'

'Dr Shapiro. Leonard, I think.'

My doctor. The one who cut off my legs. She hit all

the buttons. 'Why were you talking to Dr Shapiro?' My calf started to buzz. Threatening to go crazy again.

She wanted me to ask this. But I couldn't keep away from the accident. Even though everything about it still made me sick, I got so scared. She said, 'I was at the hospital. Why shouldn't I talk to him?'

'You looked up Leonard Shapiro when you were in the hospital?'

'I didn't have to look him up. I was there the night you were run over.' I had never heard this. I thought she just disappeared. I assumed she just disappeared. No-one told me different. Including her.

Not that it changed anything. She still took off. But I hated the idea that there was more I didn't know.

The accident was gouged into the highway. That's how I thought of it. Afterwards it was covered with a smooth layer of tar. It looked fine if nobody touched it. News from the past could come up from below like big bubbles. Then they broke, upsetting the whole thing. Splattering me with burning hot tar.

I didn't want to hear any more. My leg was screaming. And she probably wanted me to ask. But I couldn't help myself. 'What were you doing there?'

Esther opened the door. She was almost smiling now. The bitch. I thought she was going to leave without answering me. But she paused over the threshold. 'Why don't you ask the woman you love.'

'Tum!' said Jerold, as Esther wheeled him out. It seemed like her smell rushed out the door with her.

Five

I worked on Sidney the rest of the afternoon. I couldn't keep my mind on what I was doing. I packed on the inner layers of clay. They wouldn't show.

I kept thinking about what Esther said – Why don't you ask the woman you love? – She looked so happy when she said it. And so evil. Why would she show up after all this time and then say something like that?

I wished Lucy would get here. I wanted to get this over with. At the same time I never wanted to see her again. She could wine and dine a client in Bombay. And stay there. Take Esther with her. Leave me in peace.

But Lucy didn't show up that night, so I had to hold my bladder for another day. She showed the next night. And she had groceries. That was groceries twice in a row. I had to give her credit.

'Looks good,' she said about Sidney. 'A little scrawny though.'

I didn't remember Esther saying anything about him.

Lucy cooked a nice dinner. I didn't have much of an appetite.

'Are you all right?' she said.

'What do you mean?'

'I mean are you all right? Are you having pain? You look a little green.'

'I had some phantoms today.'

She took my hand. 'I'm sorry. Can I do anything?'

There was nothing she could do. It wasn't her. She was sweet and wonderful. It was the accident. After all this time I thought I understood. The wounds closed and now the scars were tough. That's what I thought. Then somebody like Esther could tear them open again.

I wanted to come right out and ask Lucy. Clear the air. But I was scared to go into it again. That got me real mad.

She said, 'I got a call today which might interest you.'

It didn't. 'Who?'

'Sanford Shoreham.' Esther's husband. The man with my tiger money.

'What did he want?'

'He's afraid that your commission is so large that it's going to make you too anxious to work. He said he's seen it before.'

'What does he want to do? Help me out by keeping some of it for himself?'

'He asked me to keep an eye out and let him know if there's any trouble,' she said.

'Why the hell didn't he call me?'

'I don't know. Maybe he figured a macho stud like you would never admit it.'

'The little prick. Did he tell you who the patron is?'

I didn't hear her answer. I was changing position and just happened to notice Jerold's shoes under the chair. The tops were sticking out. They were the only really white things in my whole apartment.

I asked Lucy to get me a sweater. When she went to the bedroom I swung across the room and grabbed the shoes. I stuffed them into my pocket and swung back.

She brought me a sweater. 'Chinese red light?' she said.

'What?'

'You just got into my chair.'

'Did I? I'm cold.' I put on the sweater. It made me bake.

She smiled. 'So what did you do today, other than work on your sculpture.'

'Not much. The usual.'

'Did you get outside?'

'The world can get their laughs from somebody else.'

'Did you read?'

'You know I don't read.'

She smiled again, the way a cat smiles at a bug on the floor. 'Want to hear what I did today?'

Are you kidding? 'Sure.'

'I had a meeting in the morning about the new ad and promotional campaign for the . . .' Was it possible that she knew something about Esther and the accident? And kept it from me? All this time? '. . . who just became the marketing VP. Now repeat any three words I just said to you.'

'Sorry.'

'What are you thinking about?'

I couldn't tell her. 'I'm worried about the whiskers.'

'Whiskers?'

'Yeah. How do you put them on a bronze? You can't make them out of clay. They'll droop.'

'You did have an interesting day,' she said. 'Did you have company?'

'I never have company. Actually, Mr Casey came in with the mail. For ten seconds. He had a headache.'

'What mail did you get?'

She was chasing me. I said, 'It was all junk. I can't even remember.'

'Any promotional samples?' She was still smiling.

I said, 'I think a catalogue of medical supplies. Trusses, braces, walkers. You know, fun stuff.'

'No samples?'

'No.'

'Come with me.'

She went to the bedroom doorway. I swung over and landed beside her. I hated to stand next to her. She towered over me. I felt like a runt.

'Smell anything?' she said.

I sniffed. It was Esther. No question about it. I should have opened the window. 'Just my BO. Do you?'

'Perfume. I know the brand. It's called Black Widow. You're sure you didn't get any samples?'

'Oh, yeah. There was one of those cards in a magazine. You tear it and the smell comes out.' Why was I doing this?

She sat on the bed. She motioned me to sit beside her. 'Well, it doesn't matter anyway.'

Now I didn't get it at all.

She said, 'The reason our relationship is so wonderful is our honesty. Don't you think?'

'Definitely.'

'I can be completely candid with you and I know you'll understand.'

'I will.'

'Do you feel that way about me?'

I said, 'Sure. You saved my life.'

'Forget that. I hope you don't ever feel you have to hide things from me. Do you?'

'Never.'

'Well, I've got to tell you, Marty. The only woman I've ever known to wear Black Widow is Esther.'

'No kidding.'

'Was she here today?'

'Here today? You got to be kidding.'

She jammed her hands into my pocket and pulled out the shoes. 'They've been sticking out the whole time. And you're such a bad liar. Why didn't you tell me?'

I felt stupid. 'I don't know why. I meant to tell you. She just stopped by. The first time. I didn't invite her. Nothing happened or anything.'

'So, what's the big deal?'

I pulled off the sweater. I was hot. The big deal was that Esther was trouble. For Lucy and me. There was no other reason for her to come around. Even if I didn't know exactly what she was up to.

There was one sure way to stop her from coming around again. Lock the front door. End it now.

But I knew I wasn't going to. And that bothered me.

It was my old weakness. My worst one. I've always been soft when it comes to getting rid of women. When I was in a romance and it started going sour, I changed the schedule. I had other things to do. That usually did it. If a woman stuck around, fine. If she left, even better. Either way, it was her choice.

That was when landing new ladies was as easy as squeezing peaches at the supermarket. Now I was down to one. Maybe two. And if it was two, the idea of telling one to take a hike made me nervous. How many more was I ever going to have?

Lucy said, 'Don't think too hard. You'll give yourself a hernia. Look, I hate to start talking about this, because that's exactly what she wants us to do. But I see no other way.' She folded her hands. 'In the old days, I did things your way. When you fell for Esther – God only knows why – I backed off, but I was still available when you wanted to see me. I didn't like it, but I never gave you a hard time.

'I don't have to remind you about her heroic departure from your life. Now her accountant takes care of her and I take care of you.

'I don't ask much from you. I make no claim on you. I'm not thrilled by the idea of sharing this unbearably sexy body, but I'm not greedy either. If you feel you have to stray, pick somebody else. Not her. She'd never try to outlove me for you. She'd get ugly. And I don't want to go through that.'

Lucy was wonderful. I felt safe with her. Now I could ask her. 'Esther said that she was at the hospital while they were cutting off my legs. She said I should ask you.'

She smiled and bowed her head. Softly she said, 'My dear, dear Esther. Yes, it's true.'

'But how?'

She got up and walked across the room. She leaned against the wall. 'How did she get there? How do you think? I called her. I thought she had a right to know. She loved you, or so she claimed.'

'She came and saw me, and then ran away?'

'I can't answer for her. If she can face you now, I'm sure she's got it all figured out.'

That killed the mood. Lucy would say it was just what Esther wanted. But she didn't say it. Because the mood was killed.

I grabbed a rope and swung over to Lucy. I was going to kiss her. She sidestepped me. I almost hit the wall. I said, 'Please don't blame me for asking.'

'I don't blame you.'

'I'm still your chimp,' I said. 'I'll prove it.'

She went and got her coat. I was trying to think of some reverse psychology to use on her. I couldn't think fast enough.

She said, 'I have an early conference in the morning. See you soon.'

She kissed me and walked out the door, leaving me dangling on the rope.

Six

I never think much about the old days. A lot of guys do. When I started going to the CRP I visited a few of them at home. They had pictures of themselves all over the place. Pulling in fish. Hugging sweethearts. And lots of trophies, always carefully dusted. Medals from the war too. Especially Purple Hearts.

I don't see the point. That life is over. This one is different. Like we're born again. On the highway. Baptized in gasoline. I would only hang a picture of myself if it showed bandages on my stumps. That would be my real baby picture. Where this life started.

I don't even dream about my past. The closest was when I dreamed about being a tadpole. I was in the middle stage. I had back legs and a tail. So did my friends. They were all talking about getting their other legs and becoming frogs. I was already a frog. I was going backwards. I was afraid I was going to lose the back legs too and end up an egg floating in slime on top of a pond. It was a bad dream.

Women were a big part of my past. Maybe the best part. Even so I pretty much stopped thinking about them. No pictures. No Purple Hearts. I didn't try to stop thinking about them. I just did. When I remember things it can make me feel bad.

But when Esther showed up, all kinds of stuff filled my mind. Not only about her. About lots of them. It was like yesterday's barge dumped too close to shore. Today the garbage washed in.

This wasn't the work of my brain. It was the work of my knees. Esther brought me the phantom pain. It didn't go away when she left. I got twinges for days after. It was weird. They felt just like the twinges I used to get after six hours on the tennis court. When I had knees.

When I had knees. Gravy days. Now I don't know what to do with myself half the time. Before the accident I was always busy. I used to teach lessons. Help out around the club. Tend the bar every now and then. Then go out. My schedule used to be booked solid. If there were cracks in it, women filled them up, like grout. This sounds like I used women. Treated them bad. But I didn't. I like women too much for that.

I liked them too much for my own good. When I met somebody new I kept thinking about the good times I had with the old one, who I should have left. It would tie me up. The other pros at the club laughed at me. They dumped women like buckets of chum.

All the women, new and old, knew they could always find me on the court. That's where they met me. It was easy to make a scene. They used to do that every now and then. I remember one time. A girl I went out with a few times. She came on to the court in the middle of a lesson, in front of everybody. Screamed that she was too good for me, and why couldn't I make up my mind, and she wasn't moving until she got an answer.

I should have called security and had her tossed out. I didn't. I was moved that she could do this for me. She was standing there all alone in her little white skirt. She didn't know that it was folded under. Showing her butt. She knew I had a new lover, who could be at one of the tables under the umbrellas, drinking a Bloody Mary. Watching the whole thing. I was moved that she could brave that. I kind of fell in love with her then.

When she was done yelling she started crying. I put my racket along her back and took her to the side of the court. I said something to make her feel better. God knows what. Then I swore I'd never get mixed up with a woman at the club again. And I didn't. Until the next time.

Years later, sitting in my apartment, looking at a skinny clay tiger, I wondered: why did I bother? Even with the phantoms eating up my legs I could hardly remember a damn thing about any of them. I remembered what was the same about them. How they made me feel. How I went after them. But I couldn't remember what was different about them.

But I used to keep doing it. Meeting women, romancing them, always looking for more. I could remember my determination. Always on to the next one. If I stopped I'd die.

There was always something I wanted to do. Something my main woman wanted me to do. Something the one who was going to replace her wanted me to do. I was pulled in every direction. There was no way to make everybody happy. I used to complain about this. If only they would back off. Or talk straight. Or make up their minds. Or decide it between them. Then I would be happy.

Now I know I was wrong. I loved the tension. The sensation. The danger. For three years I've been living a resolved life. No conflict. No decisions. I miss tension as much as I miss my legs.

Esther might have been offering me tension now. But not the kind I used to have. Esther's was the kind you feel when you're hiking in sandals and you know there are snakes and scorpions around.

Another thing in my life is missing. Friends. Almost all of them disappeared, usually after the first visit to the hospital. People don't want to be around cripples. I don't take it personally. I don't like being around them either. But I get lonely.

Now when somebody invites me somewhere, which is rare, I wonder why. Does he want to see me? Or is he acting out of duty? His good deed for the month.

When Lucy is off on business, or just off, I'm alone. I

57

have lots of time on my hands. Sometimes I don't feel like doing tigers. Then I'm in a jam. I wonder how I'm going to make it until bedtime. There's TV. The only thing I like is sports. But when I watch whole athletes I even the score with them. I think how fast they'd make it to first base running on stumps. It's not a good thing to do.

I sleep a lot more than I used to. But I have more trouble falling asleep. Sometimes I try to tire myself out at night. I sit on the floor and pull myself up the rope to the ceiling as many times as I can. It never makes me sleepy. I don't need the exercise. I exercise every day to stay strong. So my body doesn't warp. That's all. Some guys at the CRP lift weights all day long. They live for it. They get huge. They love to show off. Biceps, pectorals, whatever you want. It's really strange. You admire a guy's rippling tricep. At the same time you pretend not to notice that there's no arm on the other side.

If I didn't stop hanging out at the CRP I might have ended up like them. Superman above the belt. A Christmas turkey below it.

I don't have to make tigers. I don't have to work at all. I thought that was the bonus for being crippled. I was wrong. It would have been better if I had to get out of the house. Wheel from office to office, handing out my résumé. So I'm not qualified to do anything except to say 'Watch the ball'. And mix a Margarita. I'm a cripple. That would have counted for something.

I didn't look for work. My insurance company settled with me for the accident. It was too bad that they never found the guy who hit me. They would have nailed him to the wall. But there wasn't one piece of evidence. A very clean job.

I got enough money to live on. Enough for food, rent, oil for my wheelchair, pumice for my knuckles. Sometimes I think a chair with a motor would be nice. Or silk ropes. Social Security chipped in too. Enough so I could move up to extra-soft toilet paper.

I got a good deal from the insurance company. I figure it like this: I'd have to teach over 1,500 hours a year to make what they gave me. I couldn't do that. Not with winter coming every year. Even if I could, how long could I have kept it up? 'Bend your knees. Turn your body. Follow through.' My legs were becoming a problem. They ached every morning. They were a depreciating asset. That's what one of my students said. He knew something about money. Come to think of it, it was Sanford.

Sometimes I wonder how the insurance company decided how much to give me. Did they send some guy to find out how good my legs were? What if Mrs O'Connor, my Monday nine-thirty regular, lost hers? They look like those Greek gyro slabs of lamb that rotate in front of a barbecue and get hacked to pieces. She couldn't get from the baseline to the net without an escort. Would they be worth the same as mine? Or Sadie, with the perfect nineteen-year-old legs? They were worth a free ride from some poor bastard for the rest of her life. Would the insurance company figure that in?

There's another thing I can't help wondering. I know this sounds morbid. What if I got into another accident and lost my stumps. Would the insurance company pay me more for that? Because I would be completely out of legs. Or less? Because this time I lost less flesh.

Somebody in the hospital said insurance companies use a table for all this stuff. There's a list of everything you could lose. Combinations of things, too. Then it tells you how much they're worth. This guy didn't know many of the numbers. But he knew it was a bad break for me. I would have been better off losing an arm and a leg. Financially. And with an arm and a leg left I could still hit a tennis ball. I couldn't get much mustard on it, though.

I thought about this for days. I figured out how to

lose an arm and a leg in an automobile accident. That's what you do when you're laid up in a hospital bed.

Say you were driving down the parkway. You come to a toll. You put a coin between your toes, reach your leg out the window, and try to drop the coin into the basket. Just to try something new. Figure you had a few beers at this point. The coin gets loose. You reach out your hand and try to save it. But you're not looking where you're driving. You crash into the toll booth.

There are times I think losing my legs was the best thing that ever happened to me. Sometimes late at night I flip through the TV channels. There's a show featuring a tan man sitting under palm trees, interviewing other tan men. They all say they made their fortunes doing what the interviewer told them to. Real estates, cash flow, crap like that. It takes years.

My pitch is better. Folks, you too can find financial security. At the end of somebody's bumper.

I had another problem with all this free time. I was warned about this one by the hospital shrink. He said a lot of handicapped people fall in this trap and never get out. I thought about the guy who did this to me. I couldn't help it. I didn't get mad about it. I was curious. Who was this guy who crashed into me and drove away? Leaving me busted up and bloody.

I thought about old friends who turned into head-cases in Vietnam. And football players who tried to hurt guys when they played. These guys were sick fucks. But there was always something you could call a reason for what they did. Not a good one. But a reason.

Maybe I couldn't get past the fact that it was my body. But what this guy did to me had no reason, good or bad. Whatever he was up to, would it have killed him to put in a call to the cops? To at least get me off the pavement.

Most of the guys at the CRP can tell you everything about their injuries. They can replay them for you, second by second. 'I left the house at seven thirty-two and turned north on Elm Street. Forty seconds later I got to the crosswalk at Pine. I was five steps across the street when the truck ran the light.' Then they tell you all the things they could have done so it came out different. Little things. Tiny things. 'I tried to turn back. I slipped. If I was wearing my Reeboks instead of my wingtips . . .' 'If I stopped to kiss my wife, I would have gotten to the crosswalk ten seconds later . . .' Talking like this makes them feel better.

I hit my head during my accident. I don't remember anything about it. I can't remember anything about that whole day. I don't know where I was going, or why. At first I could hardly remember anything about anything. It took a while to come back.

One big thing was never going to come back – I would never know who hit me. So I tried to figure him out. I thought about what makes people do things. I became sure of a couple of things. The guy wasn't sober. He had no human feeling. Drinking does that to some people. He could have been high on drugs. I don't know too much about that, so I figure it was alcohol.

I was sure it was a man. I couldn't imagine the worst drunken bitch I ever met leaving me there. Actually, I could. But she wouldn't leave a stranger there.

The guy was either a teenager or in his forties. Those were the only ages I could see him. I'm not sure why. I didn't know anything about his looks.

That's as far as I got in three years. It was frustrating. The harder I concentrated the more slippery the guy became. I had to concentrate on not concentrating. To fake myself out. Kind of reverse psychology.

I remember the day I started sketching. I was still in the hospital. I was sitting there imagining I was at the stationhouse. People kept coming in. They had driven past the scene of the crime. It was nighttime. My Camaro and the other car were off on the shoulder. No-one knew there had been a crime until the morning newspaper.

Now people were coming in to try to help. I asked them for a description of the driver. They told me they were on the way to see friends. Picking up kids. Going on dates. They told me everything except what I wanted to know. They didn't see the guy. It made them feel better to keep talking.

After a while I figured out how to interpret their blabber. I watched how they held themselves, what they looked at. I drew psychological profiles of them. From these I figured out how they drove. How they observed things. Then I listened to their stories of that night again. And learned the truth.

My hand worked on its own. I didn't bother to look at the sketches. I had the guy fixed in my mind.

This went on for some time. But when I shook out of my trance, suddenly he was gone from my mind. That's when I looked at my sketches. They weren't very good. In fact, they weren't pictures of the guy at all. They were tigers.

I guess even in my trance I didn't want to embarrass myself. So I drew the only thing I could. I didn't know that's all I could draw. Not yet.

The guy was off scot-free. And I had my tigers. Just the way it's been since.

Seven

The minute I looked at Sidney that morning I knew something was wrong. I backed up. My muscles got tight. I didn't want to touch him. I picked up the broom and swept up the clods of dried clay.

I forced myself to pick up my sculpting tool. I got right up to Sidney and looked at him through the wire loop. I didn't know what to do with him.

This never happened to me with tigers. This is what happened when I tried to make anything else.

I sat down and had a beer. I don't usually do that at eight a.m. But I was all bothered. These women were getting to me.

No. It wasn't the women. I figured this out three cans later. It was Sidney. I saw two problems. He was looking back over his shoulder. He was cool. Too cool. A kid could pet him. You should never feel a kid can pet a tiger. That means it's not a real tiger. And it was too small. Ferrets are more ferocious than tigers, pound for pound. I remember that from Scouts. But sculptors don't get too many commissions for ferrets.

There was no way to fix up this sculpture. I could pack on more clay to make it muscular, but I couldn't make it any longer. It would have short thick limbs and a stout little body. Something you might see at the CRP, but never in the jungle.

The cat I had in mind was life-size. Eight feet long. Ready to strike. A real tiger. In that scale this thing might make some big bush rodent. I put a wet sheet over it. That would keep it moist. And I wouldn't have to look at it.

My first failed tiger. It smarted. Like the first time I

ever got stood up. I didn't think it could happen.

I'd have to start over. I used up all the wood and the most of the clay. I'd have to talk to Sanford about getting more.

I started sketches for the new tiger. It had to have a new name. Sidney was dead. A miscarriage. This one would be called Brute.

There was a knock on the door. It was Mr Casey. He forgot to take off his glasses.

'That's him,' he said. He took off.

A teenage boy came in. He had skin like rice pudding. He handed me a long white box. He didn't wait for a tip. He practically ran out the door.

I opened the card. *I'm sorry. I got confused unconfusing. I'll try again. Yours, Esther.* In the box was one yellow rose. My first flower since the amputation.

I didn't understand the message. Just the confused part. But my phantom leg did. It had a message: Get out of here.

I looked out the window. I didn't do that too often. Drizzle. Was I going out into that? Running away? Scared chicken-shit? Why not? I wasn't ready for her again. Not yet. Not until I did some more thinking.

I could do myself some good. Surprise Sanford at work. He would give me everything I wanted.

I wheeled to the front closet. I picked my favorite outfit. Fatigue legs and army boots with coordinated coat and hat. I got a lot of respect when I wore them.

I slid my legs into the fitted tops. They didn't fit so great any more. They were loose. Not a good feeling. They warned me in physical therapy. Stumps keep shrinking for a while. It was strange. Shrinking stumps. You'd think they'd had enough. Something else should do the shrinking.

I closed the pants and fastened the belt. I tugged at the boots. They felt secure. I opened a tin of black shoe polish. I ran a line of it under both eyes.

I knew a lot of guys who went to Vietnam. A couple got planted there. One's still MIA. I didn't feel an ounce of disrespect for them. If Uncle Sam called me I would have gone too. Now I wore fatigues so it was easier for me to get around. I didn't think they'd mind. The vets at the CRP didn't.

I left the building and came to the corner. It was a nasty day. I waited for the light.

I saw a guy staring at me. A redneck with a gray crew cut, a gut hanging over his belt buckle. I looked away. I could still feel his eyes. Just what I needed. A stump-faggot to start the day.

The wheelchair jerked. He was at the handles. 'Where you headed?' He had a deep macho voice.

'I can handle it.'

'I know you can, soldier. But it's my honor to help a fellow veteran of the Armed Forces of these United States.' That's when I remembered about the fatigues.

I let him take me across the street. Then I was hoping the rain would make him go someplace. He didn't have an umbrella.

No. He was the friendly type. 'Where'd you serve, soldier? I probably knew your CO. I got around during the war.' Might as well have asked me whether gook pussy was slit up and down or sideways. I didn't know how to start to lie. He wasn't going to take this kindly.

Then I had an idea. I turned around and stared into his eyes. My mouth dropped open. Drool ran down to my chin. I shook my head and banged myself in the temple as hard as I could. I felt it in my teeth. 'Grenade in the trench, sir. Picked it up and threw it out, sir. Can't remember anything else, sir.' I rubbed my chest. 'Except for the pin, sir.'

'The pin?'

'On the back of the DSC, sir. The general got me.' I saluted.

This was better than saying I spent the war playing

tennis, with a 4F for flat feet. I was glad when he left me at the bus stop.

The first bus came by in about ten minutes. It wasn't equipped for wheelchairs. I sat in the rain. Water ran down the bill of my hat. It would have dripped into my lap, if I had a real lap. The next bus was taking its sweet time. The first driver probably radioed back that there was a drug-crazed vet freak cripple at the stop.

I didn't used to take the bus. Sitting in the rain was one reason. I took cabs, even though they're expensive. Cabs have other problems, though. I found that out. After my last cab ride the driver reached over his shoulder for the fare. I stepped down. Suddenly he took off. My chair was still in the back seat. He left me standing in my fake legs in the street. Looking like I was three and a half feet tall and my knees bent forward. Kids started to gather round. He didn't come back for twenty minutes.

At least now I was waiting in my chair.

The bus finally showed up. The driver got out to lower the lift in the back door. He was getting soaked. He started muttering.

I wheeled on to the platform. The lift went up. I slowly rose to the level of the aisle. I felt like I was rising through a trap door on to a stage. Everybody in the bus was staring at me, all the way to the front seat. They weren't feeling sorry for me. They were pissed. I was holding them up.

The closest stop was a block away from the CRP. I got out. The rain let up.

The whole block was taken up by Harry's Cars. It was owned by a guy named Leon. It used to be Harry's Chevrolet. I wheeled by. Now most of the cars were Japanese. Then came the Chevies. They looked just like the Jap cars.

In the corner of the lot were the used cars. I went over. I liked these the best. Mean, nasty grills. Fins.

66

Chrome all over. They had character. Designed for the world, not the goddamn wind tunnel.

Then I saw a real car. A 1980 Z28 Camaro with a 427 Hemi and aluminum block. Fire engine red. Just like the last car I ever owned. The car I left my legs in. That car was junked on Brooklyn Heights Road. Flattened. Probably shipped to Japan. Came back as one of those Jap cars.

I wheeled up to this one. It was a beauty. Somebody really kept it up. The car deserved it.

I should have felt sick or something, being next to this car, considering what happened. I didn't. I felt great. I ran my hand over the side. I smelled the tires. The grease. So many good times. So many good women.

I wheeled all the way around the car. What a beauty. They didn't make them like this any more.

There was a small gash in the rear bumper. A parking lot bruise. I had something like it on my Camaro. Mine was on the front end. I was parked up on Sunrise with Esther. I just met her. She set on me like a tiger. It was amazing. Next thing I know we're rolling down the hill. Somebody kicked the brake off. The bumper caught a stump. Good thing. Otherwise we're in Miller's Creek.

I forgot all about that.

I wondered if this car took a stump. I hoped it did. And the chick was a fox.

I wondered if Esther remembered that night. If she used to be reminded of it when she saw a red sports car. If that's why she was back in the picture. That would be a good reason.

I wheeled into the office. A fancy shack. Leon was there. We used to play some ball together.

'Marty,' he said. 'My man.' He was fat. His hairline was halfway back on his head. The three years were rougher on him than me. He put up his hand. I gave him a high five. I had to. Men always do this with me. To let me know we're still in it together.

'Business looks good,' I said.

'I can't complain.'

'I was wondering about the red Z28.'

'A gem. Mint condition,' he said. 'Come anywhere near a decent offer and it's yours.'

'I was wondering where you got it. I used to have one just like it.'

He tapped his lips. 'Came in last month from a fellow named Karlin. Harlan Karlin. A local fellow. He hardly used it.'

Sure. Why didn't he just say it was his grandmother's. She kept it under a tarp. Sometimes she sat in it but she never learned how to drive.

'Why did he trade it?'

'He moved up to the engineering and economy of the new Honda. They're beautiful. Let me show you one.'

I wheeled down the block to the CRP. It's a big sturdy brick building. It used to be a school. It still looks like a school from the outside. Except they made the front steps into a ramp. Over the entrance is a big arch. I stopped under it. I do every time I come. I have to adjust my thinking.

People in the CRP are handicapped. Or disabled. Or challenged. I'm crippled. The car on the shoulder, that's disabled. Golfers are handicapped. Guys with swords are challenged. I never saw a cripple get up out of his wheelchair when somebody told him he's only handicapped.

I can say I'm a cripple because I'm a cripple. Fat Leon has to call me handicapped. But he probably wouldn't say anything. He'd pretend he didn't see anything unusual. Most people would pretend they didn't see me at all.

I felt like fat Leon in the CRP. I didn't want to offend anybody. Even though their words make me feel funny.

The world is divided into two parts – the crippled

68

and the uncrippled. That's the way it is. I don't hate people for having legs. I don't hate moonmen for being green. They come from a different world than me. That's all.

Crippled. The word describes people with a real big problem. Like mine. The word doesn't make things any easier. Or make us brothers. That's the problem I have with those other words. Handicapped. Disabled. Challenged. They're soft. They're designed to make us forget what we really are. To help other people forget how bad off we are.

But that's how people talk in the CRP. Which is why I had to adjust before I went in.

I wheeled down the hall toward the office. There were railings and ramps everywhere. The light was bright. The halls were gleaming.

The secretary had white hair and a white sweater. She smiled at me. She didn't run and hide. That was a nice thing about being here.

'I want to see Mr Shoreham,' I said.

'Mr Sanford Shoreham? I'm sorry, he's not here. He was in Monday, and he never comes in more than once a week.'

'Isn't he the accountant?'

'He is our accountant.' She spoke very clearly. She wanted me to get this the first time. 'But we are only one of his clients. He has many. He is a very busy man.'

'Doesn't he have an office here?'

She shook her head and smiled. 'Oh, no, there's no need for that.'

Why did I think he'd be sitting here? An old blackboard behind his desk. This whole big deal trip for nothing. Now I started feeling how wet I was.

I said, 'Can I leave a message for him?'

'Of course.' She slid her bifocals down her nose. 'And you are?'

I told her. She said she'd leave a note. If he called she'd tell him.

I went back into the hall. People came wheeling past. Others used crutches. One guy pulled himself along the railing. He was in a cart. Nobody even looked at me. One good thing about cripples. They don't gawk.

Inside the main hall was a big sculpture of Atlas. World on his shoulders. Atlas was the symbol of the CRP. We had the world on our shoulders. I noticed that Atlas had all his parts.

There was a big bulletin board. Lots of notices for the arts and crafts fair next month. Usually I had a few tigers showing. I didn't have anything in this show. Sidney was keeping me busy.

There were sign-up sheets for the Olympian Games. One sheet for each event. A lot of people were entering this year, from all over the county. I felt mixed about the games. It's good that cripples get out there and compete. Get dirty without somebody picking us right up. It's good to lose. It's better to win. Either way, a dose of real life.

I liked winning the 1,000 meters last year. The wind blowing across the field. The crunch of gravel under my wheels. Breaking the tape.

There were always a lot of normal people in the stands during the games. Some were relatives of the cripples. But what about the rest. Did they come to laugh at us? Did we make them feel lucky?

The games were a spectacle to these people because we are cripples and retards. Not because we're good athletes. I didn't want to be a part of the spectacle. That's why I decided I wasn't going to be in them any more.

I heard the clang of iron. Speaking of spectacles. The weight room.

I wheeled down the hall, just to see who was there.

'Yo, Hit-and-run!' It was Pepper.

Two guys were always working out. One was white, one was black. Spinal cord injuries. They both had legs, but they were no good. Just melted away, like drumsticks in chicken soup. Sometimes I wondered why they

70

didn't get them snipped. Like me. But I never asked. Above the waist these guys looked like Superheroes.

We called them the Shakers. Salt and Pepper. Thick bodies. No necks. Shaved heads. They looked like shakers.

Salt was on the bench. Pressing a bar holding wheels off a locomotive.

Pepper came up to me. 'Hit-and-run! Ain't seen you in months.' I was Hit-and-run. He gave me a high five. I didn't mind it from him.

'Yeah, I thought I'd slum for a day.'

Salt dropped his bar. The floor shook. He said, 'Pick up some iron. Man, you look scrawny. What the hell you been doing.'

I snorted. 'What size you guys wearing now. Fifty-two humungous?' And pants thirty-two pipecleaner.

'Pepper seen your old lady last week,' said Salt.

Pepper said, 'That's right. Lucy. She lost some weight. Looks real tight.' He smiled.

'Where was that?'

'A party. Some fancy man's house. Never sat down the whole time. Ants in her pants.'

'You ask her out?' said Salt. He laughed. 'You black dog.'

'Never chase my friends' skirts. Though I gotta say. She look like she could be handy with the handi-capped.'

What was she doing partying? I thought she was so busy.

I didn't want her around these guys. They scored women faster than I ever did, even back at the club. I've seen them do it. They're all muscle. Extremely powerful. But withered, strapped in wheelchairs. Extremely vulnerable. Women eat up that combi-nation. The women didn't know that next day their vulnerable guy would tell everybody in the state what flavor their pussy was. And then drop them and go after a new one.

Another guy came out of the back. He was holding two dumbbells. 'Genghis Khan,' I said. 'Good to see you.' He smiled at me. He blinked a lot. He blew a little bubble of saliva. Genghis Khan was one of the Mongoloids. They didn't like to be called Down's. Too depressing.

He was tiny, standing next to the Shakers. But he was tough. He was the reigning champion of the javelin. He could really throw it.

'You defending?' said Pepper. He chalked his hands and picked up the bar. It shook like licorice. His biceps looked like they were going to pop.

'I retired,' I said. 'Undefeated.'

'Shit. Afraid somebody gonna make the turn with you?' He was talking about last year's race. It was just me and Loid. As in Mongo-Loid. Everybody else had the flu. That's why they asked me to race. Loid wasn't too good with the wheelchair. At the first turn he kept going straight, right off the track. He turned over in the long-jump pit, in the sand.

I said, 'I had him all the way. No problem.'

Genghis shook his head. He looked a lot like Loid. Maybe they were related.

'I'm telling you. I had him.'

'Listen to this shit,' Salt said. He pulled himself over to the stationary bicycle. It was adapted for the CRP. He rested his chest on the support. He grabbed the pedals with his hands. This is an endurance exercise. It doesn't build bulk. Guys like the Shakers usually make fun of you when you bike.

'What are you doing?' I said. 'That's a faggot exercise.'

'Not this year.'

'What exercises are the faggots doing this year?' I said.

Pepper dropped his bar. I kept expecting the floor to give. 'Big field in the 1,000 meters this year, Hit-and-run. Including me and the Salty dog.'

Genghis Khan nodded.

'And the Chinaman.'

This was ridiculous. Balloon arms are no good in a road race. No endurance. These guys wouldn't make it 100 yards. As for Genghis, the javelin is a straight event. No turns.

'In my honor?' I said.

'Got nothing to do with you,' said Pepper. 'We're rolling for the dough.'

The dough. The bread? The Remarkable Picnic?

Salt was already sucking for air on the hand bicycle. 'Didn't you hear about the prize?' Pepper said.

'Money!' said Genghis. He spoke in a loud whisper.

'There's prize money this year,' said Pepper.

'In the Olympian Games?' I said. 'Come on!' Prize money in cripple games?

'Ask Pineapple if you don't believe me.'

'How much?' I said.

'A grand. Just for the 1,000 meters. The prestige event. "Fastest man on wheels".'

Salt quit the bike. He was puffing hard. 'If it goes OK there's gonna be money for more events next year.'

'What about the shot put?' I said. 'You guys entering?' They came in second and third last year. Somebody even huger came out of the sticks to take the gold. I thought they'd be hungry to try again.

'If the put is after the race, sure,' said Pepper. 'If the put is first, we gotta skip it. Can't get tired before the main event.'

'Is Pineapple around?' The chairman of the Olympian Games committee.

'He was here before,' said Pepper. 'Check the pool.' The Farnsworth pool. The happiest part of the CRP. Even if you're not worth much on land, you can still get something going in the water.

There are three pools. One is shallow all the way across. For guys who can't get up if they tip over. Most of them are missing legs. Attendants always watch.

They put me in a pool like that in the hospital. I felt like I was marinating. I wanted to take my chances in the deep pool. They wouldn't let me.

There's a regular pool. They can put extra floats and bars into it. It depends who's in it. And there's a diving pool. It's smaller. It's got a slow escalator at the back of the diving board. You can sit down on the thing. They might as well take the ladder out. Nobody uses it any more.

Pineapple was in the middle pool. The floats were out of the pool. The nets were set up at the ends. The guys were playing water polo.

Everybody in the pool was missing something. The best players were missing an arm or part of an arm. They could swim a one-armed crawl. When they got the ball they had to stop and pass or shoot. The guys missing a leg couldn't move much. They had to work to keep above water. And hope somebody would pass the ball to them.

Duck Hunter was one of the goalies. He has one leg. He was sitting in an inner tube. He couldn't leap like the other goalie. Instead he was holding a plastic leg. It might have been his own. I couldn't tell. He used it to knock down shots. Everybody thought that was fair.

Pineapple got his name from a hand grenade. He wore a hook. He wouldn't take it off, not even when he went in the water. He said without it he felt naked.

During a game he'd keep forgetting about the hook. He'd go to catch the ball and the hook would puncture it. A lot of games ended that way. Guys got pissed off. Now he wrapped the hook in foam rubber.

I didn't want to take him away from the game. I watched the diving for a while. You have to have at least one leg to go diving. They don't want people going straight to the bottom and staying there. Some guys try to dive the way they used to, with good form. Everything pointed. There was one symmetrical guy there. Gear. He lost both forearms. He was the only one

74

who went into the water straight. But his elbows didn't open the water for him. You always heard his head hit.

The guys with two legs ran down the board OK. But once they jumped they rolled toward their longer arm. When they hit the water the sound was different. It wasn't a splash. It was more like a smoosh. Unless they landed on their bellies. That sounded like cannon fire.

Most of the guys with one leg hopped to the end of the board and stopped. Then they pushed off. Simple dives. One guy, Roo, came flying down the board with tremendous hops. He could turn over in the air three times. And it was a low board. They couldn't do that in the regular Olympics. He had less leg weight. He could turn faster.

Guys were falling into the water practically on top of each other. Pulling themselves up, rolling out of the water. Flapping their stumps. Hopping to the escalator. Grinning like mad dogs as they rode up to the board. I would never do it. I look like some of them underneath. But I keep my clothes on in public. Why should anyone have to watch me.

But what the hell. The guys were laughing. Having fun. Living their lives, what was left of them. If they couldn't let their hair down here, where could they? These guys were OK.

I looked back to the water polo game. The players were getting tired. Pineapple took the ball and passed it. His teammate wasn't looking. The ball bounced off his head and went into his own net. The game was over.

The guys came toward the ladders in the pool. I could see just their heads gliding above the water. Nothing else. I never knew what I was going to see when they got out.

Pineapple was happy. The way he figured it he got the game-winner. I talked to him while he dried off. I said, 'How's it coming for the games.'

'I don't know, Hit-and-run. I went to a statewide

meeting last week. We're trying to figure out how to make the races fair. One proposal is to count fractions. You can enter a certain class if you have a certain total of arms and legs. Class three means all people missing one limb, or two half-limbs, are in that group. You have races for two limbs, two and a half, three, and three and a half.'

'What about the guys with two and three quarters?'

'Another proposal was to lump together all the arm injuries in one group and the leg injuries in the other. A separate group for people with both. In a way that's better.'

'How can the people with legs race against people without legs?' I said.

'In swimming. I'm talking about swimming. We're trying to add it to the Olympian Games, but we're not going to make it this year. Imagine trying to make the rules for synchronized swimming.'

I said, 'I heard a rumor about the roadraces. About prize money. Did you hear that?'

He stripped off his foam rubber. He got an extra towel to dry off his hook. He was very careful with it. 'It's true. We figured the best way to encourage participation in the games is prize money.'

'You know how hard it is for people to go out there. Money's going to make them more competitive. Make it even worse.'

'If it bothers you, don't race,' he said. 'The other guys love the idea.'

Why was this bothering me? What did I care if some cripple took home a few bucks? I should have been all for it. I felt it pulling me back to the games. That was the problem. It wasn't greed. It wasn't exactly pride. Whatever it was, I didn't want to go.

I said, 'Do you think that's the message the CRP should be giving cripples in the county?'

He looked at me. 'There are no cripples here.'

'Handicapped. You want them trying to beat each

other out for money? You're going to turn the games into a circus. They're going to send news cameras to cover them. You'll see.'

'Look, Hit-and-run. It's not my decision. The board decided. But I like the idea. In this world the winners take the money. That's how it should be for us too.'

In the cripple world the losers get the money. The worse off they are the more they get. Leroy Farnsworth drank a gallon of beer and tried to swim Coon Lake. During a November, wearing a football helmet. A hazing rite. He didn't make it. Who did his mother donate two million dollars to? The college? Alcoholics Anonymous? The football team? No. To the CRP. For the Leroy Farnsworth Memorial pool. And escalator.

She thought he was disabled. He stuttered. She wanted the rest of us to have a better chance.

'Whose bright idea was this?' I said.

'I don't know. Mr Shoreham dug up the money.'

'Not his own money.'

'I don't know. I don't care whose money it is, as long as the guys get a shot at it.'

Eight

When I got home my arms were aching. It wasn't really a hard day. There was no way I could race 1,000 meters in this shape. Even if I wanted to.

I wheeled into my apartment. I took off my hat and coat. They still weren't dry. I was starting to chafe. I had to get everything off.

'Marty!' The voice scared me half to death. I had one leg unstrapped. I threw it straight up. It hit the ceiling and fell into my lap. 'I didn't mean to frighten you.' It was Esther. She was sitting in Hell on Wheels. In the dark.

I waited for that icy feeling to pass. I didn't want to act scared. I said, 'Why don't you sit on the sofa. Make yourself comfortable.' Just get the hell out of my chair.

'Why do you keep this thing?' she said.

'What do you think I should do with it?'

'I don't know. Trade it in on a new model, or maybe just throw it out.'

She got up. The axle grated against the cinder blocks. I hate that sound. She moved to the sofa. I put my leg back on. I was more comfortable with her that way.

'So what are you doing here?' I said.

'I was in the neighborhood.'

'Where's Jerold?'

'With his nanny.'

'His nanny? If he's got a nanny, what do you do all day?' I was disappointed the little guy wasn't here.

'I visit you, for one thing.'

I wheeled across the room and faced her. 'So, here you are visiting me again.'

'Where did you go? I've been here for a while.'

'The CRP.'

'Did you see Sanford?'

'No. But I was looking for him.'

'Why?'

'I need more supplies. Did you tell him you came to see me?'

'Of course,' she said. 'He's my husband. I don't hide things from him.' This woman didn't make any sense to me. She said, 'You and I were finished three years ago. Enough time has passed so we can be friends. Don't you think?'

I was going to have to start locking my front door from now on.

Her face turned dark. 'All right. I shouldn't have said anything to him. He was jealous and he had every right to be. When I saw you that day on the street I swear I felt as if nothing had happened. Well, of course things have happened. But you know what I mean.'

I shrugged.

She said, 'You're making this hard for me and I suppose it's your right. I'm going to tell you now. When I saw you I realized that some of my feelings haven't faded. We didn't have an end, a parting scene to cut things off.'

'If I'd raised my head from the operating table and told you to fuck yourself, would you feel any different now? I can still do it.'

'You're angry with me.' She squatted beside the wheelchair and put her arm around my shoulder. I didn't trust her words. She always was good with them. They were just sounds. Anybody could say them.

But her smell. Nobody could fake that. It rose up all around me. I was wondering why she was squatting. Now I knew. Smelling Esther was like seeing the red Camaro. It felt great here and now. And it took me back.

Esther used to be the female center of my life. Not that I let her monopolize me or anything. But she had a hold on me. I turned down a lot of courtside invitations to be with her. She was the first one I did that for.

It was strange. There wasn't anything that special about her. I never noticed this before. I was too much in her spell. Medium height, medium build, medium brown hair of medium length, adequate tits and ass. Pretty. But nothing spectacular. She was normal looking.

She wasn't funny. Not real entertaining.

She studied to be an attorney. She became a nanny overseer. Doesn't make much of a story.

But her smell. It changed me. It was like nothing else mattered.

'Wouldn't you think I was a headcase if I wasn't angry?' I said.

'No. You have to leave your anger behind. It doesn't do you any good.'

'Don't give me that Dr Goodvibes shit. When they hacked off my legs you got married before the anesthesia wore off. I don't even know why I let you in this apartment.' I shook her arm loose. My stumps were beginning to itch in the loose legs. I couldn't take them off until she left.

'I did a bad thing,' she said, nudging her forehead into my shoulder. 'I'm sorry. What more can I say?'

A hell of a lot more than that. I didn't push her head away. I didn't want to give her that satisfaction.

Her life was all set up. Dull, yes, but all set up. What was she doing here? Confessing. Bowing her head. Offering me the back of her neck. Like I was an executioner. It was up to me to make everything right, one way or the other. That was like old times.

I could smell her sweat rising from her neck. That's why she was staying like that. Her sweat didn't say anything to me about her feelings. Or what she was really doing here.

She was sweating when I first met her. On the tennis court. I'll never forget it. There was a light breeze that day blowing from her side to mine. I smelled her every time she charged the net. I got up to the net a fair bit myself that day.

We spent a lot of time around the club. She played and drank and chatted with the rich people. I taught. Afterwards we sat in the café. She loved to watch the other people. She had a thing about physical beauty. I mean, I do too. A lot of people do. But she had it bad. She didn't have a girlfriend who didn't turn heads. Mine included. It was a test for me.

Esther divided the world into the worthy and the worthless. The beautiful and the less than beautiful. She was a natural snob. She acted like she was one of the beautiful. And got away with it most of the time. Even though she wasn't.

Knowing her standards, I should have been flattered that she picked me. I never thought of this before. I was in demand then. I didn't have to think. I never asked her what gave her the right to judge.

She showed up at the hospital the night of the accident. Lucy called her. Maybe she saw me. Maybe she didn't. It didn't matter. She found out that her beauty was going to spend the rest of his life on drumsticks. I became one of the unbeautiful. One of the worthless. And she left. I couldn't expect anything different. That's the way she was. She never tried to hide it.

I caught myself. This is the danger in smelling women. They make you want to see it their way. Make excuses for them. Just to keep smelling them.

She could have done better. She could have stayed with me. Taken care of me. We were in love. What she did was despicable.

Now I knew she could have stayed with me. She proved she could be with somebody less than beautiful. A lot less. She married Sanford Shoreham.

81

I wheeled away from her. 'What do you want from me?' I said.

She came after me and kissed me. Her taste was like her smell. Mainlined. I felt her all the way to my toes. My phantom toes. More memories flipped through my mind. The sight of her in sweaty panties. Waking at noon. Champagne hangover.

And this one. Lying on my back in the hospital. Wrapped in seeping bandage. Day after day. Where was she? What could be keeping her away? No-one said anything to me. There were probably too embarrassed. I was sure she was in an accident. Maybe the same one I was in. I couldn't remember. She was laid up somewhere. Maybe in this same hospital. Unable to visit or call on a phone. I worried about her. I called the hospital directory. I called the police. It never occurred to me to call her at home. I was a chump.

One day my friend Esme saw Esther shopping for clothes. The new spring lines were out. I swore I would never let her near me again. She made it easy. Until now.

When Esther split Lucy showed up. She wanted to take care of me. She used to be my lover, on the side. She understood that. She was my friend too. Lucy owed me nothing. Yet there she was in the hospital. Listening to me carrying on. Making me see reason. Making me want to keep living. Patient. Gentle.

Lucky for me I got mashed during a good phase for her.

'To be close to you. Somehow. I don't know,' Esther said sadly.

I wasn't buying.

'I really loved you, Marty, my dark beauty. I phantasized about ending up with you all the time. How exciting our lives were going to be. How passionate. Touring the world. Being beautiful together. To you I'm just a cruel woman who turned my back on you when you were hurt.'

'Crippled,' I said.

'There haven't been many days when I haven't put myself through the situation all over again.'

'Then you must be a very unhappy woman.'

'Maybe I am. When I saw you in the hospital I fell apart. I didn't know what to do. I didn't know how I could respond to you any more. Consciously I felt exactly the same. I still loved you. I think maybe I still do. But underneath I didn't know if I could handle it. I had to choose right away. I felt so lonely.

'You don't believe me. But you aren't comfortable with your new body, not after living in it for three years. How could you expect me to do any better?'

I hated her for saying this. The way she twisted things.

She said, 'Sanford proposed to me five years ago.'

'Five years ago?'

'That's right. I put him off to stay with you. Even though every time I tried to talk about marriage you stuck your head in the sand.

'That was your right. But I told you all along that I wanted a family. That was my right. I figured that what tiny interest you had in marriage died in your accident. That's why I got married. I didn't have to wait around another two years to hear you say it.'

'I had a good time with Jerold the other day.'

'For a few hours,' she said. 'When they're with you twenty-four hours a day it's a different story.'

'Is that what the nanny tells you?'

'It was time to be with people who share our ambitions for life.'

I never thought about this. She was thinking about it for three years. I was afraid she was putting something over on me.

She didn't answer one thing. One big thing. I said, 'Why didn't you come by and explain this to me? I deserved an explanation.'

She looked into my eyes and pushed her fingers

83

through my hair. 'Don't ask. I wish I had.'

'I'm asking.'

She walked to the kitchen and had a drink of water. She came back. 'I've explained as best I can.'

'It's not good enough.'

'All right. I wanted to come see you, but I couldn't.'

'Sanford wouldn't let you?'

'I never let Sanford get in my way. It was Lucy.' Phantoms struck my right leg. 'I'm not blaming her,' she said. 'I let her scare me off. It was a failure of nerve on my part.'

'Let's keep this real,' I said. 'Lucy took care of me when you split.'

'No, no. Lucy took care of you after she told me to get lost.'

I couldn't believe this.

'When I talked to her that night she said it was the last time I was going to see you. I had no idea what she was talking about. I thought it might be a joke. I figured when I saw you we'd straighten it out.'

'Then why didn't you?'

She sat down on the sofa. She was facing me across the room. 'There were two things. I wanted a family and you didn't. And she intimidated me. You know that psycho voice she gets? You don't want to be around her.

'Think about it, Marty. She brings you to the hospital and says she just happened to find you on the side of the road.'

'What do you mean by that?'

'I'm not sure. She saves your life and she takes you away from me, which is what she always wanted.'

'She cares for a cripple. You would never do that. You just said so.'

'I know you were seeing her when you were with me. You're blushing. At least you have a trace of conscience. Why didn't she try to take you then?'

'She didn't need me full-time. She didn't need that security.'

Esther puffed. 'I thought you understood women better than that. You wouldn't leave me for her. That's why. But now that you're in this state she could get you.'

My leg was going crazy. Almost like it had a life of its own. 'You're not saying she had anything to do with this.'

'No. But once it happened . . . You can understand how she scared me off.' Well, no, I couldn't. But I wasn't understanding anything right now. I couldn't hold the thoughts in my mind.

Esther came over and put her hand on my cheek. Even her hand smelled good. 'But look, I'm grateful that she's taking care of you. You're in good hands and that makes me feel better.' She grabbed a rope and lowered herself on to the desk. Her mood was suddenly different. She said, 'Did they ever find the man, or woman, who hit you?'

'They'll never catch him. No clues. It rained that night. The tracks washed out.'

'Isn't that unusual after a collision?'

'No clues? I guess.'

'Didn't Lucy remember anything?'

'She didn't see anything. It was dark.'

'Let me ask you a question. Think about this for a second. Would you want them to find him or her?'

'Of course,' I said, without thinking.

'And deal with facing him or her? Reliving the moment, maybe going to trial, all that stuff?'

I never thought about the actual accident. I had no memories of it. No dreams, either. Maybe she was right. Digging it up would cause a lot of grief. But how could I not do it if I got a chance. I swore to myself a hundred times that I wouldn't die until I knew exactly what happened. That was when I was in the hospital. After two or three months I pretty much gave it up.

I said, 'What do you do, sit around home thinking about things like this?'

'There's another thing I wonder. What would you do if they caught him or her? If you could do anything you want.'

'Why do you keep saying "him or her"?'

'You keep saying "him". I don't want to be sexist.' Her eyes were sparkling. Thinking about this excited her. She was cruel. I shouldn't have been surprised she split on me.

A test. I said, 'All I need is an apology. I know it was an accident. There's no undoing it.'

She jumped right off the desk. 'That's ridiculous.' A minute ago she was telling me I didn't want to know who did it.

'An eye for an eye,' I said. 'Two legs for two legs. I'd glue him into his car and drive down on him. Maybe I'd hit the brakes at the last second and go back and do it again. Just to play with his head. Then I'd hit him square and goosh him all over the road. But I'd hate to wreck another beautiful car. Maybe I'd just clamp him down over there on my work bench. Use the circular saw. Zip, zoff. What do you think?'

She squatted with me again. Her smell was stronger now. She shrugged her shoulders. But she was smiling. She said, 'I could put some brown recluse spiders on her legs and get them real mad. After they bite, the flesh rots and falls off. It's slow. It takes weeks.'

She looked at me. My turn. 'I'd take him to the Amazon and paint his legs with honey. Then stake him in the path of army ants.'

Esther put her arm around my shoulders. 'You could pack explosives around her legs and blow them up.'

'Yes, I guess you could.'

'Or lower her into a vat of acid.'

'Uh huh.'

She wrapped her arms around my neck and kissed me. She nearly pushed my teeth out with her tongue.

'We had something special, Marty. We still do.' She went for my neck. 'You taste the same. Salty, like an athlete.'

The 1,000-meter champion.

I felt her teeth. I knew this trick. I said, 'Don't mark me.'

'That's not what I'm doing. I'm not an adolescent. Anyway she wouldn't notice. She's probably lost in lithium land.'

'Just don't mark me. It's not your neck any more.'

'Don't you want me?'

Didn't I want her? I always wanted her. Since that first whiff came over the net. It was like I was fated to be with her. But it was three years now. I still didn't know what she was doing here.

'I don't trust you,' I said.

'What can I do?'

A few years ago I could have thought of a few dirty deeds. Not that they had anything to do with trust. Now I didn't have an answer. I didn't know if anything would make a difference. I was so confused.

She was waiting for an answer. The phone rang. Saved. I wheeled over and picked it up. Esther came with me. Her hands were all over me. She had a nice touch. I didn't fight her.

'Hello.'

'Shoreham here. You called?'

'Sanford.' Esther looked up at me. She smiled and went for my belt. 'I need more supplies. Wood and clay.'

'What happened to the supplies we purchased?'

I told him I was going to make a larger tiger.

He said, 'We commissioned one work, not a statuary.'

'It is for one work. The other one was no good. You wouldn't have been happy. Trust me on this.'

Esther had her hands inside my shorts. My voice was getting higher.

'We expect you to be fiscally responsible with this project.'

Both of them had attitudes. Him and his wife. The money was mine. The cock was mine. They had no business messing with me.

I said, 'Just send me the supplies. What the fuck do you know about art, you numbers cruncher. No. Why don't you tell me who the patron is. I'll call him myself. I'll wheel out to his mansion and tell him I can't work because some asshole accountant wouldn't buy me some two by fours and a few buckets of clay.'

Sanford didn't say anything for a minute. I pointed to the phone. Did she want to say hello? After all, she told him everything.

She tore my pants down.

Sanford said, 'First I have to see what you're up to.'

'Come on over.'

I hung up. Esther's eyes were sparkling, like we were sixteen and her parents just called to say they were going to be late.

We didn't have much time. Her hands closed over my stumps. Maybe there was something she could do to win my trust after all.

Suddenly she pulled her hands away. 'I've got to go,' she said.

'He won't be here for at least a half-hour.'

Her face was all tight. 'I'm sorry, Marty, but I have to go.'

I grabbed her wrist. She pulled away. She walked quickly out the door. Her hands were out to the side, like she was letting them dry.

I yelled, 'Where the fuck . . .'

Suddenly the tiger rose under the sheet. Sidney, the spurned tiger. He came straight at me. My heart punched against my chest.

I pushed myself up. I was going to run for it. For the first time in three years I forgot I didn't have legs. I crashed to the floor. I hugged it. I was too terrified to look up.

I heard the cloth flutter. The tiger didn't strike. Soon everything was still. I peeked up. The sheet was hanging limp again. Nothing moved. It was the wind from when Esther opened the door.

I looked at myself. Sprawled flat. Muscles flexed so I could scuttle across the floor, away from a clay animal. Pants twisted around my pomegranate stumps. Stuffed fatigues dragging behind.

I put my head back on the floor and cried.

Nine

The door burst open. I was still on the floor. I felt a rush of rage. Cripple rage. I never wanted that accountant to see me like this.

It wasn't him. It was Esther. 'I can't start the car.' She was scared. 'It's right out front.'

'It's dark. He won't see it.'

'It's his car, the Jaguar. He'll see it. He sees every Jaguar.'

'I thought you told him everything.'

'Please.'

I looked at Sidney, my tiger. I had an idea. 'Take the sheet. Throw it over the car, or at least over the front. Over that little statue. That's as good as hiding the whole car. Hang out in the drug store. I'll get rid of him quick. Then you can call for help.'

She shrieked and ran out the door. She didn't say anything about me being face-down on the floor. She didn't offer to help.

A couple of minutes later the door opened again. I was climbing into my chair. 'You want the sheet?'

'I almost just needed one,' said Sanford. 'For a shroud. Some maniac came down your street doing fifty easy and nearly drove me into the corner store.' He was wearing an expensive Italian suit. Italian shoes. He was tan. Every hair in place. He tried so damn hard.

He put his initialed leather briefcase on the desk. He took hold of one of the ropes. 'It's been a long time,' he said, looking to the ceiling. Not since he saw me. Since he went up a rope.

He got up to the top without much trouble. He was

90

in pretty good shape. Probably spent a lot of time at the health club.

He came down. He straightened his suit and hair. He clapped his hands. 'Let's see this masterpiece.'

'What masterpiece?'

'The tiger sculpture.'

'I told you on the phone. I need more supplies.'

'We supplied you with wood and clay and I'd like to see what you've done. That's my job.'

'If you want to see the sculpture I'm not using, it's right there. It's going to be a coyote. Or maybe a big jungle rat, or something.'

'We didn't commission a coyote.'

'I'm not going to give it to you.'

'Why are you using our supplies for someone else's coyote?'

'I'm not making a coyote. I don't do coyotes. Someone else might make that thing into a coyote. If no-one does, I'll throw it out. Understand?'

Sanford pulled the sheet away. Sidney looked completely dead to me. Like he never really existed. What was I thinking when I started him.

'What's wrong with this?' he said. 'It looks like a tiger. A little more here, a little work around here. You can do it.'

'Put the sheet back. Stop giving me gas.'

He pulled a small pad from his breast pocket and scribbled. 'I'll try to consult the patron.'

'You'll try?'

'I only have a post-office box. He's chosen to remain anonymous.'

'Great. Forget it. I'll buy the stuff myself. Nice of you to come.'

His neck grew longer, like a big bird's. 'I have to talk to you.'

'Make an appointment. This meeting's over.'

'Esther says she's been to see you.' So she really did tell him.

'Jerold too,' I said.

'Jerold too?' Now he started looking around. 'Well, of course I remember that you used to be an item.'

'Of course.' Now I knew I held up his marriage proposal for two years. I wish I'd known earlier. I would have tried harder to stay with her. Getting in his way might be very satisfying.

'Between us . . . as men . . .' He was choking. The only thing he wanted to say was the only thing he couldn't say: keep your hands off my woman. I would refuse, just on principle. What could he do? Beat me up? Sometimes it's handy being a cripple.

'Yes?' I said. 'Between us?'

'Between us . . .' His lips firmed. He looked me in the eyes. 'Between us, be kind to her.'

I wanted to laugh. But I was a bonded male. Trained not to laugh in locker rooms all over the state. 'I will,' I said.

He walked to the door. Then he turned back. 'Go ahead and order the materials. I'll pay.'

I almost forgot. 'Thanks. Listen, I heard something about prize money for the 1,000 meters this year.'

'A thousand dollars. A dollar a meter.'

'Your idea?'

'My money.'

'What are you doing? These people struggle to live from day to day. And now you're going to have them stomping each other to get your money.'

'Nonsense. It will encourage participation. It will bring out the unfortunate people who can't otherwise make up their mind.'

'That's bullshit. What are you up to? A tax write-off?'

'I believe it's a good idea. In fact, I'm entering the race myself.'

'In a wheelchair?'

'I just bought one.'

I got it. He heard Esther saw me. Now he was calling

me out. He thought we could settle the matter of her hand on the oval field.

Why did he think I'd go for it? I had mine and I was closing in on his. As far as he knew. I had nothing to gain.

It had to be the money. He thought I'd race for a grand. He probably thought I still had markers out. I didn't. My gambling debts were paid. I paid them with my Social Security. I lied about the toilet paper.

Sanford was lucky. I wasn't sure I wanted his woman back. Though I wasn't sure I didn't.

I said, 'The guys at the CRP are going to love seeing you in a wheelchair. Making fun of them. You know, the road racers are big guys.'

'I appreciate your concern. But I told them I wanted to enter and one of them came up with the idea of a $1,000 legs handicap. They know I can't possibly win.'

That was for sure. Short of another flu epidemic.

I said, 'The poor bastards. They need the money. Offer them a shot at $10,000 and they'll let you enter in a motorcycle.'

'You should race,' he said. 'It would be good for you to get out. It's awfully musty in here.'

I started sketching Brute, my new tiger. He was going to be crouched, low to the ground. Showing fangs. Ready to pounce any second. And big. Life size. You wouldn't let your kid pet Brute. You wouldn't let your kid anywhere near Brute unless you had a gun.

The wood and clay showed up the next afternoon. It took two guys about ten minutes to pile it all up in the apartment. One of the guys handed me the receipt. While I signed, he checked me out. He looked around. The ropes and everything. Not your usual delivery. He took the clipboard back. He was still looking.

'Anything else?' I said.

'You know something, mister.'

'What's that?' What could he say?

'You got a lot of clay here.'

He couldn't see it. This was a tiger just waiting to happen.

I started cutting up the wood. Brute's pieces were longer and thicker than Sidney's. This armature was going to be holding up a lot of clay.

I laid the pieces out. I started driving the nails. I used big ones to hold this monster together. There were quick echoes in my apartment.

Driving. That name kept going through my mind as I swung my hammer. Harlan Karlin. Harlan Karlin.

It took me a day to put Brute together. I stood him upright and nailed him into a base. I leaned against him as hard as half a man can lean. Every joint was solid.

Even after I stopped driving nails, the name stayed in my mind. Harlan Karlin.

I didn't think there was a Harlan Karlin. Leon made him up. I opened the phone book. I was wrong. There were three Karlins in town. Two of them were named Harlan. Now I had to call.

I dialed Harlan A. Karlin. A woman answered. I asked if he was there. She said no.

I said, 'You know where I can find him?'

'That's what I was going to ask you.'

'Did he used to have a red car? A Camaro?'

'You're looking for Harlan T. Karlin. He's got a job.'

I called Harlan T. I said, 'I saw your Camaro at the lot. I used to have one just like it.'

'I was sorry to see that baby go. But I had kids to put through school and she drank too much gas.'

'You kept it in great shape.'

'Nah. I just changed the oil.'

'Where did you get it? If you don't mind me asking.'

'No, not at all. A man loves a car he's gotta know these things. I saw an ad in the paper. It was a woman. She wanted cash. That's all I remember.'

I described Lucy. He thought it might have been her.

I said, 'When she laughed, did it look like her eyeballs were going to pop out of her head?'

It was her.

I said, 'Yeah, that was mine all right.' What a mess it must have been when he got it. 'Was it worth doing all that bodywork? It must have cost you a couple of grand easy.'

'I told you. I didn't do no body work. All I had to do was drain the gas tank. Other than that she was in mint condition.'

Ten

By the next afternoon I'd finished Brute's back legs. I didn't plan to start there. It just worked out that way. Now we had one pair between us.

I kept thinking about the feel the bronze would have at the end. I was worried about getting the texture of the clay just right. I did some experimenting. Now it felt good. I had it.

I stopped when I got to the balls. Or where the balls were supposed to go. This was a big cat. Big cats have big balls. Brute should have really big balls. I didn't want to scare anybody off. I didn't want my patron's wife telling him to stick the sculpture in the basement. I didn't want Sanford coming in here and dying of envy.

The door opened. It was Lucy. She kissed me and sat down on the sofa.

'Welcome, stranger,' I said.

She nodded. Two months ago she would have been all over Brute. Asking how the little tiger gave birth to the big tiger. Saying half a tiger's better than none. Or something goofy like that. She would have been dancing around me.

Tonight she was calm. Quiet. She had her hair pulled back in a pony tail. She looked tired. She was feeling it after not sleeping much for a couple of months.

'Something's different about that sculpture,' she said.

'It's new.'

'No, something else.'

'It's new. See? There's Sidney, the old one.'

She walked over and lifted his sheet. It looked like a

scene from a morgue. 'This one looks different too.'

She shrugged. A little smile. She fell into the chair. Right away she sprang up and yelped. She made me jump. It's a good thing Brute didn't have balls yet. I would have cut them off.

She grabbed her behind. She turned around and looked at the chair. Then she picked something up. 'What is this?'

It was my trophy. It used to be a tennis trophy. One of my buddies knocked it off the mantel in my old place and it broke in half. I kept the bottom, a big fancy base and a pair of legs up to the knees. I don't know what happened to the top. I remember thinking it was real funny. A legs trophy.

That was five years ago easy. I was glad I kept it. This was the perfect place for it.

I said, 'The supply guys cleaned out that corner. I was looking at it.'

She looked at the trophy. Lucy in gear would have told me to try it on. But she didn't say anything. She put it on the table.

'How're you feeling?' I said.

'Fine. Why?'

'You look a little tired.'

'I was looking at locations on the coast for a couple of days.'

'Tell me about it.'

'What's to tell. I came, I saw, I canceled.' She left it at that.

I smoothed Brute's flanks a little. She was quiet. I would get used to her like this again. It would take a little time.

'I gave up on Sidney,' I said. 'He just didn't look alive any more.'

'That's nice.'

'This is Brute. He's life-size. I had to fight with Sanford to get the supplies. I think this is a better pose for a tiger. Don't you?'

97

'It's a good pose.'

'I thought you liked the other one.'

'That one was fine, too.'

'Did you have dinner?' I said.

'I'm on a diet.' She gained a couple of pounds. She did this every time. It came with the mood.

'You have to eat something.'

'I'll make something for you. I'll have bites.'

She walked into the kitchen. I saw a little extra flesh on her butt. I thought she looked good. Juicier. Two weeks ago I could have told her. Two weeks ago she didn't have the padding. Too bad the way that worked out.

She came right back holding a glass of water. One yellow rose was sticking out. Really a dry brown rose with yellow highlights. I forgot to throw it out.

'What's this?'

'A flower.'

'Who gave it to you?'

I couldn't tell her Esther sent it. Wait. Why not? I had nothing to hide. It was my life. 'I bought it for you,' I said.

'Like this? I hope it was on sale.'

'I got it early in the week. That's when I thought you were coming.' A good answer.

Lucy didn't go for it. 'She doesn't come here unless she's getting something. What is she getting?'

I pulled a sheet over Brute. I had to answer. I couldn't let this hang in the air. The phantoms started creeping around my leg.

I said, 'She's not getting anything.'

'Anyone but her. Is that asking so much?'

Considering what Lucy did for me, it wasn't asking much at all. What was my problem? 'We have some things to settle,' I said. 'We never talked it out.'

'What's there to settle? Now you see her, now you don't. Are you going to believe what she says three years later?'

'I don't know.' I couldn't defend myself. 'Let me ask you something. The night of the accident you called Esther to come to the hospital. She said you told her it was the last time she could see me. You drove her off.'

She clapped and laughed. 'She said that? That's wonderful, Marty!'

'How is that wonderful?'

'What did you say back?'

'Nothing.'

'Did you believe her?'

'I didn't believe her or not believe her. I was just wondering.'

She sat next to me. She took my hand. 'Imagine that your lover got hit by a car. Try to imagine that some guy she had on the side comes to the hospital that night. Now try to imagine him telling you it's the last time you're going to see her. He – what did she say? – drove you off. Do you see how completely absurd it is?

'Let's say, because of unusual atmospheric charges, that you did back off that night. Would you stay away and leave her alone through her long horrible rehabilitation? Without even calling her?

'Then, to top it all off, would you show up years later, when she was happy with a new lover, and you were married and had a kid, and try to mess the whole thing up? Could you do that?' She pulled on my arm. 'Come on, you cold-hearted motherfucker. If anyone could do it you could. Could you? Do you believe her?'

Thinking about women really messes up my mind.

Lucy was smiling. I didn't want her to enjoy this. It wasn't funny. I said, 'You just happened to find me lying on the side of the road, right?'

'I think that's enough about the accident for one night.'

'Did you?'

'Did I? Did I? Yes, I did.'

'What did you see?'

99

'Your car. What do you think I saw? Three wise men?'

'Both cars?'

'No. Just yours.'

'All bashed in?'

'I don't remember. Yeah, all bashed in.'

Lucy was back across the room again. I said, 'Did you ever hear of a guy named Harlan Karlin?'

She crossed her arms over her chest. 'What did she say about Harlan Karlin?'

'Nothing. I called him. You sold him my car.'

'Yes. I put the money in your account. I didn't want you thinking about it.'

'He said it was in mint condition.'

'Yes.'

'But you found it all bashed in. The bodywork must have cost a couple of grand.'

She stopped. 'Please let's stop talking about this. I hate to think about those days.'

'Where did you get it done?'

'I don't remember. Somebody gave me a name.'

'Tonelli's Auto? Bucyk's Body Shop?'

'I can't remember.'

'Did you at least repay yourself after you sold the car?'

She shouted at me. 'I don't know. I don't care. Let's drop it.'

'Once I get this into my head it drives me crazy. I can't even figure out how you found me.'

She sat next to me and put an arm around my shoulder. She felt tense. She said, 'I went looking for you. You called to say you were coming to see me, but you didn't show up. You didn't answer your phone, so I started back to your place.'

'Did you hear the crash?'

'There was no crash.'

Of course there was a crash. I have the stumps to prove it.

She said, 'You were lying next to your car. That's what I saw. Your car was untouched. I didn't have any bodywork done on it.'

'But then how did it happen?'

'I didn't see it. You looked like you were standing in front of your car and someone hit you.'

I saw myself. Legs busted up like balsa wood, sticking through my skin. Knees dangling by tendons, just waiting to get snipped and tossed into the OR bucket. Blood all over my white linen pants. My good pants.

I closed my eyes. Why was I up there? Where was I going? Why the hell did I get out of the car?

I put my hand over my eyes and squeezed. I pushed back into my brain. Black and swirling. I could see myself laid out on the ashpalt. Red, white, and black. But I couldn't go ahead or back. I was frozen in time. Right there. I felt like screaming.

'I got you into my car and took you to the hospital.' Lucy said. 'I called your so-called girlfriend. She took her sweet time getting there. Somebody came out and told us what was happening to you. Esther took off. She didn't even wait to see you. But good old Lucy is still here.'

'Why didn't you tell me this?'

'I don't see that it does any good to talk about it. It doesn't change anything. That's what you always say.'

'Why was I coming to see you?'

She groaned. 'What a question. Because you love me.'

'You know what I mean. Where was Esther?'

'I didn't ask.'

'You were taking me on the rebound?'

'That's right. I have no pride when it comes to you.'

I never trusted anybody more than Lucy. But I was having trouble today. I never really trusted Esther, even when I was with her. They were all I had, as far as the accident went.

I said, 'Did I know who you were? Did I say anything?'

'You said, "Lucy, you are the most beautiful woman I have ever seen. I am the luckiest of all men."'

'Really.'

'You were unconscious. You only said one thing. When I was pulling you into the car you said, "I have Mrs Morrison at ten-thirty. What a pig. You take her."'

Damn, that sounded familiar. But I couldn't make too much of it. I probably used to say it every week.

I said, 'So, did you take her?'

'Why don't you kiss me and cut your losses.'

Eleven

I liked it when Lucy was on the way down. I hate to say it. She was easier to talk to. She listened better. She started coming by almost every day.

I worked better. I could concentrate. I stopped wondering about when I was going to eat again.

Brute moved right along. In two days I had the body pretty much filled in. I ape-walked across the room every five or ten minutes to see Brute from a distance. I could see the silhouette of his face. The tension in his body. I didn't want to let him get away from me and die, like Sidney.

It's hard to make a sculpture of a tiger. Tigers aren't famous for their shape. Like lions, with their manes and the tufts at the end of the tail. You know a tiger by its stripes. Imagine trying to do a sculpture of a zebra. You could do it. But everything would have to be just right.

With Brute I had it just right. The wide, sideburned head. Thick neck. Powerful shoulders. Rippling torso. Broad paws. Now I was concerned with the look on his face. The gleam of death in his eyes. The mouth open just a little. Fangs being drawn. Also the muscles that make him spring. They had to look hair-trigger. You wouldn't let your kid in the same zoo as this cat.

There was a knock on the door. I said to wait. I took a good look. Brute was terrific. My best tiger of all. I covered him with a sheet. I was keeping him secret for now.

It was Esther. Today she had Jerold. He was a handy shield. To protect her from what I had to say about her cowardly exit. Her latest one.

'Jerold, dear. You remember Marty.'

'Tum!' he said. He reached for me with his chubby arms.

I liked the little guy. I thought about taking the baby stroller over to my bench. Fix it up so he could push it. And visit me alone.

'What a surprise,' I said.

'Why?' She took off her coat.

'Usually women don't grab my pecker and run out the door. Except when they're scared of its great size.'

'Try to understand. I haven't touched a man besides Sanford since I was married.'

'Then what the hell are you doing here?'

'Didn't you ever fail at anything the first time and then get it right later? As a matter of fact, I do remember you failing something the first time.'

'What?'

'It's interesting that you don't remember.'

'What?' She smiled. She let Jerold out of the stroller. He ran across the room and grabbed a rope. She said, 'But I let you come back and try again. And you got quite good, thank you.'

She was turning things around on me again.

'Since we were here last, Jerold has been trying to tie his own shoes. I think he learned it from you. Jerold, darling, show Marty how you tie your shoe.'

He bent over and put his knuckles to the ground. He moved one foot and fell over. Tie his shoe. Hell. The kid was still trying to ape-walk.

'And he picked this up a few days ago. He wanted me to keep it for you.' She handed it to me. It was pebbles and asphalt. A piece of the street.

'How did you know?'

'He kept saying "Tum".'

Jerold started doing the rounds. His mom followed him to keep him from pulling things down.

If she wanted to try to make things right with me, why didn't she leave him with the nanny?

104

I said, 'Did your husband tell you about the money for the Olympian Games?'

'What money?'

'He's putting up prize money for the 1,000 meters. And he's entering the race. He bought a wheelchair.'

'That explains it. Every fifteen minutes he's been getting on the floor and doing push-ups.'

'Didn't you ask him what he was doing?'

She kept following her kid around. I looked over to Brute. I wanted to get back to work. Why couldn't I throw her out? What held me back?

'Isn't this better than being alone all the time?' she said.

'I'm not alone all the time.'

'You're not? Has Lucy increased her lithium level? She's not the tryptophan type, is she?'

'Save it.' This was weird. She knew a lot more about this stuff than I did.

'What an operator. You're so isolated that Lucy can come by now and then, and you're so grateful that you forget everything. Crumbs. That's all she ever gave you. I hate to have to remind you. She's no saint. No, Jerold. Put it down.'

'The word of an authority.'

'Why do you think you were going to see her the night of your accident?'

'You knew about that?'

'Of course I knew. And it really hurt me.'

Here it was again. The phantom calf. Esther was Old Reliable.

She said, 'I didn't stop you. I let you go so you could learn for yourself.'

'Learn what?'

'What a manipulator she is. I don't know if you remember that she called you at my apartment. She was hysterical. She convinced you she was going to kill herself. She had you set up, with all that clinical talk about depression and mood swings. I'm sorry I have to talk about Lucy like this because she takes care of you, and that's important.'

'I'm moved.'

'When I saw that woman at the hospital, I knew something was going on.'

'By the time you saw her, she had something else on her mind. My life.'

'It was more than that.'

I slammed the arm of the chair. Jerold turned around and fell. 'Stop hinting. What do you think? She had me set up to get hit? She lured me from my car? What?' The car wasn't bashed. That's the thing that kept coming into my mind.

Esther went to Jerold. He was up by the time she got there. He had my trophy in his hand. The legs. 'Tum!' he said.

She changed her tone. 'I'm not accusing her. I'm probably being too emotional. You were taken from me, and now that I see you it feels so unfair.'

This was too much. I said, 'I'll ask you again. What do you want from me?'

She sat down next to me. She put her arm around my shoulder. Her aroma came to me again. I was surprised she'd hold me in front of the kid. He didn't care. He was running around. She said, 'I want to let things take their course as if the accident didn't happen.' She looked into my eyes. She was waiting for an answer.

Watching Jerold and the legs trophy, looking at her big diamond ring and fancy clothes, seeing Hell on Wheels parked against the wall, rubbing my stumps against the wheelchair – this was the single most ridiculous thing a woman ever said to me.

The hell of it was that I knew what she meant. Put the whole damn thing aside. Get out from under it, even for just an hour here and there. With her smell I could do it. I wanted to do it. More than anything. But how could I. This was Esther. The one who left me when I needed her the most.

And what about Lucy. How could I think of doing it to her. She was great. Except that now she was going down. I was scared of what happened to me then. One of these times I knew she wasn't coming back.

But counting on Esther. What could be dumber.

It was too complicated. I was getting jumbled. I didn't give Esther an answer. She didn't press me.

I got out some scraps of wood. Jerold and I made a pyramid. He put the trophy on top. It made the whole thing come down.

Esther sat on the sofa and watched. She didn't say anything. She had a tight little smile for the rest of the afternoon. Like she had it all figured out. At least somebody did. But it made me worry. Like I was getting set up again.

At the door she stopped and pressed her chest against me. 'Smell me,' she said.

What choice did I have.

'Think of me that way. Free your mind for me.'

Now I felt her hitting me way above the phantom leg. Where I was still real.

She kissed me. Right in front of the kid. Why did she bring him?

They left. I pulled the sheet off Brute. It was nice to feel clay again. I understood clay.

After ten minutes or so I walked out front to check. I was surprised. Now Brute didn't look so good. The pose didn't have the right energy. His look wasn't frightening. I hated to think it. He was looking kind of puny. Just this morning I thought he was terrific.

It had to be Esther's smell. She mixed me up. I covered him again. I had to wait until the morning for another look.

Twelve

Lucy came by later with groceries. She cooked us a nice dinner. She stared at the wall a lot while we ate. Her mind was somewhere else. When I asked she said she wasn't thinking anything. I know what that's like.

Without Brute I didn't have anything to do after dinner. Lucy was looking at some photos for work. She used a magnifying glass on them. I didn't want to bother her. But the things Esther said were kicking up in me.

After a while I couldn't hold it down. 'Look, don't get angry. Esther was here again. I didn't invite her.'

Lucy nodded. That's all. I didn't know what it meant.

'She told me a few more things about the crash. I have to ask you,' I said.

She nodded the same way.

I told her about the suicidal call.

Lucy was very calm. 'If I was dying of a rare illness and Esther had the only vial of antidote, I would cheerfully die. Nothing could make me call there, least of all a suicide threat.

'And I would never make a suicide threat. Suicide is an act of liberation, not a threat to wield at people who care about you.' She scared me when she talked like this. 'You and I have been down the road a few times. Have I ever breathed a hint of threat?'

I said, 'It didn't sound right to me. That's why I had to ask. Are you taking pills?'

'I do what has to be done.' That was that.

I said, 'So who called who? I'm still trying to get this straight.'

'You called me. You had a fight with her and you

108

decided you'd had enough. You wanted to get out of your apartment before she came back and made a scene. I said sure, come on up.'

'What was the fight about?'

'I didn't ask. Really, Marty, I'm not a saint.'

'Why did you let me go back and forth. Didn't you want something steady?'

She kissed me on the forehead. 'I was always happy to see you. But you were wild. I knew I couldn't have anything steady so I didn't ask. But don't kid yourself. I didn't sit around waiting for you.'

I should have figured. I couldn't decide if this bothered me. Maybe now it did. I could have cared less then, when I had legs.

She said, 'And to tell you the truth I like you more now. I feel I can depend on you. Nice switch, huh?' She made a little laugh. Then she was serious again.

We went to bed early. She got tired early these days. If I wanted sex I had to start things. She enjoyed it, but now she stayed on her back most of the time. She talked less. That made me think about her changes. Especially about when she was going to change back to the way she was.

She went to sleep. I got up and ape-walked into the other room. I couldn't wait until the next day to look. I pulled the sheet off Brute.

His proportions were right. The surface was just what I wanted. But he was no good. Why? He was crouched. He looked like he could spring. But he also looked like he could roll over and take a nap. His mouth was open a little. Like he couldn't decide whether to roar or to shut up. If I had legs and he was attacking me, I wouldn't run. I'd try to wrestle him. I just might have a chance. Then again, I'm the guy who tried to wrestle a moving car.

There couldn't be any doubt about a tiger. It had to be absolutely ferocious.

109

I had to start all over again.

In the morning I left a message for Sanford. He called me that afternoon. I told him what I wanted to do.

He said, 'Just how big is this thing going to be?'

'Real big.'

'Dinosaur big?'

'Baby dinosaur.'

'How are you going to get it out of your apartment when you're done? Knock a wall down?'

'You don't have to get it out. They can make the mold in my place and take it out in pieces.'

'You and those damn tigers.'

I could just see him, shaking his head. Running his fingers through his razor cut hair. If not for Esther, that would be the end of it. But he couldn't turn me down. He was afraid of me.

He said, 'I'll tell you what. I'll get the supplies if you give me some work for the crafts fair coming up. We're short of good stuff.'

'I'm not making any more tigers. Not while I'm working on this thing.'

'I don't care what you make. Spray paint with your asshole for all I care. Make me a few pieces and show up for the opening. People will want to meet the artists. Deal?'

I was getting set up. He didn't want my art. He knew I couldn't do anything except tigers. He wanted me at the opening. With him and his wife.

What the hell. I had nothing to lose.

The next day the supplies came. The same two guys carried them in and stacked them up. I ordered twice as much wood and clay. I had some clay left from Brute. The late Brute. The same guy gave me the receipt to sign. 'Lots of clay,' he said, shaking his head.

I needed a new tiger name. Something with the right spirit. So I wouldn't go off course again.

When I was eighteen I saw a Swedish film about a

110

big blonde. She always dressed just in black lingerie, even when it was snowing. She went around catching criminals by wrapping her whip around their throat. I never forgot her.

My tiger wasn't going to be a crime fighter. Or wear black lace. But the name was right. Avenging Angel.

I didn't necessarily have to send that name along to the CRP. So long as I didn't forget.

I drew sketches of Avenging Angel. I couldn't build the armature myself. The cat was leaping. It was a big cantilever. It had to be strong enough to support hundreds of pounds of clay.

I called a friend of mine from the club. He was a contractor. He set me up with a carpenter.

I called the guy. He came the next day. A weight-lifter. He wore overalls without a shirt. Big tattoos on his arms in red and blue. I had to get him over to the weight room at the CRP.

He stopped in the doorway. 'I ain't messing with no fucking tiger, man. Is that thing tied up?'

'Of course,' I said.

He came in. He put down his tool box and climbed a rope. 'This how you get away from the tiger, man?' Finally he got a good look at me. I was in the wheelchair. 'Something happen to you?' he said.

'What do you mean?'

I showed him the plans. It was a simple job. It could be rough because it didn't show. But it had to be sturdy.

'You mean this is the tiger?' he said. 'Shit. I thought I was going to die. I told my old lady to pull out the insurance. See how much she gets if I get ate.'

He went to the hardware store for some heavy steel brackets. He knew his business. He put the whole thing together that afternoon. It looked kind of like a dinosaur.

Avenging Angel was going to go up fast. I didn't want

111

to have to stop in the middle. I decided to get the art for Sanford out of the way.

To me art was tigers. It was hard to think of doing anything else. I pulled out my paints and spread the tubes out on the table. I looked at them. I smelled them. I thought back on my days in the hospital with Angela. Great legs. I thought they might give me an idea. They didn't.

I looked over at Hell on Wheels, my old chair on the cinder blocks. I'd painted the locomotive on the back of the seat. It was the only thing I'd ever painted worth a damn except a tiger. I could give him that. Then I wouldn't have to make anything. I could get back to work.

Hell on Wheels. I thought about that day in the train station. The last time I used the chair. The day the transvestites came after me. Muscular guys. Wearing mascara and lipstick. Vaseline, or something, all over their faces. Disgusting cheap perfume blasting out of their hair. I was taking a piss at the time. They smiled at me while they pulled my wheels off. They liked their work. It only took a second. Like they did this all the time. They didn't even ask for money. They only wanted the wheels. My dick shut off. I was scared. One of the transvestites said, 'Need help there, sugar?' They left me in the seat on the floor. In the stink. I couldn't reach the urinal. Guys coming in looked at me like I was a freak. They wouldn't use any of the urinals. They went to the toilets in the back. Or they turned around and walked out.

Now I could see myself there. Falling over on the floor in front of the urinals. Dick in hand. No legs. No wonder everybody kept away. I would too.

I guess that's why I could paint the locomotive that one time. When I did it the idea of the train station was burned deep into my brain.

I was out of the hospital a month when this happened. I thought I was going to live like everybody else. That's what they told me in rehab. They never told me about transvestites in the men's room.

I couldn't give away Hell on Wheels.

Anyway, they don't go for that kind of stuff at the CRP. Disabled, handicapped, and challenged people don't end up on the bathroom floor at the Franklin Train Station. Just us cripples.

Sanford said I could spray paint with my asshole for all he cared. That gave me an idea.

I had a pad of large drawing paper. I put five sheets out.

I took off my pants and my shorts. I squeezed out some paint. Just the primary colors. I like primary colors. I smeared them on my butt, my balls, and the bottom of my stumps.

I climbed a little way up a rope and lowered myself on one sheet. I pressed down so I got a good print. I peeled the paper off. I smeared on a little more paint before I came down on the second sheet. And more for each one. I didn't want any two prints to be the same. The CRP would make more money if they were one-of-a-kind.

When I was done, all I could see on the paper was my outline. How my left ball came down a little heavier on the third sheet than the second sheet. How my hair got caked, and looked like little spikes by the fourth print. It's good I quit after five. The fifth was starting to turn brown.

Would anybody see my butt in the picture? People come to the CRP art fair to give money to the unfortunate. They don't want some guy's asshole winking at them. Even though it would be good for them to see it. They should know what being Remarkable is like. It's not poetry. It's worrying if you can get up the curb and into the men's room before you have an accident.

Sanford had eyes of stone. He wouldn't see my butt.

He would put the prints right out there in the fair. Front row. The next day he'd catch hell from the board of the CRP. Serve him right for making me do this shit.

That would be fun. But if he got mad he could try to cut off my money. I couldn't risk Avenging Angel making it to bronze. She was going to make me live forever.

I decided to doctor the prints. What else could they be? It was hard for me to see anything but the truth. Buttocks. A little blob on top of them. Long drumsticks.

Then I saw it. The scrotum was a little head. The butt was his big chubby body. The stumps were his arms, up and out. A victory pose. The arms were mighty big for the head. What the hell. It was stylized. Modern art. That's what everybody would see. Big arms. No legs. Amputee art. The way a handicapped person sees the world.

It didn't take much to finish the prints. I drew hands at the end of the stumps. A little hat on the top of the scrotum. A little muffler around the base of the scrotum, where the fellow's neck would be. Two of them got a little corncob pipe. That was taking too long to do them all.

I decided to call them 'Fans at the Olympian Games'. A series.

If anybody pointed out the buttocks I would act shocked. I'd say it must have been one of those powerful subconscious urges of the challenged.

Soon the paint started to dry. It pulled at my flesh. I felt every hair at the root. I went to the closet for the paint thinner. Then the drawer. Then the kitchen. I couldn't believe it. I didn't have any.

I wiped off as much paint as I could with rags. Most of it stayed on. This was ridiculous. I couldn't sit down. I didn't want to ruin my clothes. But I couldn't stay like this. I was getting goose bumps. They pulled the paint tighter.

114

I tried everything I could find. Vinegar. Olive oil. Witch hazel. Shampoo. 3-in-1 oil. I still had a butt in primary colors. I finally put on some old shorts.

Lucy came home. She was quiet again. A little sad. I wanted to tell her what happened but it didn't seem right. She wasn't in the spirit.

I turned off the lights before I got into bed. She snapped on her light to check the alarm.

'What's this?' she said. She pushed a finger into my back.

I still had my shorts on. But the paint was all over me. 'A little art accident.'

'Let's see.' She tugged my shorts off. 'My, my. Bright blue and red buttocks. They're divine. Aren't you a handsome fellow tonight.'

Her eyes were lighting up. It was a while since I saw this. She got behind me and snuggled up. She opened the braid in her hair and shook out her golden mane.

I said, 'You're going to get paint on your gown.'

I felt her hand pushing between my stumps. I reached for the light. She stopped me. She said, 'I want to admire this. You know who else has buttocks like yours?'

'A guy sitting in a salad bar.'

'A mandrill.'

'What's a mandrill?'

'A big African monkey. Its butt is bright red and blue. Its snout too. Mother Nature's way of color-keying. We do things like this at work all the time. Just not quite as exquisite as this.'

She was yanking me around with her hand. She was talking right into my ear. I could feel her wind.

'Mandrills are ferocious animals,' she said.

'You'd better be, walking around with an ass like that.'

'They get everything they want.'

'What do they want?'

'What everyone wants.'

'Which is?' I asked.

'Me.'

I didn't understand how being out of paint thinner could do this to her. After being meek all month. I wondered if this would work every time. If I'd found the cure for depression.

'I suppose mandrills swing on vines,' I said.

'I suppose.'

'So I better get up this rope.'

'Yes, I think you better.'

Thirteen

I started working on Avenging Angel the next morning. There was going to be no doubt about this baby. Leaping forward off her back legs. For the kill. Head about six feet off the ground. In flight. Like an arrowhead. Mouth open and roaring. Fangs like sabers. Front legs reaching. Back legs thrusting. Tail straight back like the stick on a bottle rocket.

I worked up the back legs. I laid on clay by the bag. The legs were pushing hard. Almost horizontal. I made them ripple with power. I ran my hand over the surface. They made me feel tickly. Like they could jump right off the armature.

I got up to the abdomen. Now I had a big problem. Balls on a cat this big you could bowl with. That would make Sanford feel real bad. But the cat would look pretty stupid without them.

Then I thought of something. This was going to be the perfect sculpture. I didn't have to sacrifice anything. Avenging Angel was female.

I filled in the underside of the body. Then I started on the front paws. I did as much as I could from the ground. It took me three days.

The rest I had to do from the ropes. I couldn't hang very long by one arm, especially carrying twenty-five-pound bags of clay. I had a chair in the bedroom I never used. I turned it over and cut out the webbing. It was in pretty good shape. I stitched it over a couple of pieces of rope. A sling seat. I could hang from the ropes in it.

Up in the sling seat I started on the left shoulder. In ten minutes I used up an entire bag of clay. I didn't want to go down for more. I fixed a noose at the end of the drawstring from the bag I just used up. I lowered it over a bag on the floor. It closed and I pulled up the clay. I wouldn't have to go down again all afternoon.

This is how intense I was. Every two bags I got out of the seat and got down anyway. Ape-walked across the room to take a look. This wasn't so easy any more. Avenging Angel took up most of the room. Still I had to do it. I couldn't let this one get away from me. This was my last chance.

Sidney and Brute didn't let me forget. They were pushed up against the wall under crusted shrouds. Sad. Pathetic. In the scale of Avenging Angel Brute looked like a fox at best. Sidney was just a big squirrel.

I worked longer hours than ever before. Even longer than when I worked at the tennis club. Avenging Angel kept my heart pounding. When Lucy showed up I came down for dinner. Afterwards I went back up for a few more hours. Until I was too tired to get my arms over my shoulders. Lucy didn't bother me. She was keeping to herself.

The day I started working on the head Mr Casey came in. It was the first time I saw him since I started this sculpture. He had his hand on his nose. Another headache. His glasses were in the other hand, with a bill for me.

He looked up. Avenging Angel had some kind of impact. She knocked him two steps back. Even without his glasses. He quickly put them on. After a closer look he got control of himself. But I remember the first look on his face. Fear. This was a tiger.

Esther showed up that day. She was alone. Too bad. Jerold would have gotten a kick out of the tiger. I didn't think he'd be scared.

'Wow!' she said.

'Think your old man will be happy with it?'

'Who cares.'

'It's going to be in a garden. Should keep the birds out, don't you think?'

'Sanford says you're coming to the opening Friday.'

I said, 'That's right. We made a bargain.'

'You don't have to bargain with him.'

'He controls my money. I want this thing done right. It matters to me.'

'He's just a go-between. A flunkey.'

'I have to deal with him. If I knew the patron I wouldn't have to deal with him.'

'You know the patron.'

That made me stop. I looked down at her from my hanging seat. 'You know who it is?'

'Yes.'

'He told you?'

'He doesn't know.'

'How did you find out?'

'I have my ways.'

'Why didn't you tell me before?'

'I didn't want it to distract you.'

'It won't. Tell me.'

'Don't you know?'

'Does it sound like I know?'

'How many people do you know who like monochromatic tigers?'

'Plenty of people. People with taste.'

'How many people care about landing you a big commission?'

'The commission isn't for me. It's for whoever makes the sculpture. It doesn't matter who.'

'It does this time.' She raised an eyebrow. Then I knew.

'You?'

'Me,' she said.

'You did it for me? Not the cat?'

'I did it for you and the cat.'

'Is this supposed to be charity or something?'

'Not at all.'

'I don't need no fucking charity. I know what I'm doing.'

'It's not charity. I believe in you. Don't get so defensive.'

'I don't take charity. If this is charity I don't want it. Take it back.'

'You've made your point. It's not. OK?'

I was furious. I said, 'Where did you get the money?'

'It's Sanford's. I transferred it into another account and drew a cashier's check from it.'

'He's going to kill you.'

'I was very careful. I hid it with the credit card payments. He'll never find out.'

This was too much. Sanford's wife was taking his money and giving it to him to give to me. Sometimes it frightened me what she could do.

'Why didn't you tell me?' I said.

'I didn't want you treating me a certain way because I was funding your project. I want things between us to run their natural course.'

I looked at Avenging Angel's huge teeth. They were sticking straight up all by themselves. There was no head around them yet. If I was going to make a sculpture of the natural course, this was it. I climbed out of the sling seat and down the rope.

I said, 'I guess you felt bad for me when you saw me that day outside Harry's. With my shoe.'

'Actually I offered you the commission first and then I went looking for you.'

That's right. I got it the next day. 'What do you mean you went looking for me?'

'Jerold and I were around this place for two weeks. I thought we'd never run into you.'

'You said you didn't know where I live.'

'Oh, please, Marty. That was easy. The hard part was getting you out. I was worried you would never come out.'

'When Lucy's around I don't.'

'Then I guess I should thank her.'

'I'll tell her,' I said. 'Why didn't you knock on the door like a normal person?'

'I didn't think you'd let me in.'

But I did. I never really thought of turning her away. Though I probably should have.

I said, 'Were you going to tell me about the commission eventually? Even if I didn't force it out of you.'

'No.'

'Then why do it?'

'I wanted you to have the money, with me or without me. With me, I hope.'

This wasn't the way I thought of Esther. 'You did that for me?'

'Who else?'

'Really?' Still I couldn't help thinking she was putting something over on me again.

'Really.' She came over and squatted with me. Her smell was all around.

I said, 'Want to take it into the back room?'

She kissed me. 'You satyr. Let's keep talking for a while. We're finally getting it right.'

Too much talking was wrong, no matter what you said. 'So what do you want to talk about?'

She said, 'I almost forgot. I brought you a present. You'll like this.' She dug into her purse and put something cold into my hand. It was a bronze tennis player. With a little bronze racket. He only went down to the knees. The rest was missing. It was the top of my legs statue.

'Where did you get this?' I said.

'Off the floor of your old place. I cleaned up after that party. I completely forgot about it until Jerold picked up the bottom last time we were here.'

'Why did you keep it? It's junk.'

'I don't know. I guess I can't let you go.'

I put my arm around her and hugged her. I felt great. Just like old times.

'You're crushing me!' she said. I let go. 'Boy, you're strong.'

'It's those good wheelchair arms.'

She got the base of the trophy off the floor and put the two pieces together. They fit perfectly.

'You see that?' she said. 'I can put the broken tennis player back together again.'

She turned around and put her butt on the arm of my chair. She slid into my lap, or my excuse for one. No-one ever did this before. Not since I used the wheelchair. Her buns fit my cock like styrofoam packing. I stuck my nose into her chest. It was like wearing a hospital mask with her smell under pressure. My heart was pounding so hard I could hear it in my ears.

I started wheeling both of us toward the bedroom. We had to make this official or I was going to die.

As we went by the table she said, 'Stop.'

No way. She grabbed the brake on the side of the chair and jammed it on. I stopped short. I almost lost her out the front.

'What is this non-tiger art? Is it for the opening?'

She got up. It was a bad feeling. She spread out the prints. 'Not your usual. What do you call them?'

'"Fans at the Olympian Games".'

'The view from under the bleachers?'

'What do you mean?'

'You probably still have paint in your crack.'

'I don't know. Maybe we'd better go check.' I tried to pull her back into the chair.

She shook me off. 'Why go to the opening with these, when you could wait for your grand entrance with that wonderful cat?'

'It would look funny if I backed out now.'

'To who? An accountant? Do you care what he thinks?'

I didn't want any trouble with the bronze. Just in case it wasn't really her commission. Or she had lost control of it.

I said, 'I want to meet my public.'

'He's got his hooks in you. You don't like the CRP, and you probably don't like parties.' She was right. But why did she care if I was there?

I said, 'You're afraid Sanford's going to make a scene.'

'There's nothing Sanford can do to scare me.'

I thought about the night of the opening. Lucy would be standing next to me. In a nice dress. Great legs. She'd look like a million. She would know it too. It would show in her smile.

No. These days Lucy didn't smile. Sanford would come up to us. In a tux. Smiling. Esther would be wearing lots of jewels. She'd look at me. At Lucy. Lucy would look away. Lucy can't stand her. She wouldn't deal with her.

What could Sanford say that would be so bad? I couldn't think of anything. Not with all of us there. Esther was the one who could do damage. Because Lucy wouldn't rise to meet her. And because Sanford was a wimp. Esther was the one to be scared of.

'The opening could be a big moment for you,' I said.

'Then let me have it alone. I'll take your prints in.'

'You're going to have a great time.' This was reverse psychology. She didn't go for it.

Now I had to go for sure, to see what this was all about. I wouldn't give her the prints. She put the top of the tennis player back in her bag. She could put him back together, and she could take him apart. She kissed me on the way out. But she was pissed.

I had to protect Lucy. Over dinner I told her I was going to the opening alone. I knew she had only offered to go to please me.

When I said this she cried.

123

Fourteen

The place was mobbed. Wheelchair heaven. Rubber screeching all over the floor. They waxed it just for tonight. Canes and crutches smacked against each other. Every now and then somebody caught one in the shin. Everybody kept saying 'Excuse me'. They needed a lot of room to get by.

I was dressed nice. Lucy pinned up the legs of my suit. The thing was so out of date it was back. She was carrying a portfolio with my prints. She was wearing a straight suit. Slit. She looked good. Professional. Guys looked at her. She didn't smile.

We made our way to the main desk. Pineapple was working there. He was big on committees. He looked at a chart and pointed with his hook. 'Table three. Third one from the end.'

We had to fight through the crowds around the tables. God knows what they were so excited about. Usually the art was shit. No better than kids did at day camp. But you couldn't let on here. Just like you couldn't let on in front of kids.

I put the prints on the table. There was just enough space. On my right some guy had log cabins built out of toothpicks. Actually they were pretty nice. I couldn't tell what his problem was. Probably one of those weird diseases. He had a lot of spare time.

I felt a paw on my shoulder. I turned around. It was Pepper. The weightlifter.

'Well, Hit-and-run. Don't you look sweet.' He reached for my tie.

I pushed his hand away. 'So do you.' He was dressed cool. His pants were fitted so you couldn't make out how bad his legs looked. He was wearing sunglasses even though it was night. 'Pepper, this is Lucy. Lucy, Pepper.'

He gave her a big smile. 'Sure, I know you.' I forgot. He saw her at parties.

She looked blank. She didn't remember. I could tell she wasn't faking. Maybe memories from up days didn't make it to the down ones. He shouldn't have felt bad. Her memories of me didn't always make it either. She was polite. She smiled back.

'Killer suit,' he said to her. 'Slay me dead.'

She nodded. She looked good. I would say hot, but in this mood she didn't get hot. Her hair was in a bun. Somebody like Pepper wouldn't pick that up.

He said to me, 'What you got?'

'Take a look.'

He wheeled up to the table. 'Oh, man. You sat down in some paint. You call that art? Man, I rather look at tigers, and I'm sick of tigers.'

'Is it obvious?'

'What do you mean? Is it supposed to be something else?'

'"Fans at the Olympian Games". See, this is the head. These are the arms. Never mind.'

'Woah. Here comes Mr Dollars.'

Sanford came up. Just like I imagined. He was working a cigar. Smiling. Dressed in a tux. His wife was next to him, a step away. She wasn't really with him. That was clear. She was wearing a short, tight black dress. Way too fancy for the CRP. She was showing some tit. Great legs too. She had a glass of wine in her hand. I could see in her face it wasn't the first.

Sanford pumped Pepper's hand, then mine. He said, 'I'm happy you came.'

'Me too,' said Esther.

'Let's see what you got here.' He looked at the prints. 'Very nice. What are they, psychedelic clouds?'

Esther took Lucy's hand. 'I'm so glad you could make it.'

Lucy looked her in the eyes. She was calm. Esther was smirking. She was loaded. Lucy said, 'I wouldn't have missed it for the world.'

Phantoms started to grab my calf. Danger. I took Lucy's hand. 'Let's look at some of the other stuff.'

Esther was still holding Lucy's other hand. She wouldn't let go. 'Don't bother. It's the same as it was last year, and the year before that. Pisspots and paintings. Stay with us. Sanford and I are better entertainment. Aren't we, dear?'

Sanford was still looking at the prints. 'Are they really clouds? Maybe they're just abstracts.'

'They ain't abstracts,' said Pepper.

'Maybe not,' said Sanford. 'They remind me of something, but I can't put my finger on it.'

Esther took the print from Sanford. 'You got this upside down. Like that. Makes you kind of want to jump right in. Don't you think so, Pepper?'

He laughed. 'I don't know nothing about that.'

'That's what they all say. What do you think, Lucy?'

We all looked at Lucy. I couldn't read her face. She took her time. Finally she said, 'I think they're clouds.'

'That's what I said,' said Sanford.

'There's Amal,' I said. I pulled Lucy away from the table. Not that I wanted to talk to the guy. Right away my phantoms felt better.

'Mr Champion,' he said. He offered me his real hand. I wondered what would happen if he greeted Pine-apple. Would they shake hooks? 'Have you brought us some more art?'

'I don't know about art. But there's a few prints over there.'

'Does this mean you have changed your mind about handicapped activities? Like the race?' He smiled. He always sounded formal.

I looked at Lucy. She was looking back at the table. She wasn't listening to us.

I said, 'I retired.'

'But this year there is prize money!' Even the shopkeeper knew. Sanford was applying the squeeze.

I said, 'It's going to ruin the games.'

'Oh no. Money does not ruin anything. It is people who ruin things.'

Tar Man wheeled up. He used to work for the road department, shoveling out the asphalt in front of the steam roller. Until his accident. 'You talking about the race?'

'Yes,' said Amal. 'Marty thinks the money will spoil its flavor.'

'No chance. It's only going to happen once,' said Tar Man.

'How do you know?' said Amal.

'The field is so big that guys are going to go off the starting line in waves. They're going to cut for the front.' He showed this with his hands. 'It's going to be a mess. I wouldn't be surprised if people get hurt.'

'You really think so?'

'Yeah. It's going to be great. You should get in on it, Marty. I'm going for it myself.'

I left them. Lucy was still looking back at the table. Esther was hanging all over Pepper. She was looking at me. Her husband wasn't there. It was all for me.

'Want to go?' I said to Lucy.

'If you want. Or we can stay.'

'Let me tell Sanford.'

I wheeled over to him. He was showing people a sculpture of yin and yang, welded out of two bed pans. 'Ever seen anything like it? Anywhere? At any price?'

I told him we were leaving. He said, 'So soon? You just got here.'

'I can't stay away from that tiger.'

'She's a big one, eh?'

'A beauty.'

'Wait here for a second, would you?'

He disappeared through the door. The place was really jumping. There were guys around since Vietnam, Korea, World War II. Even a couple from the Great War. Not to mention all the automobile and industrial accidents, the diseases, and the birth defects. I was nothing compared to a lot of these guys.

Someone took my arm from behind. Roughly. It was Esther. She was angry. 'If you're going, go.' Her breath smelled flammable.

'Your husband asked me to wait.'

'I'm telling you to get out of here.' She shoved the back of my chair. She was trying to push me across the floor.

I grabbed the wheels. 'What the hell are you trying to do?'

Sanford passed back through the doors. Esther disappeared. 'I got somebody who wants to meet you,' he said.

'About the tigers?'

'You'll see.'

'Another commission?'

I followed him into a room. A woman was standing against the far wall. Just looking at it.

'I'll leave you two alone.' Sanford carefully closed the door.

I wheeled into the middle of the room. She didn't turn around. I said, 'Did you want to sign me up?'

She turned her head. She was hard-looking. Angry. Long, wild black hair. But she was absolutely gorgeous. She was tall, too. Real tall. Six feet easy. Maybe not. Since my accident all women looked tall.

'For what? Laboratory experiments?' she said.

So Sanford set me up. That's what this was about. What would she want with roadkill like me.

At first I thought she was in on it. Then I didn't think so. She was too angry. She wasn't having fun.

I said, 'Sanford said you wanted to meet me.'

'I've met a thousand like you.' She was still facing the wall. It was like she was afraid if she turned toward me she'd go crazy. I would have left. But I couldn't stop looking at her. The little she showed. The tall elegant body. Great, endless legs. Perfect profile. How did she end up with pondscum like Sanford?

I wasn't going to grovel. Not that I have anything against groveling. It's just that it wouldn't work with her.

I wheeled to the door and turned the knob. 'Wait,' she said. So she was in on it. Probably just the way Sanford and her planned. I figured she was going to say: I didn't mean it.

'I didn't mean it.'

I opened the door. Now I figured she'd start weeping. Maybe tell me she was rude because she was scared of me. All six feet of her.

'Shut the door, you mutant.'

That did it. I wheeled toward her. I was going to grab her legs and take her down. See how tough she talked cut down to size. Now she decided she'd better turn around. From the front she was even more gorgeous. She had no business being in the CRP. Especially not in an ugly set-up like this.

She wasn't afraid of me, the way most good-looking women are. She looked me right in the eyes. She didn't move out of my way. She was still. Except for her sleeves. They swung a little.

I looked for a wedding ring. A habit from my days at the club. I couldn't see her hands. She had them pulled up in her sleeves.

I grabbed for her. I expected her to push me away. She didn't. She let me take her around the waist. One of the sleeves swung into my face. I grabbed it. It was empty. I felt it up to her shoulder.

I rolled back. She looked blank.

She had no arms. The man with no legs meets the

129

woman with no arms. Sanford was one sick bastard.

'I'm sorry,' I said. 'He didn't tell me.'

She didn't answer.

I said, 'I guess you didn't want to meet me. This was his idea. I didn't know.' I turned back for the door.

She said, 'Stay. Please. I'm sorry.'

I looked at her. I wasn't going to be played for a sucker. She looked softer. I believed it. I have this sense about women.

I said, 'I'm Marty.' I offered my hand. A reflex. By the time I realized, it was too late.

She nudged the end of my stump with her high heel. 'Daphne,' she said. Great legs.

Right away I felt open to her. Cripples can say things to each other they can't say to normal people. 'They call me Hit-and-run. Automobile accident.'

'Explosion. Ceramics factory. They call me Miss Daphne.'

'OK, Miss Daphne. I've never seen you here before.'

'I've never been here before. Sanford asked me to come.'

'To meet me?'

'He didn't say why. I didn't care. I just wanted him to owe me.'

I wouldn't want to owe Miss Daphne. That could be like owing a black widow spider. I said, 'Don't think I'm being fresh. I'm just observing. I never saw a cripple anywhere near as nice on the eyes as you.'

'Thank you I'm sure. Handicaps are so hard on most women that they don't have the energy left for their looks. It's not fair. A lot of you disabled men look quite good.'

'What's your secret?'

Now she smiled for the first time. Beautiful teeth. 'I'm too angry to give it up. I was a model when I was younger. What could I model now? You look athletic. You must have done something when you had legs. Don't you miss it? Aren't you angry?'

I thought for a minute. 'I guess I miss it. I don't think about it much.'

'That's amazing. I'm angry every second. I'm angry when I sleep. I'm angry when I get the blood checks from the insurance company. As if they really compensate me for my loss. How can you not be angry?'

'Because this is the way it is. The legs aren't going to grow back. Why not try to make the best of it?'

'What could be the best of this?' She twirled. Her sleeves flew into the air. 'I don't even know what that means: the best of this.'

It took me a long time to get past that one for myself. And I never looked nearly as good as her.

She said, 'You must be Mr CRP. Handsome, athletic, artistic. And most of all, you accept your lot. Maybe Sanford wanted us to meet so you could teach me attitude.'

'What do you get out of being angry all the time?'

Her eyes were flaming now. They were the dark blue you see in the middle of a lake. They were great with her black hair. 'I'll tell you what it gets me. It means that I haven't forgotten. I haven't forgiven. I don't have little art shows and little Olympic Games to convince myself that everything's all right in my new little world.'

'I still don't see what that gets you.'

'It makes me feel that I'm not a collaborator. I'm a freak in the real world. I'm not a star in a freak world.'

I knew just what she meant. I used to feel that way. I didn't want to go through that again. I didn't want to go back and feel like they were just cutting off my bandages. I said, 'Your men friends must have their hands full with you.'

'Just what a man would say.' She moved closer to me. Only to stand over me. To remind me how much bigger she was. 'I don't have any men friends.'

'I can't believe that. You could have anyone. Maybe even me.'

131

'I could have anyone, before. Believe me, I did have anyone. Now the guys I can have want to push around someone beautiful who can't push back. The real tough guys. What do you think Sanford sees in me?'

The thought of him pushing this woman around made me sick with anger. I said, 'You wouldn't let him touch you, would you?'

'Bothers you, doesn't it?'

'Yes, it does,' Why? She wasn't mine. But she was crippled. One of us.

Sanford's wife was outside the door. And my main woman. 'What the hell is he up to?' I said.

'Don't you know?' I didn't. 'This is how he gets his kicks. Right now he's probably out there making up a joke: what has two arms, two legs, and two heads?'

'What?'

'You and me fucking. Don't even think about it. Just think about what he's thinking.'

Too late. I could see my arms and the two long beautiful legs. I thought about the bodies all covered with paint. Primary colors. Making gorgeous pornographic prints, no two the same.

I said, 'Why does he need to put us together? Can't he use his imagination?'

'Sanford has the imagination of a cobblestone.'

My imagination kept running. I wanted her on her back. I wanted to look into that face. But she couldn't pull me down when she came. Or rub and scratch me. If she took the top she might have trouble with her balance. Hell. I'd find a way. I was sure of it.

She said, 'I told you. Don't even think about it. That's just what Sanford wants you to do.'

'What?'

'Think about screwing me. He wants you to lose interest in his wife.'

'How do you know? You just said you didn't know why he wanted you here.'

'Listen, you seem like a decent guy. I don't know

132

exactly what's going on. But I know Sanford. My advice to you is my advice to all mutants: take whatever you can get. If you can take that bastard's wife, if she's good to you, do it. No matter what these do-gooders say, they wish we would all just go away. They're never going to give us anything we really want.'

'Bless you, Daphne. I knew you weren't in it with him.'

She bent way down and kissed me. Big, firm lips. Nice taste. 'And if you ever get caught with her, tell him I said it was OK,' she said. Then she was out the door.

When I got into the main room the crowd was thin. I couldn't find Lucy.

Sanford found me. Now I liked him even less. He said, 'Lucy went home. I told her the negotiation might take a while. Esther went too. She brought her own car.'

'You bastard. Then call me a cab.'

'I have to talk to a few more people. Then I'll take you.'

I went back to table three. Three of the prints were gone. Pineapple said, 'They sold. I told people you called them "Rainbow Nightmare".'

'Why did you do that?'

'It was the only way to talk them out of seeing what they already saw.'

'It's a guy in the bleachers. See? This is his head. This is his pipe . . .'

Sanford made me wait another hour. We were two of the last ones to leave.

I folded up my wheelchair. He put it in the trunk. I settled into the seat of his Jaguar. It felt like an expensive glove. Smelled like one too. The car had every accessory I ever saw. Even a baby fax machine.

He drove too fast. He gave me a big grin. I told him to watch the road.

'So what did you think of her?' he said. 'Isn't she great?'

'Yeah, she's great.'

'I was surprised you came out of there so fast. I got rid of Lucy right away. You had plenty of time.' This guy was out of his mind. 'Just think of the possibilities,' he said. 'The two of you could be one of the greatest couples since Sodom and Gomorrah.'

'I got an old lady, Sanford. I'm happy with her.'

'Lucy. Sure. Great lady. But you're not married. There's nothing stopping you from looking around a bit.' He patted me on the shoulder. As long as I didn't look at his wife. Meanwhile he could try pushing Daphne around. I felt like tearing his arm out.

Suddenly there was a terrible squealing sound. 'The phone,' he said.

'Aren't you going to answer?'

'I'll let the service get it. So, are you going to see her again?'

'Who?'

'Daphne.'

'No, Sanford. There will be no freak show for you.'

'What, freak show? I set you up with a gorgeous babe. I thought I was doing you a favor.'

'I don't need your favors.' I had to watch what I said to him. I didn't want to risk the bronze. Even if it was Esther's commission.

He said, 'I know how hard things are for you guys. I thought a woman like Daphne would understand. I thought she'd relax you.'

'You hear a few stories from those meatheads in the weightroom and you think I sit around all the time thinking about slamming babes, right? You don't know anything about being crippled. Maybe you should pay attention. Instead of putting your head down and counting your money.'

'Correct me, then. Tell me what you think about.'

'I'll tell you what I think about. I think about standing in the waves in the ocean. I think about rounding the bag at second and kicking up dirt with my cleats. I think about bumping a pinball machine with my hip. I think about hearing my piss hit the ground from the right height. You want to do me a favor? Give me back one of those.'

Actually I don't think about those things. Not any more. I trained myself to keep away from them. A lot of guys weren't that smart. No way Sanford could know I wasn't one of them. It was reverse psychology. Shut him up for the rest of the trip.

I watched the chrome jaguar at the front of the hood. It was ridiculously big. I wondered if he ordered it special. Had it flown in from England, with its trainer. The streetlights played wild tricks with it. It was so shiny. Sometimes I was sure the thing was running on its own.

Sanford dropped me off. I wheeled into the apartment. Lucy wasn't there. It was too late to call.

I wasn't tired. I changed my clothes. I pulled the sheet off Avenging Angel. She startled me. I was nearly done. I put the sling seat up next to the head. I decided she couldn't be perfect. It wasn't realistic for a jungle animal. She had to have a wound. I took off part of one of her ears. Lost to an angry male. Maybe she wasn't putting out.

I climbed down and took a look. Now the beast looked like she knew what she was roaring about. That made her even scarier. But something felt so damn familiar about her now. Did I copy her off a photo somewhere without realizing? Or off another painting? It bothered me.

I sat and closed my eyes. I paraded every tiger I ever saw through my head. I couldn't come up with it.

I opened my eyes. The light was bright for a second.

Wait. The flash of light. On the cat's body. Sanford's car. The jaguar on the hood. The streetlights flashing on it. I saw a scrape on it. In the front, where the ear would be. The same ear I just cut off the tiger.

My stumps started to shake. Then my stomach went crazy. I just made it to the bathroom. I puked my guts out.

I lay on the tile floor. It was cool. It felt good. I was sweating like I was in a jungle.

Now I understood. For three years the tigers were trying to tell me something. I wasn't paying attention. These weren't tigers. They were jaguars. Actually, they were one jaguar. The one on the front of Sanford's car.

I had seen it once before. Three years ago. It roared at me while the car broke me in two.

Fifteen

I was the only one in the reception area except for the sergeant. He was sitting at a desk. It was ridiculously high. When I looked up at him I felt it in my neck.

'Excuse me,' I said.

He leaned over and looked down at me. He had a name tag on. Katz. I didn't like it. 'Can I help you?' he said.

'A guy tried to kill me . . .'

He moved some papers around and interrupted. 'Name?'

I told him. '. . . I just realized it . . .'

'Address?'

I told him. '. . . I came right over . . .'

'Where did the incident occur?'

'Brooklyn Heights Road. Somewhere past Shiloh.'

'What time?'

'I don't know exactly. About eleven at night.'

'What happened?'

'A guy tried to kill me with his car.'

'You were on the side of the road?'

'No, I was in a car.'

'He drove you off the road?'

'No, he smashed into me.'

'What makes you think he was trying to kill you?'

'I know he wants me dead.'

'You know him?'

'Yes.'

'Why does he want you dead?'

'He thinks his wife is hung up on me. We used to go out.'

'Has he threatened you?'

'Actually, he's been OK to me. But that's because he's setting me up.'

'You seem to know him pretty well.'

'Professionally. My money runs through him. I'm a sculptor.'

'Did he confront you after the accident?'

'I'm not sure. I was unconscious, so I doubt it.'

'You were unconscious? Did you go to the hospital afterwards for treatment?'

'Somebody took me in.'

'Usually they hold head injuries at least over-night.'

'They held me for three months.'

I heard Sergeant Katz's pencil drop to the desk. He said, 'Look, buddy. I've been on duty twelve hours. One of the vans carrying the circus was repossessed today, and I'm not in the mood for any more shit. Now, when was this accident?'

'Just about three years ago.'

'Three years ago. And here you are at five-thirty in the morning reporting it.'

'I just figured out who did it. It was a hit-and-run.'

'Three years ago. Hold on.' He disappeared and came back a minute later with a file. 'The statement says you were picked up along Brooklyn Heights Road and taken to the hospital. Both legs were crushed. The driver of the other car never surrendered. A copy of this file was submitted to your insurance company.'

'Never surrendered? Why the hell would he surrender? You're supposed to find him. You're the police.'

'If somebody brings you in after an accident, all we know is what people tell us. We don't go to the scene unless there's a fatality.'

'Is the case still open?'

'It's as open as it ever was.'

'Did you have any suspects?'

'"Hit-and-run. No witnesses." What kind of suspects could we have?'

'That's why I'm giving you the suspect right now. His name is Sanford Shoreham. He's an accountant. He drives a gray Jaguar.'

'And why are you telling me this now, instead of three years ago?'

'Like I said. I just remembered it. I was hit on the head during the accident. Everything's coming back slowly.'

'You just remembered seeing him in the car as you were hit?'

'Not exactly. But I remembered it was him.'

'What exactly did you remember?'

'I have this image of a big cat. It's burned into my mind. I know it sure as I know my name. Today I realized the cat is the jaguar on the front of his car.'

'So you have an image of a big cat, and this cat is the jaguar on the front of the car, so you're sure this fellow hit you and was trying to kill you.'

'It's hard to explain.'

'It's hard to understand.'

'I was riding in his car when I saw it. I'm sure it was him.'

'So this fellow was giving you a ride in his Jaguar and you looked out and saw his hood ornament and decided he had tried to kill you three years earlier. Could it possibly be another Jaguar?'

'It was his Jaguar. It has a scrape on the side of the head. Just like the image of the cat in my mind. I made a sculpture of it.'

This time he didn't answer.

I said, 'Just put it into the file. How soon can you get him picked up? I know where he is.'

'We'll send the information to the DA's office. It's up to them.'

I heard him close the file. He wasn't going to do anything. He probably thought I was just another case from the circus.

'I want something done. This is discrimination

against the handicapped,' I said. 'I'm going to get the Feds after you.'

'Tell them the name is Katz. K-A-T-Z.'

When I opened my front door, Avenging Angel scared the hell out of me. For a second I tried to yell but nothing would come out. This was a real tiger, all right. When I calmed down I remembered about the car. Then I couldn't really see the tiger part any more. No, I could see it, but it didn't matter to me. Now I saw the jaguar. That was the scariest of all.

I was glad it was finished, or pretty much. There were some details yet. I could get somebody else to do them before they made the mold. I couldn't work on the sculpture any more, now that I saw what it was. I could never do another tiger. It had jumped out of me.

I covered it with a couple of wet sheets. Avenging Angel. A sculpture for money. Compliments of Sanford. Or was it Esther. The monument to the life I lost.

But the monument wasn't enough. Not nearly enough. There was the matter of Sanford himself. Things had to be made square.

Remembering about him and the accident was a big thing for me. But timing was a problem. If I'd remembered this right after I got out of the hospital I would have known what to do. I would have gone to his office. Barged right in. I would have locked my arms around his throat and choked him to death. Even if he dragged me out of my chair and across the floor. Even if the board of directors of some company was in the room and hit me on the head with umbrellas. That's how mad I would have been.

If I'd remembered six months after that I might have gotten myself a gun. I would have shot off his legs. Eye for an eye style. It would have been satisfying. I was cooler by then.

Now I didn't know what to do. I was a mellow

140

guy. Mr CRP. That's what Daphne said. I didn't have the blood urge any more. I trained myself away from it.

I remembered the conversation I had with Esther. If they found the guy, she wanted to put spiders on his legs. Or dip him in acid. Or blow his legs off.

I remember wondering why she was so excited about it. Now I knew. She knew Sanford did it. She was excited about watching spider bites rot his legs away. She couldn't stand the guy. But if she knew this, why did she keep trying to make me think it was Lucy's fault? Why didn't she just tell me? Or turn him in? How could she be with him at all? How could she have his kid?

Lucy knew Esther was making all this stuff up. Why didn't Lucy say something? Why were they protecting him?

It couldn't be that. Lucy probably didn't know. She must have showed up after he drove off. I can't see her letting him get away with it.

Esther might have been waiting for the perfect moment to nail him. Or maybe she was holding it over him. Squeezing him for money. Maybe he was worth more to her this way than if they got him. She could be that cold-blooded.

I could ask Lucy and Esther. They would never answer me. They didn't do anything for three years. They weren't about to start now. I had to do it myself.

But what the hell could I do? The law was no use. Sergeant Katz didn't think I had a case. He should have looked at my stumps. Pretty good evidence.

I could go ahead and get the spiders. Through mail order or something. But how was I going to put them on Sanford? Or wrap him with dynamite or dip him in acid?

Wait. What did I want? If I got a chance to run him down with a car was it important that he knew it was

141

on purpose, because of what he did to me? Or was it good enough just to run him down?

I finally knew I wanted him to know that I knew what he did. And that I was the one who was holding the scales of justice. Pushing them with my thumb.

Sixteen

I woke up late in the morning. I didn't have any more work to think about. I tried to read, but it's too much hassle. Anyway, the magazines were all turning yellow. I turned on the TV. All garbage.

When Lucy showed up I was brooding. I learned how to brood in the hospital, from the guy in the next bed. He smashed up a hip skiing. His walking days were over. He went four weeks without saying one word. And he had lots of visitors.

'I'm surprised you're not working,' she said.

'It's done.'

'It's done? That's terrific!' She reached for the sheets.

'Don't.'

'Why not?'

'I don't want it to dry out.' I didn't want to look at it again.

'You should feel wonderful about finishing. What's wrong?'

I said, 'Nothing. I'm a little tired, I guess.'

'What time did you get home last night?'

'Not late.'

'What were you doing back there?'

If I told her about Daphne, she would figure Sanford had a reason for introducing me. Esther. What else? I didn't want to get into that. I didn't want to tell her about the jaguar either.

I said, 'Some collector. Two of them. They were asking me about the tigers.'

'Why couldn't I wait for you?'

'You could. You could have been in on it. It was no big deal.'

'Sanford said you were involved in a long, complex negotiation. That's the only reason I left.'

'Well, who knows what that guy's thinking.'

'His wife made sure she left just as I did, and in the parking lot she cut me off with her car. I came this close to slamming into her. She rolled down her window and stuck out her head, right in my lights. She had a big loopy smile. She was plastered. She yelled, "They weren't clouds, Lucy. Shame on you. You're not doing your job." She was so loud that everybody in the parking lot could hear.'

I said, 'They weren't clouds. They were fans.'

'Am I doing my job?'

'How do I know. They pay you a lot.'

'Tell me.'

'You're not king of the mountain these days. I don't have to tell you that.'

'I know. But do I still get the job done?'

'What job? I don't like to think of myself as a job.'

'The job Esther was talking about.'

'You mean the night job? You made it with the mandrill. Don't you think that's getting the job done?'

She sat down with me. She put a hand on my chest. 'You remembered,' she said softly.

We didn't talk for a minute. I couldn't get Sanford out of my mind.

Then she said, 'I don't know why I'm letting her get to me now. She's usually so easy.

'She came right after me, to be sure to make a scene in front of all those people.'

'You were on her turf at the CRP. She's the Queen Accountant.'

'Once she'd made me stop and she'd said her piece, she looked positively triumphant. She straightened her head, threw her shoulders back, and rode off. Like Ben-Hur.'

'Ben-Hur?'

'When he came in for the victory at the chariot race.'

144

I said, 'It's hard to think of an accountant's wife as a chariot driver. Especially in a parking lot.'

'You know what I mean. She had the same attitude.'

I knew what she meant. That's what made it so ridiculous.

Lucy went to bed early. I stayed up. Sanford rode my brain like Ben-Hur behind a team of horses. The thought of him made my mind gallop. He didn't have to whip me. I was pre-whipped.

In a way it helped me. I was narrowing my options. I decided I didn't want to kill him. That would be too quick. I wanted to maim him. I wanted him to live with it. That ruled out bombs and poisons. Too bad. They would be easiest. The next easiest would be to shoot him. I used to be able to shoot up a Stop sign at sixty m.p.h., holding a beer and the steering wheel. I was pretty sure I could hit him from a moving wheelchair without killing him.

I had to get him alone. Without anybody else knowing. Maybe I could lure him outside of town. Tell him I was thinking of racing, but I didn't want anybody to know. He'd go for it. But the cops would get me. They'd get the tracks of my wheelchair. Or knuckleprints, if I tried to ape-walk out of there. Sanford could splatter me all over the front of his Jaguar and they couldn't find any evidence. Didn't even bother looking. But they would get me. I just knew it. There was no use thinking about it any more. I was driving myself crazy. I climbed up a rope and swung across the room a few times. I still liked feeling the wind. I owned my little rented world. Outside, that belonged to Sanford. So be it.

I dropped down into the seat of Hell on Wheels. The axle crunched against the blocks. Dust flew. I'm not the greatest housekeeper.

There wasn't much to see from this chair, the way it was turned. Only the back of the three sculptures. First

145

little Sidney. Then Brute. Beside it, mighty Avenging Angel. All draped in white.

It didn't seem right to kiss them off after all that work. Even if they weren't tigers. They should be something. It would be nice if they could run around the apartment. That would make it more exciting in here. I didn't have to think of them as tigers. They could be horses. I grabbed one of the ropes and lashed at their behinds. 'Yah!' I yelled. Then I remembered Lucy was asleep.

I listened for a minute. She didn't get up. She was so funny. That story about the parking lot. Three months ago she probably would have smashed into Esther and then sued her for damages to her car. Now she was worried about Esther's drunken garbage. 'They weren't clouds, Lucy. Shame on you.' Esther driving off like Ben-Hur. It was too much.

Ben-Hur. The Great Circus of Rome. I still remembered that stupid movie from when I was a kid. I saw it about ten times.

And here I was. Parked in my chariot. Hell on Wheels. Behind my white steeds. There were only three of them. A handicap. Not only that. The first one was ten times the size of the third. The team wouldn't be so good on the straightaways. But on the turns, look out. The little one would take the inside. We would be great. Everybody knows the Great Circus is won on the turns.

Hail, Caesar. The consul drops his hanky. The race starts. It's a crowded field. Chariots turning over left and right. Guys flying through the air. Stretcher-bearers running in and out. But we're solid. Sidney holding tight to the rail. Brute high-stepping outside his shoulder. Avenging Angel thundering around the outside, keeping everybody else away. We hurdle over broken chariots. Maybe a rider or two disappears under their hooves. It's so fast it's hard to tell. The air is filled with the sting of whips. My steeds don't need one. An easy victory. The consul places the wreath on my head. 'I crown their god,' he says. The fans scream. They love me. 'Whose?' I say. He says, 'The cripples. God of the cripples.' I am honored throughout the land. My last celebration is a procession through the great hall of the CRP. Cripples toss flower petals in my path and over my cape. Daphne kicks them at me.

I let this ridiculous fantasy go on for a while. The point of the whole thing was staring me in the face and I didn't see it. Lucy would say I wasn't letting myself see it. Maybe not.

After five or six trips to the emperor's chair, it finally hit me. I wasn't in a chariot. I was in a wheelchair and there was a race coming up in a month. Not nine laps in the Great Circus of Rome. The 1,000 meters in the Olympian Games.

My enemy was going to be in it. Just like Ben-Hur's. I could deal with mine like he did his. It was the perfect situation. We would be racing as equals. He wouldn't suspect anything. He couldn't get away from me. No-one could protect him. And if I did it right I wouldn't be blamed.

I could feel my heart skipping around. I was so damn excited. Probably scared too. I couldn't remember what happened to Ben-Hur after his victory. All I remember is that at the end of the movie he found Christ. I could handle that, as long as I got to leave my enemy face down in the dirt. First.

Down Eros. Up Mars.

Seventeen

You don't use a regular wheelchair in a race. It makes you sit up straight over the wheels. That's fine for tooling around. But you don't get much leverage. You can't move out.

A racing chair is different. The seat is lower, behind the wheels. You can really get hold of the wheels and drive them forward. Long strokes. Your legs, or whatever's left of them, hang in a sling in front of you. It sounds weird, but it's comfortable. You feel balanced so you can push even harder against the wheels.

I borrowed a racing chair last year. I got up some good speed in it. Even though the way the race went I could have won on rollerskates.

This year there was a big problem. I had to get hold of a chair without Sanford knowing. If he found out I was racing he'd know exactly what I was up to because I kept refusing and suddenly I changed my mind. He's a clever guy.

The CRP was the only place to borrow one. But he knew everything that happened at the CRP. I could buy one. Not that I wanted one. They're expensive. I didn't want to park another chair in my apartment. And it wasn't like I was going to use it to go jogging after the race was over. Anyway, he'd hear about it if I bought one. He was the money man. He had his hand on every cripple supplier in the county. Maybe even in the state. Those places are all hooked up by computer.

There was only one way to get a chair without him knowing for sure. I had to make it myself. I needed supplies. Mostly tubular steel. Or plastic. And wheels. I could buy two pairs of wheels without seeming suspicious. They get damaged and have to be replaced. No big deal.

I made a few sketches. I didn't realize how tricky it was to put the damn thing together. I didn't know the angles for the structural pieces or where they crossed. Or how the whole thing balanced. I tried to remember what the chair I raced in looked like. Too bad I never bothered to look at it like that.

It was no use. I had to have plans. Without them my chair would be a lemon. I would come around the first turn of the race and the thing would shake into pieces, leaving me sitting with my butt on the cinders. Just like in the train station.

But I couldn't get plans. A racing wheelchair isn't your regular project in a how-to book. I had to start with something put together, and adapt it.

I didn't want to use my chair. What if I messed it up? I'd have to buy another one. I'd be stranded in the house until it came, relying on Lucy. There was no telling how long she was going to stick around.

The only other possibility was Hell on Wheels. It was in great shape. I only used it a few times before the incident. I could lower the seat. Move it back. Get a new set of wheels. Put in a sling.

I wasn't easy with that idea. Hell on Wheels meant a lot to me sitting there parked in its spot. It kept me clear about me and the world. If I cut it up I might lose it.

On the other hand, Hell on Wheels was the worst humiliation of my life. Now I had a chance to turn it into my greatest triumph.

Before I could change my mind I put Hell on Wheels on my workbench. I cut the verticals underneath the seat with a hacksaw. There was no going back.

I put the chair back on the blocks, resting on the axle. I experimented with the balance. I got a pretty good idea of what I wanted to do.

It took a few calls to find the material. I chose steel

149

because it could be bent and welded. I had a welding torch. The wheels were no problem. The guy who answered the phone knew my name. I was the champion.

Everything was delivered in two days. I sawed off the front of the chair. I welded on two long pieces of steel tube. I cut them down slowly, testing each length. I did the same with two pieces running out the back. I kept putting on the seat and the wheels and taking them off, to check the balance. I got it just right.

Some of the supporting pieces were trickier. I made some mistakes. I cut off some tube I should have left. The frame got wobbly, so I welded in more tubing. I took it slow. I still had almost a month to go.

Lucy stayed with me every night. Hell on Wheels was out there in clear view. She didn't say anything about it for a week. One night she came in before the smoke from the torch cleared. She smelled it. Then she asked.

I said, 'I'm making a racing chair.'

'Out of Hell on Wheels? I thought you loved that chair. I thought it was sacred.'

'I'm making it faster. That's all.'

'But why?'

I didn't want to tell her about the race. Maybe I was afraid she'd figure out the real reason and try to stop me. Or warn him. God knows why.

I said, 'I get bored sitting around all day.'

'You bought all this stuff to soup up a chair you never use.'

'I'll use it when it's done. You'll see.'

'It's not like you. You decided to enter the race, didn't you.'

If I denied it she would have nailed me. 'I might. I'll see how fast I go.'

'You swore you'd never be in the Games again. You said they're a spectacle. Normal people come to watch you so they can feel lucky.'

'Handicapped people should get a chance to win. And get their reward.'

'"Handicapped people"? Did I hear you right?'

'I'm practicing. I don't want to offend anybody over there.'

Lucy said, 'What changed your mind? Did Sanford offer you another commission so he can yank you around some more?'

'He's got nothing to do with it.'

'Like hell he doesn't. It's his money. He's not what you'd call a generous man.'

'He's trying to get people interested in the race.'

'He was trying to get *you* interested in the race. But it didn't work. The money wasn't enough.'

'Damn right,' I said. 'I can't be bought.'

'Which means that you're entering for another reason.' Lucy felt like a big noose closing around me.

I said, 'I thought it might be fun. A lot of guys are entering because of the money. I think I can beat them.'

'You don't give a rat's ass about them. It's Sanford. You want to beat him.'

The noose was getting tight. She knew. She continued. 'The issue between you is bigger than money. I know what it is and I'm not going to take it lying down.'

I believed her. I needed a minute to think. 'I don't know what you're talking about.'

She said, 'Oh yes you do. It's her! You're fighting over her. Two little boys on the playground, playing in your little chairs, trying to impress the girl. What a spectacle you're going to be. I feel sorry for both of you . . . What are you smiling about? You think this is funny?'

I was smiling. I didn't mean to. It was relief. She didn't know the plan. I was happy she thought I was racing to impress Esther.

Lucy burst into tears. 'I've been with you for three

151

years. Three years when she didn't so much as send you a Get Well card. Don't you care about me at all? How can you humiliate me like this.'

Suddenly she had runny makeup all over her face. With her braids pinned to the top of her head she looked like an aging schoolgirl. She ran into the bedroom.

I felt bad. But I didn't know how to soothe her without telling her everything. I could hear her weeping. I ape-walked into the bedroom. 'All right. I admit it. I want to beat the guy. I don't like him messing up our race with his money. I don't think a guy with legs has any business being in our race. Do you blame me?'

Her head was on the pillow. She was looking the other way. She wasn't moved.

I said, 'Esther's got nothing to do with it. As far as I'm concerned, the two of them got their just deserts. Each other. I mean it.'

Lucy still didn't move.

'I don't have to prove anything to him. Or her. Or anybody. I'm my own man.'

'Are you?' she said.

'Nobody tells me to do nothing. I do what I want.'

'Then don't race.'

'Why? I don't get it. Because of Esther?'

'As a favor to your lover. Because you want to please her.'

She was making this hard. I sat beside her and stroked her hair. We didn't talk for a while. I leaned over and kissed her. She put her arm around my neck. I spoke to her in lover-voice. Which is kind of like baby-voice, only a little lower. It always makes me feel like an idiot. 'The race only lasts a few minutes, snuggly. You can handle that. Can't you?'

'No.'

'I want to beat the guy. I can use the money.'

'I'll give you the money.'

152

'I got to do this.'

She dropped her arm and turned away. I sat up. She was getting me mad. How many ways were there for me to get satisfaction any more? When she got depressed did I tell her not to mope? Did I take her to parties and make her do the Bunny Hop?

I looked at her behind. In her straight skirt it looked like a big, juicy plum. The weight she had gained filled her out just right. And those long shapely legs.

Cripples don't have much of a life expectancy. I had to do what Daphne said. Take what I wanted. I pulled up her skirt and yanked off her panty hose and panties. She didn't try to stop me. But she didn't help me.

I pulled off my pants. I rolled her over and fell on top of her. I stuffed myself in. She wouldn't look at me. She was silent. Her cunt was betraying her. It was giving me little squeezes.

I'm not rough with women, but I liked this. Served her right giving me a hard time. She knew it too. Or else she would have said something. And she wouldn't be sopping wet.

Soon I was ready to come. I wasn't waiting for her. Suddenly she pushed me off.

'What the hell . . .' I said.

She rolled on to her knees. 'Up the rope.'

She wanted a Tarzan. I said, 'This isn't the time.'

'Up the rope.' It came through her teeth.

I climbed. I was too charged to argue. She was fiddling with something in her bag. She grabbed my stumps and guided my cock in.

'Feel good?' she said.

'Oh yes.'

'Getting close?'

'Oh yes.'

She put a hand on my stomach and pushed me out. I swung back on the rope. The cold air made my cock ache.

I started climbing down. I was going to have this out

with her. No woman did this to me since I was fifteen.

'Stay there,' she said. Her voice was like steel. I stayed.

She pulled my stump toward her pussy.

'What the hell are you doing?' I said.

'If I have to suffer being with a cripple, at least I should get the benefits.'

My stump was slick. She had a lubricant in her hand. She put the stump at her opening.

'I don't want to do this,' I said. It felt kind of sick.

'You started a rape. What's wrong. Lose your nerve?'

'It's got nothing to do with nerve.' Maybe.

'Do you think stumps are repulsive?' she said.

'No. But they're not roses either.'

'Then hide this one.' She backed into me. She was making me feel cold all over. Like after all this time I didn't even know this woman. She said, 'Come on. Push. I thought you were a big-time athlete.'

'Not any more.'

'Sure. That's why you have to be in the race. Nobody tells you to do nothing.'

'This is about the race?'

'That's right, lover boy. Before you do this to me in front of five hundred people, I want to see what it feels like alone with you.'

She bucked back into me. My stump sunk into her. I could feel that this was no pussy. She took me in her ass.

I thought the whole thing was disgusting. Or I thought I thought the whole thing was disgusting. My cock was hard as bronze. She was pushing back and forth. She said, 'First time in three years I've been filled up.'

That made me mad. I drove the stump into her like a vaulting pole. She screamed. I knew she didn't mean to. That made it sweeter for me. She stuffed her head into the pillow.

She kept moving. Sweat rose on her butt. The bitch

was getting off on this. I could tell. Her hips bucking like crazy, then slowing until they stopped. Then twitching just enough so I could feel it with my stump. My shrunken, ugly, atrophied leg. I hated her for this. But my cock felt like it was going to explode.

She put a hand on my stump and started pulling me out very slowly. I jerked away from her. She screamed and fell to the bed. She rolled up like a baby, holding her ass. I looked down at her. I wanted to fuck her lights out. But I didn't want to touch her.

She gave me a steely smile. 'Now I know. Enjoy your race.'

Eighteen

I finished the chair by the end of the week. I sat in the seat and strapped myself in. The balance was great. The wheels were right in my powerhouse. I felt like I could fly.

I went over the frame one last time. There were scratches. Discoloration from the heat. I wanted it to look sharp for my ride to glory. I decided to paint the whole thing black. Except for the back of the seat. My painting of the locomotive. Hell on Wheels. I touched up the lettering. I wanted the guys to be able to read it from a long way back. That's where I planned for them to be.

I had to get myself into racing shape. I did like Sanford. Every time I thought of it I dropped to the floor to do pushups. I could do them by the hundred. They weren't hard for me because I didn't have much weight to push. I also worked the ropes. Up and down. Sets of twenty-five. You do that ten times a day and your muscles feel like they're radioactive.

I was in good shape. The guys from the weight room might be stronger than me, but they just had bulk. They didn't know what to do with it. I'm an athlete. I have coordination. Timing.

What worried me was my wind. That's not like riding a bicycle or catching a ball. If you don't exercise you lose it. The last sustained exercise I had was doing a Tarzan. I didn't do them very much. And I bet I wasn't going to get the chance to do one for a long time.

There was no way to work on endurance inside the apartment, the kind I needed for pushing the chair. Not in the exact muscles. I couldn't take more than two

156

strokes in the chair without running into something. Usually Avenging Angel. She still took up most of the room.

I wanted to see how bad my wind was. I wanted to test my wheelchair. I wasn't sure it would feel as good rolling as it did still. But I had the same problem. If I went outside somebody would tell Sanford. He'd know what I was up to.

I got edgy because I wasn't getting into real shape. I couldn't stand the idea of being unable to catch Sanford on the track. Watching him cross the finish line ahead of me. Him with his legs. Keeping his prize money. Thinking about it killed me.

I had to take a test run. Late at night was the only safe time. Then I could run in the street. No traffic. I didn't want to use the sidewalks. Bumping in the cracks every second. That could chew up my new wheels before the race.

I asked Lucy not to come around that night. I told her I wanted to be alone. She said she understood. She was lying. I took a nap late in the afternoon and ate a late dinner. At two in the morning I eased Hell on Wheels out the door.

I rolled down the ramp of the building. The chair was silent. No scratching or scraping. No thumping. A good sign the wheels were balanced.

I got into the street. The street lights were on. I could hear them buzzing. Everything else was silent. Asleep. I used to love the night. The cool. The quiet. Making my rounds. I tried not to waste the night by sleeping. I started sleeping at dawn. But I changed my ways, three years ago.

I started moving out. The chair glided. It didn't lose speed. Good bearings in the wheels. Better than in my regular chair. Every push made me go a bit faster. I could feel the wind. My hair blew up off my neck. It was like old times. I could feel goose bumps on my stumps.

I stopped at the light. There weren't any cars going either way, but I waited for it to turn. I could hear the mechanism clicking in the box at the bottom of the pole. I never heard it before. I was always inside a car, listening to the tape deck. Then I crossed. I felt like a high-speed vehicle. Something too dangerous to just blow through intersections.

Soon I was up to speed again. I loved the motion. Looking down at the street and watching it fly by. The zip when I passed over a manhole cover. I loved making long, powerful strokes with my arms. Much more satisfying than pushups. I loved feeling my pulse in my neck. Hearing it in my ears. Like I was alive again.

It didn't take me long to go what I figured was about 1,000 meters. It was a short race. Almost a sprint. I was breathing hard now. Sweating. But I wasn't tired at all.

I had to keep going. That's how you train. You go a longer distance than your race. That way the race seems easy. I turned away from the center of town. Too many lights. And there might still be traffic.

Everything was clear the other way. I picked streets that had some lights out. I disappeared into a stretch of blackness. Without them I couldn't see anything. I hit bumps now and then. I had no idea what they were. Asphalt patches. Squirrels maybe.

When I came out of the black stretch and into the light I felt like I could see everything. I saw houses for the first time. Houses I saw a hundred times but never noticed. I saw people's lives. The trouble they took keeping their places up. Painting. The lawns. The flower gardens. I always thought that's what I'd do with my spare time too, once I got married. I kind of liked the idea of drinking beer with one hand and holding a leaf blower with the other. But a leaf blower in a wheelchair. That didn't make it.

I couldn't feel bad about that now. I couldn't feel bad about anything. I was still moving out. My arms had a dull ache deep in my muscles. There was a little fire in my lungs. Like a cigarette lighter. Still, I felt like I could keep up this pace forever.

I saw a couple of teenage boys hanging out on a corner. Leather jackets. Acne. I thought I looked like a good target for a hold-up. A cripple in a wheelchair. Then I realized they'd have a hell of a time catching up with me.

I swung on to Shiloh. I took the turn on to Brooklyn Heights Road. Somehow I didn't think about where I was going until I got there. A short way up Brooklyn Heights Road. The site of the crash.

After I got out of the hospital I had Lucy drive me up here once. I just looked and went home. I didn't remember anything. It was the only time I came by here until now.

I felt sick at first. Thinking my wheels might be right on the spot where Sanford's wheels ran me down. Thinking that if the street lights went out I could run down somebody else. Or another car could get me.

I got really intense. I looked all over the place. Like I was going to find something to prove it was him. Something monogrammed. Or a reminder of me. Three-year-old blood stains. Or legs lying in the weeds behind the shoulder. Bones in shoes.

I didn't see anything. No surprise. I didn't know the exact spot where I was hit. It could have been anywhere along here. All I knew is what people told me. There's nothing special about this piece of road. Two lanes. Double yellow line. Asphalt with patches. A good-sized gravel shoulder. It was like that up and down, as far as I could see.

I thought about my red Camaro. It was night. I was driving west. Up the hill, toward Lucy's place. I guess. That's what everybody said.

I wheeled into that lane now. West. Up the hill. There was no traffic. I pretended I was driving that night. What did I know about that night? Esther was being a pain in the ass. That part was easy to believe. I wanted a break, even for just a night. I wanted to be with a woman who knew how to take care of me. That was Lucy. That used to be Lucy.

So here I was. Tooling up the road. Was I not paying attention? Unlikely. Worried? Probably a little. Esther believes in putting brown recluse spiders on people who cross her. But overall I was probably happy. Excited to be free. To be seeing Lucy. I wasn't seeing much of her any more. I expected that any day she was going to meet Prince Charming and walk out on me for good.

I was moving pretty good in my wheelchair now. Could I have been speeding that night and lost control? No. I once totaled a car driving too fast. A T-bird. A beauty. I walked away from the wreck. I swore: never again. Was I drinking? Probably a little. I had a beer holder attached to the glove compartment in my Camaro. But I knew when to stop. Anyway, I'm sure they took blood from me in the hospital to measure alcohol. The insurance company was probably praying I'd come out higher than the magic number. It would have saved them a fortune. I never heard anything about it.

I was forgetting again. I had such a hard time with this: I didn't crash. My Camaro was in Harry's lot. Untouched. I must have gotten out of the car.

I kept wheeling up Brooklyn Heights Road. What could have made me stop? It wasn't a good road to stop on. Traffic moved fast. There were too many curves. Too many blind spots. Even the shoulder didn't look safe.

Maybe I had car trouble. Maybe I was down-shifting and my transmission stripped. Or I ran out of gas. Maybe. It was hard to believe that I could forget something like that. Even if it happened that day. My Camaro was like a part of me. I kept her like a queen.

I would have remembered easing off to the side.

Limping out of traffic. Hearing gravel crunch. Feeling crippled. It would have been my first time.

I must have seen something. Maybe on the side of the road. A person? An animal? Or maybe I saw somebody in a car. I turned off the road to hook up with him. Or her. Somebody else had to pull over too, or else I wouldn't have gotten out of the car.

I wheeled on to the shoulder to get the sensation of slowing and stopping on this road. I didn't like it. I felt so vulnerable. Like somebody could come up and do anything they wanted to me. I felt that now, when there were no cars.

So I pulled over. For whatever reason. Sanford comes up the road. He sees me. I see him. Maybe in the rearview mirror. It's hard to believe I would pull over for him. I had nothing to say to him. He was just a nerd who was in love with my girlfriend. Anyway, I walked out in back of my car. He pulls off the road behind me. I think he's going to stop. But he keeps going. Maybe he's smiling because in a second he's finally winning Esther.

I still can't believe it. There were other ways to get her from me. He could have waited me out. Things weren't so great between us.

I see him coming. I try to run but I can't. Or I run but I don't get far. My bones are crushed between the bumpers like nuts in a nutcracker. Bone pieces rip through my skin. Blood fills my pants and socks and runs down my shoes into the gravel. The pain is beyond anything I ever thought was possible. I swing my fists at the air. I scream so hard his windshield shakes. He backs up his car. I topple like a tree. The jaguar on the front of his hood looks like it's leaping at me. Actually I'm doing the leaping. Downward. The jaguar is the last thing I see before my head smashes against his hood. The next thing I see is a bedpan on the dresser. In the hospital. After surgery.

And then Sanford drove off, leaving me here. I

wheeled up the shoulder. Filthy gravel smelling of exhaust and gasoline. Old tar bubbles. A crushed can. A piece of a tire. Some newspaper caught in the weeds. It was Godforsaken. He left me lying in this. Blood pouring from my shattered legs. Helpless. God.

My face got hot. I closed my eyes. I couldn't hold it back. I cried. I couldn't stop. It was a good thing it was night and I was alone. I saw myself pitched face-down on the asphalt. Trying to get up. Crying for help. Trying to wave at passing cars. They couldn't see me. I couldn't even get to my knees. My knees were gone. I was hemorrhaging. My life seeping away into the filthy gravel. Into the cracks in the road. I was becoming just one more piece of roadside garbage. The life I used to have was already gone.

How could he do this to me and drive off? How could anybody do it to anybody?

Just then I heard a roar. I turned my head. I was blinded by headlights. I froze, just like a deer. The car came right at me. How did it get so close before I heard it? I couldn't wheel my chair. I could barely hold my bladder. The car might have nicked me as it blasted by. It didn't matter. The wind was so strong that I spun around and fell over. Here I was again, three years later. Face down in the gravel.

Now the car honked. The driver just saw me. The brake lights went on. The car stopped. This guy wasn't like Sanford. He was coming to help me out. He was probably looking for me out his rear window.

He didn't turn around. Maybe he couldn't see me. I was flat on the ground. The chair was on its side. The car just sat there. The back-up lights didn't go on. Soon the brake lights went out. The car drove on.

I managed to get up and back into the racing chair. I wheeled into the street. I was worried that the fall bent the chair or knocked it out of balance. But it was OK. This was my lucky day.

I started back. The wind blew my tears dry. I could

feel them pulling at my cheeks. I was hardened now. All I could think about was Sanford Shoreham.

I sprinted down Brooklyn Heights Road. Faster and faster. My hair straight back. My sleeves rippling like a flag. I was going to win the race. I was sure. It didn't matter how many people entered. Even if I had to race in the outer lane the whole way. I was going to explode across the finish line. Then I'd raise my fists and look back to see how far behind me Sanford was.

Fifteen minutes later he'd hand me the winner's check. Shake my hand. Everybody would clap. It would be for him. The generous guy. The gracious loser.

What kind of victory would that be?

I wheeled back down Shiloh. I thought about Ben-Hur coming across the finish line and getting the victor's wreath. He didn't just beat the Roman. He left him in the dust. To die. That wasn't Ben-Hur's plan. He just wanted to win the race. It was the Roman who showed up in the war chariot, with the big blades coming out the axles. Their wheels got locked. Ben-Hur's wheel cut the Roman's axle. It was an accident.

Ben-Hur was a tougher guy than me. He lived three years as a galley slave. I lived three years in a wheelchair. And at the end of it he looked a lot better than me. He had faith. Jesus gave him water. I don't have faith.

The Roman drove black horses. My wheelchair was black. I was going to race in a war chariot. I was going to fix blades to the axle of my wheelchair. I was going to let Sanford have Jesus and all the luck.

When I got back to my place my arms were shaking with fatigue. I was relieved to ape-walk. Different muscles.

It was really late now. Almost morning. I was wide awake. I started toward my work bench. I wanted to start designing the axle blades.

I noticed something on the table. I turned on the

163

light. It was a cake. There were three candles in it. Two plastic figures on top. One was a nurse. The other was a guy in a wheelchair. God knows where she found it. The icing said Happy Anniversary.

So today was the day. Three years to the day since the accident. Three years to the day since I became hers. I had to pick today to tell her to get lost.

I felt bad. I almost called her. But it was way too late. She knew I would feel bad. That's why she left the cake.

That's how things were going between us. A little weird, ever since the night of the Tarzan stumping. I felt kind of dirty. I didn't know how she felt. She didn't say anything. That was another problem. A lot of the time she didn't say anything.

This was a good time to spend some time apart. I wanted to prepare for the race without distractions.

Nineteen

Sometimes I used to watch TV late. Usually after a night of carousing. I never just stayed home the way I always do now. I came in and had a couple of beers. Watched a little tube. Then I went to bed.

I like the late-night commercials. They're real bad. You know you can make better ones in your basement. The same commercials run over and over. You get to know every word even though you don't want to hear them at all. The actors feel like your friends. Like they're the only ones except you still up.

One commercial stuck in my mind. Not that it was any better. The set was cardboard. We weren't supposed to know. The lighting made it look like there was an escalator moving on the collar of the guy's shirt. He talked fast like he knew it was late. He wanted to get home. The commercial was for knives. Foreign knives. Maybe Japanese. I forget the name. Probably made from scrapped Camaros. Anyway, they take one of the knives and bash it with a hammer. Then they drop a cinder block on it. And cut a tin can in half. You think the knife is history. Then they bring out a tomato. It goes through like a razor blade.

I had to slice things up sometimes. Nothing gourmet. Bread. Salami. Stuff like that. I tossed my knives into the sink, even from the living room. But they weren't tough like the one on TV. After a few months they had trouble getting through a Danish. But who wants to spend money on knives.

This commercial ran for months, twice an hour, every night. Then one night a new commercial ran. This time they drop the knife out of a plane and into a pit. Then they dump a ton of gravel on it. Then a tractor comes and runs over the gravel. They dig the knife out. They bring out another tomato. It slices right through.

That did it. I had to have them. They were delivered about two months later. I bought a tomato. I don't like tomatoes. It was just for a test. I pulled the first knife out of the box. I sawed a little. That didn't work. I pressed harder, a lot harder than that guy did. Finally I got through the skin and the damn tomato exploded all over the place. Maybe they use special tomatoes on the commercials. Maybe you're supposed to hit the knife with a hammer and use it to cut a tin can first. Then cut the tomato. I tried that. It still didn't work.

I tossed the box of knives under the sink. That was in my old place. That's the last I saw of them. I figured they were here somewhere. The mover wouldn't bother to steal them. I found them in the back of the kitchen cabinet.

The axle of the Roman's chariot, the one Ben-Hur raced against, had four blades. All facing out from the center. I wanted it the same way. I cracked the handles off four knives with a hammer. Cheap plastic. Then I welded the backs of the blades together. When the cutter cooled off I spun it in my hand. It felt like it could cut through anything.

I couldn't show up at the Games the way the Roman showed up at the Circus with the blades shining in the sun. Pulling up next to Sanford's chair. Maybe smacking him with a crop. They would pack me off to the state asylum.

I could design a base for the cutter to fit over the end of the axle. I could reach down and put on the cutter during the race. But I was worried it would be tough to attach the thing when the axle was turning so fast. I wouldn't have time to slow down. One thousand meters isn't long enough. If the blades fell off – perish the thought – I was in deep soup. That would be it for me and Sanford. I could never touch him the rest of my life.

The cutter couldn't fall off. And I wanted to hide it inside the axle. When I got home after the race I would take it out and lose it. No-one would ever know. Just me and Sanford.

I cut into the chair with a saw. I fixed a lever next to the seat that made the cutter slide out and lock. Then slide back in. When it was in you couldn't see it. I put in only one cutter, on my left wheel. I figured I'd be coming at him from the outside of the track.

Late that night I took another spin to practice popping my cutters in and out. And swooping with my chair.

There was one more thing. I thought about the minute I caught Sanford in the race. What did I want him to think? 'There's Marty. I can beat him.' No. He had to know I was there to make things right. Finally. I didn't want to tell him. I wanted him to see it for himself.

I could think of one sure way to do this. Wear a Roman helmet. Guys at the starting line would think I was being stupid. They didn't know I was racing at all. They'd think I was goofing on the race. That's what Sanford would think too. Down the backstretch I would look different. Coming right at him, where he couldn't get away. He would see I wasn't kidding. He would see the helmet and think of Ben-Hur.

What else could he think? Everybody knows the movie. Everybody knows what happens at the end of the race. I wanted him to have that feeling.

Where do you buy a Roman helmet? You have to be a movie star. Or live near a school with a team called the Romans or the Trojans. Our local college is the Woodchucks.

I had to make one. If I could make a chariot I could make a helmet. I still had my football helmet from high school. I dug it out of the closet. The Farmers. I sawed pieces of it away. Soon you couldn't tell what it used to be.

I needed a plume for the top. I found my old feather duster in the same closet. It was pretty grungy. I knocked the dust out of it. Touched it up with a little red and pink paint. I wanted it to look like a plume from a long way away.

I stuck the plume to the helmet, with a piece of wood in between. I painted the whole thing black, except for the plume.

The last few days I kept doing pushups and climbing the ropes. I ate a lot of spaghetti. Carbo loading. It was good for endurance. Also, that's all I had in the apartment. Lucy didn't come by.

Twenty

Race day. I got up early and ate a last bowl of spaghetti. I finished four hours before the race. It didn't go down easy. I was kind of nervous. I never used to get nervous, not even before a big match. Probably the difference was that this time I was mad. Really mad. This was it for Sanford. Finally I get even. After three years.

I oiled Hell on Wheels. Not that it needed it. I ran a rag over the frame. It was black and shiny. It looked good. I slid out the cutter. I went over the blades with a little oil. When they came out during the race I wanted them to gleam. I polished the helmet with black shoe polish. I fluffed up the feathers.

That was it. Nothing more to do. Killing the last hours was the hard part.

I kind of expected Lucy to show up. She knew this was a big deal to me even if she didn't understand why I was doing it. And it was a good excuse for her to come by. I didn't think she'd want to stay away for so long.

An hour before the race I gave up on her. I called for a cab.

I got out at Flanders Field behind the grandstands. First I pulled the chair out of the car. Then I paid the guy. No-one was going to drive away with Hell on Wheels in the back seat.

Flanders Field wasn't the best name for the setting of the Olympian Games. The vets always complained. The CRP tried to get it changed. But Joe Flanders wouldn't do it. His family owned the land for a hundred years.

There was a big crowd in the grandstand. A lot bigger than last year. I couldn't see the field yet. I was in the back. But I could hear the oohs and ahs.

Then I saw the guys getting ready for the 1,000 meters out at the end of the turn in the track. I knew it was my race, not the 10,000 meters, because these guys looked serious. They were checking each other out. That never happened. Only money could do that.

I started toward them. There was a big scream from the stands. All the racers looked out over the field.

I felt a hand on my shoulder. I turned around.

'It is you,' said Esther. She had a camera hanging around her neck. 'You're not racing, are you?'

'Sure, why not. Take some of your old man's cash off his hands.'

Now I saw Jerold. He was behind her in the stroller. He leaned over for his wheels. 'Tum!' he said.

I said, 'See that? He wants to race too.'

'Why are you doing this? So Sanford can try to make a fool out of you?'

'If the race is such a bad idea, what are you doing here?'

'I'm the Games' photographer. I don't care. Let's go, I'll drive us all someplace. We can go out to the lake.'

She got behind the chair. Like I was going to let her push me off. I didn't know what this was about. I pulled her out in front of me. I said, 'I'm racing. I made this chair just for the race. I'm going to win. Then you can take me and Sanford's $1,000 someplace.'

'He set the whole thing up just to get to you. I thought you knew that.'

'Hey, I used to be a sports pro. This guy's an accountant. I'll spot him two legs and I'll still beat him.'

Esther said, 'So what? So you beat an accountant in a wheelchair race. Will that satisfy you? Is that how low he's pulled you?'

'That and $1,000 will satisfy me.'

'You're so pig-headed. Go ahead. Let him beat you at this too.' She pushed Jerold's stroller toward the front of the grandstand.

'Too?' I called after her. 'What else?'

I joined the other guys on the field. There were a lot of them. Twenty-five easy. All sizes. All accidents. All diseases.

'What's the word, Hit-and-run?' said Pepper. 'What you doing here?'

Salt was there too. They were still limbering up. 'You said you'd never do this again.'

I laughed. 'Live and learn. What the hell. You know all these guys?'

I recognized Sanford. He was in a Spandex suit. Red, white, and blue. Looked like Captain America. A mask would have made it complete. Nicer to look at too.

Salt said, 'I know a couple more spinal cords here. The guy without the shirt is Tank Top. The one with the tattoos is Fire Plug. He's got the whole zodiac on him, six on each arm. Tell him your sign and he'll show it to you.'

I passed on that.

A few of the other guys looked familiar. Probably from the CRP. I could see most of them were here for a good reason. They were cripples. A few of the guys looked fine. Healthy. But you can never tell. Some diseases come and go, at least for a while. Like multiple sclerosis. Race today, in the cat scanner tomorrow. One guy was all twisted up in his seat like some old tree stump. A twisted branch hanging on to his wheel. All gnarls and knots. Cerebral palsy. My heart went out to guys with diseases like that. Compared to them my accident was a bee sting. These guys didn't have a prayer of winning and they knew it. They weren't brain damaged. So what the hell were they doing out here? If they thought racing was such a good idea, they would have come out last year. The flu didn't take down the whole county.

171

It was the goddamn money. Sanford was humiliating these guys, bringing them out like this. He should give them his money. Let them go out and try to have a good time. If they still could.

The guys started clapping. Genghis was running through the infield. He had a funny run, more side to side than forward.

Pepper said, 'The Chinaman won the javelin again. Put out a guy's tire with one throw. Brought down a pigeon with another.' That must have been the scream before. 'Good thing they moved the field events down the open end. He woulda killed people.'

Genghis ran over to a racing chair and strapped himself in.

I said, 'Did you just win the javelin?' He nodded. He was blinking fast. 'Then why are you racing? You don't use a wheelchair. You could be in the regular race.'

'Money,' he whispered. He smiled.

It was time to make sure Sanford knew I was in the race. The helmet was in a bag on my lap. I put it on. Now he'd know what his fate looked like.

Sanford was off by himself at the far end of the group. He was spinning in his chair. Popping wheelies. Like a kid.

'A wheelchair isn't a toy,' I said.

He turned. He cracked a big grin. 'Well, Marty. Now my day is complete. Tell me you're in the race.'

'I'm in the race.'

'Splendid. From the look of that duster on your head you must be planning to clean up out there.'

'Joke while you can, my friend. This time you're not getting away from me.'

'Why on earth would I want to get away from you? I expect you to come in second, unless Loid slips in there ahead of you.'

I didn't see Loid.

'Hey, boss hat,' said Tank Top. Some of the other

guys were coming over. 'I used to be in a gang too. Who'd you ride with?'

'It's not from a gang. It's Roman.'

'Roman Catholic?' he said.

'Roman. Like Ben-Hur. Did you ever see that movie?'

I looked over at Sanford. He was still spinning around, wearing that ridiculous outfit. He didn't look worried. He would later.

Fire Plug reached for the helmet. Snakes and crabs all over his arm. He made me feel creepy.

I made a mistake with the helmet. It was drawing everybody's attention. On the track I didn't want anybody looking at me. Just Sanford.

I wheeled over to Genghis. I took off the helmet and put it on his head. 'I crown you javelin champion.' A couple of guys clapped. Genghis smiled and turned pinker.

I went back to Sanford. I said, 'Be sure to fasten the belt. You get better support. It's better for pushing.' His brand-new chair had a thick nylon belt. New government regulations.

He looked at me funny, like he didn't know if he should believe me.

I said, 'I don't want you to have any excuses when you lose.' Reverse psychology.

He bought it. 'That's sporting of you, Marty.' He fastened the belt.

Somebody told us we were the next event. We started moving up to the starting line. There were so many chairs that we had to line up two deep. It took a couple of minutes to get everybody in position. Pineapple was the starter. There was trouble with the gun and he was trying to fix it.

Sanford was next to me, in the second line. He said, 'I'm glad you're here, Marty. Finally I get a chance to kick your ass.' He was taking this bluff to the end.

'To try, anyway,' I said.

173

'How about a side wager.'

'Name it.'

'If I win, you get out of my life.'

'And if I win?' I said.

'I didn't even consider that. What do you want from me?'

What did I want from him? Before I could answer there was a bang. The gun went flying backwards off Pineapple's hook. Right into the track.

Hail Jupiter and give me victory!

The first line surged forward. But most of the guys didn't get far. They were driving in each others' way. Wheels getting jammed up. That's what happens when you put amateurs into a wheelchair race.

A few guys got loose and took off. I wasn't one of them. I couldn't move until the guys in front of me did. Sanford was lucky. He was behind Pepper, who wiggled loose and broke free. Sanford got out way before me. I was stuck behind the cerebral palsy guy. Finally I pushed his chair to the side. I felt real bad for the guy. But he had to get the hell out of my way.

Soon I got up to pace. The race was four times around the track. I didn't plan to do anything at least the first two. Then things would thin out.

Guys started dropping out fast, especially the rookies. They coasted off to the side, holding their arms or catching their breath. Wheeling was harder work than it looked. Some of them started up again, but they didn't last.

Halfway through the race the regular wheelchair guys were in front. A few others were still in there, like Sanford and some of the gorillas. Sanford moved out much faster than I expected. He had trained hard. What did he think it was going to get him? We didn't close that bet.

I had to keep in striking range. It wasn't easy. He was moving. My arms started aching during the second lap. I didn't train enough. I should have gone out a few more nights. If Sanford wasn't in the race I might have quit.

I didn't forget what I was doing out there. I was thinking of going after him in the second lap. But he had fifty yards on me.

Battle speed.

I closed it during the third lap. Just on bigger arms and smaller legs. I got so there was nobody between me and him. I was still twenty yards back. I yelled, 'Captain America! Captain America!' He turned his head to the right. I rode off to the left so he couldn't see me. He whipped his head the other way. His chair wove on the track and kicked up some gravel. He might have learned to wheel, but he didn't know how to wheel and do something else too. It cost him ten yards.

'Marty. At last,' he said. He was talking straight ahead, but I could hear him.

I lengthened my strokes. My hands stayed on the wheels almost to the ground. I was breathing hard. I felt good. I could keep it up to the end.

Attack speed.

I sprinted all the way up to him. He smiled. He said, 'It's been a long time. I was worried I wouldn't see you until the victory ball.' He was red and sucking for air. But he didn't break his rhythm. He wanted this bad.

'Here I am,' I said.

'Where's your helmet? I was looking for the helmet.'

'Did you know who I was supposed to be, wearing that helmet?'

'A Trojans salesman,' he said.

'Ben-Hur. Remember that movie?'

'Yeah. Christ dies so Ben-Hur's mother's face will clear up.'

I said, 'But first Ben-Hur evens the score.'

We were getting near the grandstands. I couldn't go after him until we were on the backstretch again. No witnesses. I had to wait. I looked into the infield.

Esther was standing out there with the camera in her hands. She looked worried. I guess she really did get it.

Sanford set his jaw and pushed on his wheels. He tried to leave me behind. I was real smooth now. He couldn't get away.

'Does that bother you?' I said.

'You bother me.'

'The part about evening the score.'

He said, 'The only thing bothering me is that Buddha thirty yards ahead of me.'

'You really think you can win?'

'Why not? You cripples all think you're something special.' He bowed his head. This time he took off. I didn't know he had it in him. He was a tough guy. No wonder he didn't mind running me over.

It took me a good fifty yards to pull next to him again. We passed the grandstands. I pulled the lever under the handle. The cutter slid down the axle and stuck out the end. I locked it in place. The steel blades glistened. Ready for anything. Except a tomato.

I looked over at Esther.

Ramming speed.

I moved right next to Sanford. He didn't see the cutter. He was ignoring me. I dipped in. The cutter caught one of his spokes. Ping! They ought to put this in the commercial.

'Watch where the hell you're going,' he said. 'You know how much this thing cost?'

I dipped back in and cut a few more. Sanford looked down and saw the spokes. They were flying every which way. He looked at my chair. Finally he saw the cutter.

What a look. His eyes were popping like Genghis's. His face was red a second ago. Now it was more like scar color. When you're in a wheelchair and something goes wrong, your instinct is to get up and run. It took me a long time to get past that even though I didn't have legs. Sanford had legs. He pushed off the arms. He couldn't get up. He was strapped in. All he had to do was free up his hands. Let go of the wheels. He could get out easy. He didn't think of that.

He was a frightened man.

Sanford wheeled for the inside of the track away from me. I followed. All my practice in the chair paid off. I was much more agile than him. I put the cutters on him again. His wheel sounded like a pinball machine.

He pushed hard across the track. The other way, to cut me off. I let him go. I didn't want him to feel helpless. Not yet. He was working like mad. His mouth was wide open. He was soaked in sweat. I bet the Spandex wasn't making it any easier.

I still had a reserve in me in case I had to sprint with him. Now I knew he was mine.

He started thinking. A white-collar guy. He kept on the outer edge of the track. I could only cut him from the outside. He was safe there. I swooped underneath him, to the inside. Then I got right in front of him. I slowed way down.

He yelled, 'Get the hell out of the way. What the fuck are you doing.'

He bumped me. Then he rammed me. It was nothing. The way the chairs were built he couldn't hurt me like this.

He couldn't take it. He cut back to the inside. All this weaving was wearing him out even more. I was back on his shoulder in no time. We were on the far part of the track, away from the grandstands. It was time.

'This is it, Sanford. Tell me why you did it,' I said.

'Get away from me!'

'Tell me or I'll cut you down. I mean it.'

He screamed. 'I'll tell you. You can't stand a little competition, even when it's fair and square. You never could. Sports or women. You fucking prima donna.' He looked back, like somebody was going to help him.

Help him, a regular person. Against me, a cripple. In a cripple race. Anyway, nobody was there.

I said, 'So you're not talking?' I couldn't wait. Pretty soon we'd be in front of the stands again. I cut in. Ping. Ping. Ping. I pulled away. His wheel sagged.

If I was him I would have stopped and undone the belt. But he panicked. He kept pushing the wheels as hard as he could. The chair bucked. He was bouncing around in the seat. The wheel was breaking down. It got flatter and flatter. The other one kept rolling. His chair started turning toward the outside of the track. Then the wheel gave out. He spun and stopped, facing me.

I came right up to him. Face to face. I was going to ask him one last time. He surprised me. As soon as I got close he took a swing at me. Grazed my cheek. The wheel gave under him, or he would have caught me square. I gave my wheels one hard push and jumped for him. I wrapped my arm around his neck. I could always say I was trying to save him. Stop him from going down. In case anybody was watching.

I was strapped in too. My chair came after me on to him and his chair. We both crashed down to the track on our sides. I could feel my elbow tear up on the gravel. I might need stitches. At a hospital. I hate hospitals. That made me real mad.

I still had my arm around his neck. I pushed my weight on top of him. I was in his face. I could have snapped his neck right then and gotten away with it. I would have been done with him. Gotten on with my stinking life.

His mouth was open. His eyes were popping out. He wasn't even moving. I figured he'd be pounding me. Scratching me. Lying to me. A man ought to put up a fight when he's about to get snuffed.

It was no good. I didn't want him getting off this easy. I had to have a confession. After that I'd decide what to do with him. At this point I didn't really care if

178

he lived or died. As long as he owned up.

'Speak,' I said.

'What do you want from me?' His voice was hoarse.

'Tell me why.'

'Why what?'

'Why did you run me down?'

'Run you down? You ran me down!'

'Three years ago. On Brooklyn Heights Road.'

'I can't feel my arm. Get off it.'

I didn't think I was on it. If I was, I wasn't moving. I pulled his head back by his hair. His razor cut hair. He said, 'You mean your accident? You think that was me? You dumb bastard. Is that what this is all about? Why didn't you just ask me. You asshole.'

'All right. I'm asking.'

'I wasn't even in town that night. I was in Anaheim on business.'

'Don't fuck with me. I'll break you in two. It was your car. I saw it.'

'I left my car here. Ask Esther.'

'How would she know? She was with me that day.'

'She drove me to the airport in the evening. You had a big fight that day, didn't you? What did you expect her to do, sit home and cry while you were off porking Lucy?'

'Esther had your car?'

'That's right. Why don't you try to pin it on her. Now get off my arm.'

I believed the guy. I'm not sure why. Maybe his pain. It's hard to lie when you're in pain. When the Roman guy was in pain he finally told the truth about Ben-Hur's mother and sister being lepers. I would have preferred hearing that than this.

If this was true, I'd fucked up bad. A good thing I didn't break his neck. Maybe not. If I broke his neck I wouldn't have heard it.

I had to get out of here. Go home. Think about this. Talk to Esther.

I was still all wrapped up with Sanford. I got my arms loose. The rest wasn't so simple. The chairs were locked together. He wasn't helping at all. I had to try to rock mine to get free. I put weight on my left wheel. It was on his leg. He didn't say anything. I started moving my chair back and forth. His broken spokes started pulling free of something. They twanged. It was a weird sound.

People were finally coming to help. I could hear their steps on the gravel. I pulled my head up and looked down the track. There was a whole pack of them. Running like people who don't run. All over the place. Joe Flanders was out front. Big fat guy, cigar in his mouth. Must have smelled the lawsuit. There was our nurse, Mrs Bustard. Built like a 250-pound turkey. Good thing we weren't bleeding.

Somebody in the pack fell. Then somebody else. Something was going on in there. Then I saw it. A wheelchair cutting right down the middle of the runners. The race was still going on, at least for the stragglers.

Amal was one of the runners near the front. He didn't know to get out of the way. The front wheel of the wheelchair clipped his heel. He threw out his arms and went down. His hook skidded in the gravel.

Now I could see who was in the chair. From his red plumes. It was Genghis. He looked great. Right out of the movie. His head was down. He usually looked at his toes, even when you were talking to him. Like he was always embarrassed. Now he was looking at his lap. I bet he didn't see Amal or anybody else. As he got closer I could see his face. Pink. Dripping sweat. Eyes bugged out. Nostrils flared. I loved this guy. He was so intense.

He was coming toward us. Maybe he was going to pull me up, like a tow truck. And get Sanford off the track before he got hurt. I yelled Genghis's name. He still didn't look up. Maybe it was the helmet. I should have cut away the part around his ears.

I called him again, as loud as I could. I liked the idea of him saving us. With his feathers whipping in the breeze. Better him than the people running behind him.

He was close now. His lane made a turn. He left it. He was coming to me.

'Maybe you want to back it in,' I called to him.

He wasn't slowing down. He was probably going to skid or pull a wheelie, or something. Like Sanford did before the race. Spray us with gravel. Guys with legs got no class.

Now I could really see his face. I realized what was going on. Genghis didn't see us. He didn't hear a word. He was off in Mongolia somewhere.

I called him one more time. The people running down the track were calling him too. He wasn't going to stop.

I turned Sanford a little bit so his head was behind the top of my chair. To protect him from Genghis's chair. Then I drew myself into a ball. If he had to hit me, he could have my back. I closed my eyes.

Genghis bashed into us. The force of his chair smashed us back across the track. When I opened them Genghis was above us. His wheelchair was on top of ours. Our wheels were on their sides. His wheels were caught in them.

Sanford swore and grabbed his neck. Genghis stopped for a minute. He was shocked by the impact. Now he was trapped. Good thing help was on the way. Genghis didn't want to wait. He started pushing on his wheel again. The guy wasn't too bright.

'Race is over,' I said. He pushed harder. 'It's over. Stop,' I said. I grabbed his hand.

He pulled away. Maybe he would listen if I got the damn helmet off his head. I reached for it. My belt was holding me down. I couldn't get it.

If you push the wheels on a wheelchair it goes

forward. If the wheels don't move, something's got to. The seat. It goes back. That's what happened. He pushed and the chair started tipping back. A foot at a time. You think he would have felt himself going over. It didn't stop him. When he got halfway the chair fell over backwards.

He was stuck in the chair, belted in. His legs flopped on top of his head. He kneed himself in the face. Which is what should happen to all people with legs who use wheelchairs. There he was just above us. Upside down. Still wearing the helmet.

'You moron! You nitwit! You cretin!' Sanford yelled. He still had his hand on his neck.

Genghis looked at him like that was the first thing he heard. His lips started quivering. His face was getting darker and darker. He whispered, 'The money. I win?'

Sanford screamed all kinds of things at Genghis. Stuff you're not supposed to say to somebody like him. Genghis started to cry. Hanging there upside down. He started choking on his snot. His tears ran up his forehead.

Soon people were all around us. Picking up Genghis and me. Brushing us off. Asking if we were all right. Joe Flanders was one nervous guy. Sanford stayed down. He said his neck was bothering him. And his arm. He probably wanted to see Joe sweat. Genghis was still crying. He wouldn't let anyone take off his helmet. Mrs Bustard finally showed up. She painted my elbow with Mercurochrome.

The ambulance came up. They put Sanford on a stretcher. He was talking. He was fine. He was probably trying to get out of paying the prize money.

My chair was scratched up pretty good. But the spokes were straight. The wheels still turned without making noises. It was a miracle. The cutter stayed inside the axle. Nobody saw it. I took the chair back on to the track. It was clear now. I guess the Games were over.

I got up some speed. Felt the wind. It cleared my head. I thought about what Sanford said about Esther and the car. Even if it was true it didn't matter. She was at home during my accident. Lucy called her there to come down to the hospital. They both said that. Esther might have made that up. No way Lucy would cover for her.

The ambulance turned on its flashing lights. It went down the track real slow. Sanford waved. He was just taking a ride.

Twenty-one

When I wheeled past the grandstands I saw Esther.
Most of the people were gone.

'Are you all right?' she said. 'What happened over
there?'

'A little accident.'

'There's blood on your arm.'

'It's nothing. They just took your old man out in the
ambulance.'

'I heard.'

'You did? Why didn't you go with him?'

'I was going to. But what good could I do now? I'd
only be in the way. I'll go see him soon. I was worried
about you.' She put her hand on mine. I didn't like it.
Not with her old man in the ambulance. I wheeled out
from under it.

Jerold was still trying to move his stroller like me. He
couldn't reach his wheels. He shimmied his body back
and forth. The stroller rocked a little. He was getting
frustrated.

'Give him to me,' I said.

'What are you going to do?'

'I want to take him for a spin. What's wrong with
you?' Something was. She handed Jerold to me. I sat
him on my stomach. It was the only level place. I didn't
design this wheelchair for two.

I moved away from Esther. I speeded up slowly. I
didn't want him to get scared. Every time I pushed the
wheels down my chest knocked into him. He didn't
seem to mind. He kept looking straight ahead. Taking
the wind in his face. His hair flew back. Pretty kid's
hair.

Soon I was up to cruising speed. As fast as most people could run. 'Tum!' he said.

'Tum. Fucking Ay Right!' I felt great. The best since I got stumps.

Esther was back in the infield, taking pictures. I kept moving. Jerold said 'Tum' every five or ten seconds like he was my cox. The wind smelled sweet, coming off the cut grass. I did four laps. 1,000 meters. Then I remembered I didn't finish the race. Well I did now. I was like those other assholes. I had legs aboard my wheelchair too.

I wondered who won. Just for a second. It wasn't Sanford, and that's all that mattered.

I stopped in front of Esther. Jerold cried when she took him. 'You're not going to see life this way,' I said. 'You're going to run. Or drive a Jaguar. Or maybe your rich daddy's going to buy you a plane.'

'Don't talk nonsense to him,' Esther said.

He stopped crying. His face was long. Cute kid.

'We'll give you a ride home,' Esther said.

'Aren't you going to the hospital?'

'Your place is practically on the way.'

Fine with me. I didn't want to risk another cab. We loaded the chair into her car. The Jaguar. The ornament had a big scratch on the side, just where I remembered.

She said, 'Sanford took the wagon today because he was bringing his wheelchair.'

We drove. Jerold fell asleep. Esther didn't say anything for a while. Then she said, 'You know, if I go to the hospital right now, I'm going to be sitting in a waiting room for three hours.'

'B t you should go.'

'Yes, and I will.'

We pulled up in front of my place. 'Thanks,' I said.

'Before you go, tell me something. What were you and Sanford talking about out there?'

'The role of the handicapped in modern society. That's what I always talk about.'

'Really.' She was worried. This was an opportunity. If I asked her what she wanted to know, she wouldn't tell me. She was slippery that way. A good time for reverse psychology. Trick her into telling me what I wanted to know.

I said, 'We were talking about his trip to Anaheim. The night of my accident.'

'Why on earth would you be talking about that?'

'Something about the wheelchairs, I guess.'

'What did he say?'

This was my shot. 'He said you were dying to go with him.'

'To Anaheim?'

'He said when you drove him to the airport you were trying to talk him into taking you to Disneyland.'

'I dropped him off. That was it. I never even got out of the car.'

'How did you end up with him that night?'

'As you'll recall, you had gone off in search of cheap thrills. What was to stop me from doing whatever I wanted?'

'Did you drive this car?'

'Sure. Wouldn't you?'

So Sanford told the truth. It wasn't him. I thought about him stretched out at the hospital. Maybe waiting for some gruesome procedure. I felt bad.

She said, 'What else did he say about me?'

'He thinks you're a good driver to the airport.'

'Tell me.' She didn't care about the car. She wasn't making alibis. That settled it. Sanford and her were clear.

'He said he thinks I was the best tennis player he ever saw. Except for Jimmy Connors.'

'Is that what he said?'

'Also he used to wonder if you were good enough for me.'

'Get out of here! He would never say that.'

'Hell he wouldn't. He said you wouldn't have left me except for the accident. And what you like best about him is his money.'

She turned red. She looked out the windshield. 'I don't believe you for a minute. Did he really say that to you? That shit!'

I don't know why I never did this to her before. It felt good. 'Hell, I know it's true. I owned you. But you didn't want to be with a cripple.'

She looked back at me. 'You still own me.'

'What?'

'Why do you think I've been coming around to see you? Why do you think I bring my boy?'

'You're bored. With your husband and with your nanny.'

She said, 'I want to see how you like being with us. How do you like being with us?' She was trying to reverse my reverse psychology.

I said, 'I like the kid. He's got heart. What are you trying to pull?'

'I want to be with you again.'

'What do you mean: with me?'

'With you. Live with you.'

My first thought wasn't about her and a split level. Pie in the oven. Me hobbling around with a leaf-blower. It was about those months in the hospital when I never heard from her. I didn't think about them much. Now they came back to me in living color. I hated her for them. My phantoms were waking up.

I said, 'One man in the hospital. And you choose another man for your future. Doesn't that sound familiar?'

'Somehow I know he's all right. You just said so, didn't you?'

'No I didn't. I don't know he's all right. He might be messed up bad. Is that what you said to him about me? "Marry me, Sanford. Marty's all right"?'

'That was different. I knew you were hurt.'

'Yes I was. If you knew that, why did you leave? And not even call.'

She had her hands on the steering wheel. She put her head between them. The horn gave a little honk. When she looked up her face was all wet. 'I know you think I'm a hideous person for walking out on you. I told you the truth. I didn't know if I could deal with it. If I tried and failed I would have made everything worse. I knew if I left right away Lucy would take good care of you. I thought I was doing the right thing.'

I didn't know what to say to that. It kind of made sense. Even though I knew that wasn't her reason. She left so Sanford would take good care of her.

She said, 'I couldn't get you out of my mind so I came back for you. I want to see if you can stop hating me. Can you?'

I didn't hate her. Only for moments now and then. I was already cooling off. Hating took too much energy. But did I want her any more? I was sitting in her car. Windows closed. Smelling her. It got to me every time. But did I want her living with me? With a kid? I didn't think about a home like that any more. About normal life with a family. Now I think about whether pizza can live eight days in the refrigerator so I don't have to go out. That's my home life.

I guess Lucy came in here somewhere. I never knew exactly how. I said, 'Suppose I could stop hating you. You don't work. I don't work. Who's going to support the happy household?'

'You have some money. I could work.' She turned to look at the back seat. Jerold was sound asleep. 'Sanford would contribute, though that would be more difficult if you maimed him.'

'Maimed him?'

'I saw the whole thing. I have it on film.'

'It was an accident,' I said.

188

'You gave Sanford an excuse for not winning. That was nice of you.'

'Why didn't you say something to me before?'

'It was between you and him.'

'If I was doing something to him, didn't you wonder why?'

She said, 'I can think of lots of reasons and I don't really care which one it is. I just hope you didn't hurt him.' She didn't care now, as long as I went along with her plans. If I didn't it would be glossies on parade.

I said, 'Did anybody else see?'

'No. The winner was coming across the line just as you nailed him.'

'I guess I wasn't going to win today anyway.'

'I'll get money from him no matter what happened.'

'What if he's hurt?'

'He isn't. But if he is, he's insured from head to toe. Sanford is a survivor.'

'He's an accountant. He'll hide the money. Stick it in offshore oil rigs or something.'

'I know how to handle him.'

'He'd fight you for the kid.'

'I'd talk him out of it.'

'No way. You don't understand men.'

She laughed. 'You don't understand me.' It was creepy the way she said that. Like she had control of him. And I bet me too.

I couldn't give her an answer about whether she could have the rest of my life. I said I had to go.

She said, 'Where does that leave us?'

'In front of my apartment.'

'Will you consider what I said?'

'Of course.'

'You don't trust me, do you.'

I thought about telling her what she wanted to hear. But she'd know. It would make her mad. 'No.'

'You should, you know. I've been looking out for you for a while now.'

'How?'

'I got you the commission. I mean, I am the commission.'

I said, 'I made you a hell of a sculpture. You won't regret it. Where are you going to put it?'

'What?'

'The bronze.'

'I froze that money. I'm going to move it into another account and then take it back. That will be our stake.'

'The money for my statue?'

'I told you I look out for you.'

I said, 'But I want the bronze made. It's very important to me.'

'Silly boy. Casting that thing will cost $50,000. Think what we could do with it.'

'We could cast a statue. This is the last one I'm ever going to make. You can't do this.'

'Why can't there be another statue? I'll help you finance it. Don't be so dramatic.'

I said, 'It's the finest thing I've ever done. Please.'

'That's just what I was going to say. This is the finest thing I've ever done.'

Twenty-two

I wheeled into my apartment. I tried to park, but the new Hell on Wheels was longer than the old one. It didn't fit in the old spot. I pulled myself out of the seat by a rope and swung across the room.

I pulled the sheets off Avenging Angel. What a chump I was to think somebody really wanted this thing. In bronze! A ferocious tiger. A real man eater. I used to think it looked like it was almost alive. Now I saw what everybody else saw. A big stupid clay cat that the guy with stumps made. He makes cats. Isn't that nice.

For three years I worked up to this twelve-foot hood ornament. Now Sanford was in the hospital because I ran him down. Because of what I thought this cat meant. And I was wrong. Esther commissioned it. But she didn't want it. She just wanted us to have the money. Sanford's money. Our stake. If we did just what she wanted.

Face it, Marty old man. You went wrong with this sculpture. In lots of ways.

I went to the refrigerator for a beer. Then to the closet for my tennis racket. I climbed back up the rope.

Get a load of this nose, I thought. I bashed it with my racket. Little squares of clay went flying like snot from a sneeze. I hit the tiger again. Knocked her teeth out. Smacked in the fur on the sides of her head. Mashed the ears down. Soon all the fur texture was gone. The big jaws looked like a waffle iron.

My arm got tired. It was three years since I'd swung a racket. I moved over to the next rope and swung with my left arm. Clay kept flying. Soon I turned the head

191

into a big ball. I moved down, mashing the legs, the body, the tail. When I was done you couldn't tell what it was. It must have been modern art.

I dropped to the floor. My shirt was soaked. I brought out the rest of the six of beer. I sat on the sofa and drank. The beer didn't last long.

I looked at the sculpture. I let my mind go. What would I call it now? Velcro Mutant. Swamp Girlfriend. No. There was something else. I couldn't get my hand on it. I put my head down on the sofa. I watched the sculpture as I dozed off. When I woke up I was still looking at it.

Then I saw it. The big oval head. The stubby legs. The stocky body. How did I ever think this thing was frightening. It was pathetic. I could almost hear it crying.

It was a baby. A human baby.

Great. A baby living in my apartment. A lot of my old girlfriends would get a hoot out of this. Say it's what I always wanted. I was just too dumb to know it.

Of all the things I didn't know, that was the one I didn't know the most. How many yards of sheep intestines did I use up to not know it.

I followed up every time when somebody said she was late. Except for my hair, it was the thing I was most careful about. Nobody was going to pop a kid on me now. No way. Old Marty wasn't born yesterday. I felt a lot better. No baby for him. I don't know how long it took me to remember that the baby was here. I was staring right at it.

What was this? I didn't want a baby. I didn't have a baby. I didn't even know any babies. Then I remembered. I did know a baby. Jerold.

But if this was Jerold, just what the hell was he doing in my living room? Twelve feet long? His mouth was open. His arms were up. Maybe he was hungry.

No. He wouldn't come to me for food. Not unless he liked eight-day-old pizza.

He was jumping. Maybe he was jumping ship. Running away from home. I couldn't blame him there. But that wasn't it. What could have made it inside my brain about Jerold? I didn't even meet him until a couple of months ago, when I was starting Sidney.

I don't believe in previous lives. I don't always believe in this one, the way mine's gone. But I knew something about this kid. I knew it before I met him.

Suddenly I had it. It raced through me. I crushed the can in my hand without thinking. Suds jumped on to my shirt. Jerold was reaching for me. The way any kid reaches. For his dad.

Jerold was mine.

I had to do some quick figuring. The accident was three years ago. Jerold was two. More than that, I bet. I couldn't tell. I didn't know anything about babies.

I had to find out. A little more reverse psychology. I called Esther. I asked how Sanford was. I let her carry on for a while. Something about his spinal cord. Then I told her I found this great thing for Jerold. Was his birthday coming soon? She said that was very thoughtful of me, but I'd have to think of another event to celebrate. I was right. He was two years, three months old.

No wonder Esther showed up. No wonder she brought Jerold. She wanted to see if I liked being with him. How could I not like being with my own kid? Not that I had to like any kid that was mine. But I couldn't dislike him yet. Not until he had time to go bad.

I was so excited. I went flying around the room on the ropes. I didn't know what to do with myself. Which was strange. If she had told me she was knocked up back then I would have dragged her to the clinic. Or gone after her with a hanger. She said she was on birth control so this wasn't supposed to happen. Maybe she did it on purpose to trap me. Then I lost my legs. The joke was on her. And Sanford.

Me. A dad. That was my kid in the car. I made him.

The only thing I made in my whole life. Except for a few tigers. And they were him too.

I felt new. I smiled. If Mr Casey walked in he would have thought I was wacky. When I was into my third six of beer I decided to think of what to do now. I was a dad. Things were going to be different.

First I would marry Esther. The mother of my child. Just like that. I would marry Esther. For years I fought it. I had more fights over that than anything in my whole life. More than over if Mohammed Ali could beat Joe Louis. Now I would just do it. Move in with her someplace. With my child. I'd let her take care of the finances. Commission a few more sculptures. She'd have to adjust a bit. Learn to live with wheelchairs parked in the living room. Ropes hanging everywhere. Jerold would be using them in a year or two. He'd be one strong little kid.

I called Esther again. For the second time in three years. I woke her up. I didn't realize it was three in the morning.

She came by the next afternoon. Jerold was with the nanny. It was time to get down to business.

I covered up Avenging Angel. Avenging Jerold. I didn't want her to know I'd figured it out.

'How's Sanford,' I said.

'Half of his body is paralyzed.'

'For good?'

'They don't know. There's a blood clot pushing against his spinal cord right in his neck. It might go away on its own, but it might not.'

She sat next to me. This was supposed to be our big moment together. Sanford found a way to show up. Half-paralyzed. I ran through the accident again. He swung at me. I pulled him down. My arm was wrapped around his neck. But I didn't break it. I was sure of it.

Genghis. He ran right over Sanford's neck. That's what gave him the clot. I tried to get Sanford out of the way. Not that it was Genghis's fault. It was an accident. There were too many people in the race. It was Sanford's money.

Or maybe it wasn't an accident. Maybe Genghis was pissed off at Sanford for tossing money to the cripples like slop for the hogs. So he nailed him on purpose.

I pulled Esther to me. She kissed me. She tasted like honey. We were getting over Sanford's accident in a hurry. Just like they got over mine three years ago.

I took her hand to take her to the bedroom. I said, 'Let's make it official.'

'Wait,' she said. 'Let's talk.'

'We can talk in there. In between takes.'

'Let's stay here.' She put her hand on my shoulder. 'Things are moving very fast. I have to catch my breath.' She had three years to catch her breath.

I kissed her again. 'Smelling you lights me up. Come and lie down. We'll go slow.'

She jumped up. 'Don't. Don't push me.' She sat. 'I'm sorry, I'm trying to put it together in my mind. Being back with you, while my husband is so badly hurt. I wonder if I'm doing the right thing.'

'In the old days you used to pull me into the bedroom the minute you came in. That was the right thing.'

'I'm a mother now. I have responsibilities. I don't pursue personal pleasures the way I used to. I'm more mature.'

'I guess I'm still immature. You don't plan on living with me and being mature, do you?'

'I think that when you're around a child the same will happen to you. That doesn't mean there won't be time for us.' Time for us? Why was she talking like this?

I said, 'You're not worried about me and Jerold, are you?'

'No. He likes you and you seem to like him.'

'He's a good kid.' She smiled. She had a special

Jerold smile. I said, 'You sure you don't want to lie down?'

She smiled again. I didn't get it. If she didn't want to lie down why did she want to be with me?

I said, 'You had Jerold right after my accident. Didn't you?'

'It was a blessing. He gave me something else to think about.'

'You must have started sleeping with Sanford right away.'

'I married him right away. I wanted a family, as you well know.'

'Didn't it seem like you should wait? Maybe until I stopped bleeding?'

'You didn't die, Marty. You didn't require a period of mourning.'

'The kid was born nine months after the accident. What did you do, ball the guy while I was lying on the highway?'

She made a face. 'How disgusting. If you must know, Jerold was premature.'

'How premature?'

'Three or four weeks.' I thought she'd come out and tell me he was mine. To make me want to stay with her.

I said, 'Was it possible that you got knocked up before the accident?'

'You mean by you? You didn't want children, remember?'

'Why are you so sure you could get him away from Sanford?'

Esther said, 'My son stays with me, no matter what I have to do.'

Then I saw it again. That steel in her eyes. She could do anything to anybody. Even go to the hospital and tell a half-paralyzed guy that his kid wasn't his.

I said, 'Sounds like it's my kid.'

'It shouldn't make any difference. You have to come to love him for who he is.'

'Even if it's Sanford's kid.'

'Of course. I love you in spite of your father and I expect the same of you. This is my child. That's what matters. What do you want, medical proof?'

Bingo.

Twenty-three

There would be proof about Jerold's father. Definite proof. But it wouldn't come for ten years at least. Could the kid come over his backhand when he hit cross-court? Could he drink two beers without drawing a breath? If so, he was mine. If not he was Sanford's. Or anybody else's.

There was no way to get proof now. I couldn't bring Jerold to the hospital or a clinic. I'm a medical celebrity. The guy with the Betsy Ross stitching on the stumps. They all know me. They know I don't have a kid.

If I could get blood from him and me I could send it into a lab. That would be medical proof. I could gouge open my face to get some. I did that often enough just for the hell of it. But Jerold would need a syringe. The thought of blood doesn't faze me a bit. But the thought of sticking a needle into that pudgy little arm made me shiver.

There was only one way to get proof. From Esther. This was really going to take some reverse psychology.

I made a date with Esther and Jerold. I wheeled next door and asked Mr Casey to call me fifteen minutes after they were supposed to get here.

They showed up. The phone call came on time.

I said, 'Hello.'

'This is Mr Casey.'

'Yes I do, Doctor. She's right here. Is anything wrong?'

'This is Mr Casey.'

'Did this just happen?'

'This is your neighbor Mr Casey.'

'She'll be right there.'

Esther ran out. Mr Casey stopped in a few minutes later. I thanked him. He shook his head and left.

I told Jerold we were going to play a new game. Tattoo. I took out my old India ink. Dark purple. With a pen I drew a big scar on the inside of my elbow. Jerold pulled on my sleeve. He wanted one too.

I gave him one. The ink sank into his skin. I put more on, until it crusted. It looked good. Almost real. It wouldn't wash off soon. When it dried I covered it with a bandage.

Esther was agitated when she came back from the hospital. She said, 'Who was that who called for me before?'

'She didn't leave a name.'

Esther took Jerold and went home. She didn't notice the bandage. The nanny would. I left my phone off the hook that night. It was good for her to stew.

I went off to see Sanford in the morning. It wasn't easy for me. I hated going into that hospital. The smell of it. The fluorescent lights glaring off the floor. My phantoms were slithering around even before I got in the door.

Sanford's room was only two doors away from my old room. I didn't bother looking in the old one. I wasn't nostalgic. There was a crowd of medical students and residents around Sanford. An old doctor was pointing to things on his body. I couldn't see which. They stayed a long time. Not a good sign.

When they left I wheeled over. Sanford was lying flat. He had on some super-duper neck brace. He couldn't move his head, not even his jaw. He could only talk through his teeth.

'So how you doing?' I said.

'Fuck,' he said. It didn't really sound like that, but I figured it out.

'Can you move?'

He punched me with his right hand and kicked at me with his right foot. The foot hit the metal bar on his bed. Then his right hand picked up his left hand and made it swing. He reached for his left leg. His left side was still dead. Like there was a highway stripe down his middle and traffic was only moving one way.

I said, 'I get the idea.'

His left arm fell off his chest on to the bed. Like a snake uncoiling.

I said, 'Does it hurt?'

'Fuck.'

'A blood clot, huh? Those things usually go away.'

'Fuck.'

I didn't know what to say. I noticed a bulge in the sheet over his cock. The bag hanging from the bed. The catheter. I remembered that. Like a big steel ring shoved into your mouth all day and all night. Only it was more humiliating.

I said, 'Any good looking nurses?'

'Fuck.'

'How long are they going to keep you?'

'Fuck.'

'I'm going to get some water.' I wheeled into the hallway. I wanted to leave, but that didn't seem right. I stopped one of the nurses. She remembered me. I asked her about Sanford's chances.

She said, 'There's a lot of swelling associated with the injury. We're trying to control it with steroids. When it goes all the way down we'll know.'

'Can you guess?'

'Off the record. He's about a fifty-fifty for full recovery.'

'How long would that take?'

'Could be months.'

The wait was the worst part. I wanted to know. I didn't make anybody wait. Plop, plop. Into the bucket. Story's over.

I wheeled back into the doorway. He didn't look good. One hand behind his head. One leg up, bent. The other side lying there. White. Flat. Poor slob. He might be like that for the rest of his life. He couldn't wheel, couldn't use crutches. Maybe he could still work if they propped him up. I couldn't help wondering which side of the line his pecker was on. Or if he could only use half. Or use it only half the time.

I couldn't leave. I had to talk to him first. I wheeled next to the bed. 'Look, Sanford. You and me got to come to an understanding. You put up the prize money to get to me to race. Didn't you?'

He thought for a minute. 'Yes.'

'All right. So it was your fault I was in the race. I cut you down. I shouldn't have done it. I was sure it was your car. That was my fault. I admit it. But when we went down you were all right.'

'I couldn't feel my fucking arm.' Suddenly he could talk.

'I pulled your head out of the way. Genghis drove over your neck.'

'He did not. He went right over the top. You hurt me, motherfucker.'

'You don't remember. You were out of it. He drove over your neck. And you remember why he was in the race. It was the money. He said so. That was your fault. You don't go offering prize money for a cripple race.'

'So I win. Two faults to one.'

'I just don't want you holding this against me.'

'Great.'

I felt bad for him, lying there in that brace. 'Look, nobody knows what's going to happen to you. One way or the other you're going to need rehabilitation. I know all about that. I can help you out.'

He kind of chuckled. It didn't come through his teeth too loud. 'You going to teach me how to make tigers?'

I laughed, but I didn't like that. It made me want to ask him if he knew his wife was knocked up when he married her. If he knew Esther and the kid were going to split. But instead I began wondering how I could take his wife from him. A woman is supposed to stand by her guy when there's trouble, not run to the next one. And his kid. How could I tell this guy his kid was mine and I was taking him. Jerold could be all he had left.

'You take it real easy, Sanford.'

'Fuck.'

I shook his live hand and started down the hall. Now I was drawn to my old room. I went in the doorway. Some guy was asleep on my bed, all wrapped in bandages. I started to cry even before I knew what I was thinking. Images started flooding me. Nurses. Doctors. Medical students. Waking me up in the middle of the night. Always sticking me with needles. Making me drink disgusting things. Pulling up my sheets. Squeezing my stumps. Prodding them. All the blood. The pain. The feeling that my world was shrunk to the size of a bed. It was awful.

I came by to see Sanford. Sanford didn't come by to see me when I was here. He knew my life had turned to shit. No fifty-fifty for me. One hundred per cent for sure. And he took my girlfriend. It didn't stop him.

Dog eat dog, Sanford. It wasn't going to stop me either.

I knew Esther hadn't come to visit yet. I asked the nurse. I knew she'd come, at least for appearances. I waited.

When she saw me she gave me an angry face. She wheeled me down the hall. She didn't want to talk near Sanford's door.

'What did you do to my boy?' she said.

'What are you talking about?'

'You know what I'm talking about. There's a big scab on his arm.'

'Oh, that. I took some blood. Don't worry. The syringe was sterile.'

'You what? Are you totally deranged?'

202

'That's what I had to find out. I sent his blood and some of mine to the lab to see if there were any similarities.'

I looked at her. I was waiting for the confession. She was looking at me. She said, 'Well?'

'Don't you know?'

'Of course. I was just wondering what the lab said.'

'You don't know?'

'I know, Marty. He's my baby.'

'Then you know the truth.'

'That's right.'

'You know who the father is.'

'Of course,' she said.

'Who?'

'What is this, a quiz? I know. What did the lab say?'

I said, 'Why do you care? You know who it is.'

'That's right. So why are you sitting here? Just to ask me these ridiculous questions?'

'I came to see Sanford.'

'Were you sensitive enough to bring up the subject with him too?'

'Why would I? He knows.'

Twenty-four

When I got home I climbed into Hell on Wheels. I put my stumps in the sling. Racing position. I wanted to pretend I could go anywhere. Even though I was parked, facing the wall. It was like sitting in my father's car when I was a kid. In the driver's seat. In the garage.

It was my thinking chair now. Things were happening fast. Now this thing with Jerold. Maybe he was mine. Maybe he wasn't. Maybe Esther knew. Maybe she didn't.

Living with my kid would be great. No problem there. But living with Sanford's kid, how would that be? Doing all that work. Changing diapers. Reading the same books over and over. Wheeling out to the ballpark. Dealing with the PTA. All for some other guy's kid.

Here I was resenting the guy, like I was going to be doing him a favor. I was a jerk. I was taking his kid. A good kid. Jerold would grow up thinking I was his father. Sanford would be nobody to him. Just some bitter old accountant. Sanford might try to get him back. I'd offer him a wheelchair race with Jerold as the prize. But I would be yanking his beard. No way I would give Jerold up.

I couldn't see Esther making trouble. If Jerold was mine, we would be a natural family. Just starting three years late. If he was Sanford's, she would keep that real quiet, or the whole thing could go up in her face. And if she didn't really know whose he was, hell, even better. She'd think if she ever let that out, we'd both get rid of her. Sanford and me.

It was going to work out fine, whoever's sperm. But

204

just look at Sanford and me. Who had a better chance of striking the flint. Bring on the leaf blower.

Esther came by the apartment a little later. She kissed me on the mouth. A good thing she left the attitude back at the hospital. She sat down on the sofa. She looked at the dried clay all over the floor. I couldn't get it together to clean it up.

'It looks like your tiger is shedding,' she said. It was under the sheet. She still didn't know what I did to it. Some day she'd pull the sheet off. Boy, would she be surprised.

I said, 'She could go bald. What difference does it make.'

'You don't want a big bald tiger in Echo Lake Park.'

'There's no tiger in Echo Lake Park.'

'Not yet. That's where this one is going. I got a letter from the parks commissioner yesterday.'

'What are you talking about? You said you weren't going to pay to cast it.'

'I thought about that. You were right, it is important to get your tiger out into the world. The parks department agreed to split the cost of the casting with me. That way you and I still get to keep half our stake. I think I was panicking a little the other day. I always meant to have it cast. Why else would I commission it?'

I felt like ripping her head off. The great Avenging Angel, turning into dust on my floor. I could have been bronze. Eternal. I could have been an inspiration. Guys parking up at Echo Lake Park at night with their dates would have looked out the window. Avenging Angel would have reminded them that women are wild beasts needing to be tamed. Now they could come look at my dust. I guess there was a message in that too.

Parking at the lake. It was kind of a funny thought now. I could see the bus coming up there at night. Letting me down the back elevator. Wheeling under the trees. Looking at the moon. Trying to cop a feel off somebody in the next chair. Hoping she still had what I was feeling for.

I used to get a kick out of parking. Watching the sun go down and the sky go dark. Drinking a few beers. Testing out the shock absorbers. One of the reasons I bought the Camaro was because the seats go all the way down.

I said, 'Do you remember the night we went parking on Sunrise?'

'What made you think of that?'

'You remember? I didn't think you knew where you were that night.'

'Oh, I knew.'

'Did you have a good time?'

'It wasn't bad.'

'Then why did you hustle us out of there?'

She said, 'What do you mean?'

'When you kicked the brake off.'

'Me?' she said. 'You're the one who kicked the brake. I wasn't anywhere near it. Don't you remember what you were doing to me?' Didn't I remember? Actually, no, I didn't.

'Never mind,' she said.

I'd get it out of her later. 'I thought we were going right into Miller's Creek.'

'That would have been something. We would have had to swim out of the car.'

'Once we found our clothes. We could have put you out on Sunrise in the buff. We would have got help in a hurry.'

'How about you?' she said. 'One of your little students would have come by, driving an expensive car that daddy gave her. What an opportunity, seeing Mr Macho standing there swinging in the breeze.'

'I think somebody would have seen your headlights first.'

'You're far too modest.'

'Yeah. Probably.'

She squatted next to my chair and hugged me. She said my name softly, the way she used to. She smelled the way she always did.

'I'm glad you're back,' I said. It was true. My mind was clear.

'Me too.'

'Where do you think we should shack up with Jerold?'

'Oh, I don't know. I haven't even thought about that, with everything else going on.'

'So, think about it.'

She closed her eyes. 'I can't. You think about it for both of us.'

'How about a mansion. A big old one. Something with high ceilings. I'd put in some long ropes. There'd be columns outside the front door. Lots of land all around.'

'I want to raise horses. I always wanted to do that.'

'You have to tell me these things. I have to know what to look for.'

She said, 'I'd like the house to have a marble front and big working fireplaces. And a pond with statues, with water coming out of their mouths.'

'And nipples.'

'I want a huge rose garden with roses climbing up high brick walls. Yellow roses too. And a big lawn that looks like a putting green on a golf course. Jerold would like that.'

'We're going to need help keeping up this place.'

She said, 'A maid, certainly. Maybe a gardener. Maybe an overseer. But I don't want anybody except the nanny living in the house with us.'

'I'll total up the bill. Then you can ask Sanford to cover it.' I was just kidding. But I killed the mood.

She said, 'I don't know why I feel so bad about Sanford. I didn't do anything.'

'He got hurt. Nothing wrong with feeling bad about that.'

'It's not that. I feel guilty, as if I'm supposed to do something now.'

I said, 'Like what?'

'I don't know. It's not an emotion. It's a responsibility. Am I supposed to take care of him now, even if I didn't plan to before he got himself messed up?'

I shut her up with a long deep kiss. A kiss with ambitions. It was amazing how good she tasted every time. When I let go we both reached for breath. I was totally turned on. This time I was going to go slow. I didn't want to scare her off.

'So what do you think?' I said.

'I don't know.'

'Do you love me?'

'Do you have to ask?' she said.

'Why don't you stay for a while and get comfortable.'

That stiffened her right up. I thought I was pretty gentle about it.

She got up. 'I have to go. I have to get my son.'

'He's fine. He's with the nanny.'

'I'm going to take him to see his father.'

I didn't answer.

She looked at me. 'What's that face for?'

'Taking him to see his father?'

'Oh, please. You know what I mean.'

I said, 'I'm not sure I do know what you mean. I can't figure you out. You're here, there, all over. You're moving in, but you don't stay for fifteen minutes.'

'Be patient with me.'

'Sometimes I think I'm too patient.'

'Next time I'll stay as long as you want. I promise.'

'Fine.' What was the point of arguing.

She kissed me and stuck her tongue in my mouth. Right away I felt better.

Twenty-five

I hadn't seen Lucy since the night I took Hell on Wheels for its test run. The third anniversary of my becoming short.

When I was getting ready for the race I was happy to be alone. I was feeling real intense. After the race my apartment felt empty. It was weird not having Lucy there. Even though I'd finally made my plans to live with Esther. I guess Lucy would have been uncomfortable coming by if she knew that.

Now I had to talk to Lucy about my plans. She was going to hear about them from somebody. I thought if I talked to her she might understand. Also, I still had some of her underwear and stuff. I didn't want to stick them in a box and mail them. I cared too much about her to do that.

I tried calling her for days. Nobody answered. I even tried calling her at work. I hate that. People kept putting me on hold and forgetting about me. Finally I got her secretary. She said she was out of town. She wouldn't say where or when she was coming back, even after I told her who I was.

This wasn't like her. Lucy likes everyone to keep in touch. That is, when she's feeling right. Obviously she wasn't feeling right. Lucy has seasons, just like the trees. Only she doesn't go by the calendar. And she doesn't turn color. That makes it harder to tell what's going on with her.

I've been through the cycle with her a couple of times. I've learned some of the signs. Last time I saw her I would say she was on the way down. No, the last few times. By now she could have hit bottom. If that happened she couldn't work. She didn't care about it any more. She had to get away. I bet she wasn't out of town on work. That secretary was lying.

There was a place she liked to go. Cedar Knoll Estate. It was like an old resort, up in the hills. Only it was filled with loonies. People there took long walks. Or hid in their rooms. Or stayed in one of the big living rooms. Even there they kept to themselves. Except that sometimes somebody would start screaming at somebody who wasn't there. Like their husband or wife. It might be just another inmate standing there, or nobody at all. Lucy said it was the only thing about the place that almost made her laugh.

I called Cedar Knoll. They wouldn't tell me if she was there. House policy. I thought about calling back, pretending to be her boss. But what the hell. I had time. I could go myself.

Getting there was a problem. It was a long way. Too far for a cab. It wasn't far from the train, but no way was I ever going back to Franklin Station.

I called Esther and asked her for a favor. Anything for you, she said. Then I told her. She was stuck. Anyway, I figured it would be her moment of triumph. Replacing Lucy, and leaving her behind at the booby hatch.

Esther had the Jaguar again. She said, 'I feel so bad for her. I wish I had had a chance to bake her some cookies.'

We pulled up at the place. I pulled out my wheelchair and got in. My regular one.

Esther started walking with me.

'Where do you think you're going?' I said.

'With you.'

'No way. This is private.'

'Private?' she said. 'Then what did you bring me up here for, to be your chauffeur?'

'I thought you'd want to be here for this. I got to talk to her a few minutes. You can't sit there with us.'

210

She gave me a look and went back to the car.

There were old stone walls leading up to the entrance to the main house. There were lots of holes in the walls. The dirt around them was fresh. There were animals living in there. I hated the idea of wheeling around little animals. Getting them in my spokes and everything. I got inside fast.

I stopped at the desk. I said Lucy was expecting me. The woman checked the list. She let me right in. For once the chair comes in handy.

So Lucy *was* here. I wheeled into a huge living room. There was a fireplace big enough to rent. Windows a couple of stories high. Like a cathedral, but without the colors. Overstuffed chairs and sofas all over. An oriental rug the size of Utah. It was great to look at, but hell to wheel on. A couple of people were sitting there. Not reading or watching TV. Just sitting.

I didn't like her being there. Of course, that's what she probably thought when she came to see me in the hospital. But I had to stay there. I was crippled. She could get up and walk out. Not that I didn't take her seriously when she was feeling low. I could see she changed. She cried a lot. She gained weight, and all that. I tried to treat her nice until she felt better. But that's not the same as being hurt or sick. There's nothing anybody can do about those. Lucy could have treated herself by getting tough. Pulling herself up by her lapels and giving herself a good talking to. She never did it, not that I saw. I would have been more sympathetic with her if she tried as hard as I did during my rehabilitation.

I wheeled around the room, looking into all the chairs, behind the bookcases, even into the fireplace. They weren't using it. I couldn't find her. I was thinking that maybe she heard what I was thinking. Telepathy or something. And she was upstairs packing.

Then I heard her voice. 'Marty.' She was in the corner, in the shadows.

211

I wheeled over. She looked the same. It surprised me. I don't know what I was expecting. Like she'd be hanging upside down from the ceiling like a bat. The room had that feeling.

No, something was different. It was her hair. Her mane was chopped off at her shoulders. A big mistake.

'Aren't you surprised to see me?' I said.

'No.'

'I was worried about you.'

'That's nice of you.' There was no expression on her face or in her voice.

I wanted to tell her about Esther and get moving. But I couldn't get it together to start.

Lucy didn't say anything for a while. Then she just started talking. 'It's funny being here in my retreat. I feel like a character out of *The Magic Mountain*, taking my cure. Men cry cure, cure, but there is no cure. I feel like a flounder, pressed to the bottom of the ocean by irresistible force. One day I'll wake up with both eyes on the same side of my nose. Then I'll know for sure there's no hope of rising. Flounders don't think about rising, you know. They've adapted to the bottom. Up near the surface the other fish would humiliate them because of their looks, and they would long to return. Woe is me, Marty. Sometimes I still see little dancing flecks of light far above. They're enough to tell me that something bad has happened. I may not belong up there, but I don't belong here either.

'That sounds grim, doesn't it. I don't mean it to. I'm not in pain, really. I don't feel much. And I can say this for depression – it frees me of worries. There is something refreshing about the bottom – you can't go any lower so you don't worry.

'But you've come a long way to ask, or say, something. I'll tell you anything. You probably think that when I'm flying, and blabbing, I'm telling you everything. No. During those times I have nothing to say. I'm moving too fast to feel. I'm lost in the speed.

It's probably a wonderful feeling. I wish I could remember.

'But then I lose speed and it all catches up with me, all the feelings I neglected to have. The weight crushes me. I sit here, in the corner, feeling nothing.'

She lost me five minutes ago. I was thinking about my first Little League game. I must have been seven or eight. I walked up to the plate. The pitcher wound up. The ball came steaming over the plate before I could get the bat off my shoulder. The catcher's glove sounded like a rifle. I felt the same way next to Lucy. Both times, out of my league.

Esther was in the car. I had to do this. And I had the feeling Lucy was seeing right through me. No sense delaying. 'I've made some decisions. I wanted to tell you.'

'Do.'

My chest got real tight. 'I'm going to marry Esther. She's leaving Sanford.'

'Congratulations. You must be very happy.'

'You're not mad?'

'Why would I be? But tell me more.' This was creepy. I thought she would throw me out.

'I don't know exactly what to say,' I said.

'She must love you very much.'

'I think so.'

'You had a lot of catching up to do.'

'Yeah.'

'Has she explained why she left you after the accident? I know that's been bothering you for a long time.'

'She couldn't handle my stumps and everything. I can't blame her. I had a bit of trouble myself. I give her credit for being honest. It was better to do it right away than later down the line.'

Lucy said, 'Better for who?'

'She thought right away was the best time to go.'

'Why?'

'She knew you'd take care of me.'

'Me? How could she possibly know that? I didn't know it myself.'

I said, 'I don't know how she knew. But she did. You took care of me.'

She paused. She made an expression with her face. The first one today, even though I couldn't really tell what it meant. 'You believe Esther knows me well enough to know that? All she knows is through you.'

'I told her a lot about you. All good stuff, of course.'

'Did you think I was going to take care of you?'

'By the time I thought about it you were there.'

'Suppose you thought about it earlier. Would you think I'd take care of you?'

Hell, I can't see why anybody would want to take care of somebody with stumps. 'No,' I said.

'Then how could she?'

'Look. I'm real grateful that you did. I don't care how it happened.'

She said, 'If I were you I would suspect something unusual. These were extraordinary circumstances. Did you ever think that maybe she struck a deal with me: I'd take care of you if she got out of our lives.' Those last words were just what Sanford said at the starting line.

I'd play. 'Sounds like it's right out of a horror movie.'

'I couldn't argue with you there.'

'And since she's breaking the deal you're entitled to something.'

'Her firstborn,' she said.

Jerold. This was getting a little out of hand.

'Now what about the stepchild?' Lucy said.

'He's mine.'

'I'm sure he will be, but Sanford will remain part of his life. And yours.'

'No, he's mine. I knocked her up before she married Sanford. That's why she did it so fast. Didn't you wonder about that?'

214

'No, that didn't surprise me. Esther cannot survive without a man at her side. But if she was pregnant, why wouldn't she have an abortion? I'm sure she's had them before.'

Damn. I never thought of this. The obvious solution. Then she could have had his kid. 'Maybe she's against abortion. I don't know. All I know is she said she can get him away from Sanford. How else could she do it if it wasn't my kid?'

Lucy said, 'Did she ever say Jerold is yours?'

'She didn't have to. I could tell.'

'Of course she could have been sleeping with him.'

'What? When she had me?'

'Why not? You were sleeping with me.'

I said, 'Yeah, but only now and then.'

'Yes, I remember. But it only takes once. That's what they say. It doesn't sound like a modern man to up and marry a woman without taking a few test rides. Would you?'

'Beggars can't be choosers. He takes whatever she gives him.'

Lucy said, 'But what did she give him?'

I didn't know.

'Let's suppose she loves you, and the child is yours. What makes you think she can deal with you now? She left you because of your handicap, and you still have it.'

'She knows that. Why would she come around, except to get over it.'

Now Lucy almost smiled. 'Maybe she's comparing to see if she'd rather have a guy who's divided north/south than east/west.'

'That's gross. Hey, how did you know about that?'

'We at Cedar Knoll are intimate with matters in the medical community. Now tell me, have you slept with her?'

I looked at Lucy. It was impossible to read that face. 'Don't ask me that.'

215

'Marty, this is hardly the time to start worrying about hurting my feelings.'

I didn't want to discuss it with her. It was personal.

'You won't tell me? I'll guess. Knowing you, I'm sure you tried. It was her smell that made you do it. You told me about that once. Let me give you a hint for future happiness – never tell a woman you were incited by another woman's smell.

'If Esther wants to marry you I'm sure she tried to respond. But you know what? I bet she couldn't. She probably put you off by telling you how confusing it all is, how fast her life is changing. But when all is said and done, I'll bet she hasn't dropped her drawers for you.'

'You know, you come and sit around in this fucking place and you think you know everything.'

'So, I'm right. I knew it. She's in love with the old Marty, the jock, the guy who could cover the court so gracefully in his little white shorts. Handsome, strong, tan. That guy she would lie down with until the cows came home. And who wouldn't. But she doesn't feel the same about the guy who won the 1,000 meters in a wheelchair, the guy who swings to the bathroom on a rope. She's hoping it's going to be the same. She has no idea who you are now.'

I said, 'How could she know yet?'

'How could she marry you before she knows?'

All I could think was that she wanted to get away from Sanford. I didn't like the way that felt.

Lucy said, 'I liked you as a jock, Marty. You were a stud. But I like you more now. Didn't you ever wonder why I was more available to you after the accident than before?'

I thought it was because I never asked her to be more available before.

She said, 'It took me a while to figure this out. Amazing what sitting in the dark for a few days will do for you. I love you as a cripple. You're more empathetic.

216

You listen better. As for your body – you looked good before, but you excite me more now.'

I couldn't believe she was saying this. 'That's disgusting.'

'Is it, Tarzan?'

'It's all right to want a guy in spite of his being a cripple. Not because he's a cripple. That's sick.'

'But I love you because you're a cripple. That's what you are, and I love you. I really do. Don't get me wrong. I wouldn't love just anyone without legs. I'm not a CRP groupie. What awful faces you're making. You tell me – would you rather be loved as something you are, or as something you're not, and will never be again?'

This sounded like something a shrink would put her up to. To keep her mind off what was wrong with her. I said, 'Let me tell you something. I'm just a dumb jock who had an accident. That's all.'

Lucy said, 'That's fine, if only Esther could accept the part about the accident. How will she handle the disappointment, and then the guilt, of getting into bed with you night after night? But enough about this. Tell me what you've been doing. Did you finish your big tiger?'

'I'm done with tigers.'

'But why? You're so good at them.'

'I did enough of them. I'm all tigered out.'

'Did you ever figure out what they were supposed to mean?'

I said, 'You thought they meant something?'

'I thought they were modeled after the little statue on the hood of a Jaguar.'

'When did I tell you about that?'

'You never said a word. When I was there last you didn't even know.'

I said, 'Then how do you know?'

'I watched you work. I watched the forms change. When you started the last one it became clear to me.'

It felt spooky that she knew this. 'Sanford drives a Jaguar,' I said.

'And Esther. What do you make of it?'

And Esther. Now sitting in the same car in the parking lot. I said, 'I had this idea that by making the tigers I was remembering getting run over by the car. I thought it was Sanford's car. That's why I went after him in the wheelchair race. Did you hear about that?'

'Yes. As I told you, at Cedar Knoll we hear just about everything. You'd be amazed at the number of alumni in the community.'

'But he wasn't even in town. He was in Anaheim.'

Lucy said, 'And Esther had his car that night.'

'She was at home. You called her at home to come to the hospital. You told me that.'

'Yes I did. Did you believe me?'

'Did I believe you? What the hell is that supposed to mean. Hey, how did you know that she had the car that night?'

Lucy said, 'She drove him to the airport. What do you think she did after that, took a cab home?'

'You think she was anywhere near me? Is that what you're getting at? You'd have to be a liar, for starters. Your whole story would be a lie.'

For the first time Lucy smiled. It was a very sunny smile. It made her gorgeous again. It made me nervous. 'Suppose I am a liar. Suppose I'm anything horrible that you like. Suppose I'm a liar and she was anywhere.'

I had half a mind to bring Esther in. That would knock the smile off her face. 'All right. Say she was still driving that late. What would she be doing all the way over on Brooklyn Heights Road? There's nothing over there.'

'You were. She knew, or easily guessed, that you were coming to me.'

'No way she'd go to your place. It's not her style. But

all right. Say she did. If she was driving that way and I was driving that way, how did we hook up?'

She said, 'Let's say your car broke down. You were looking at the engine, or the transmission. Whatever.'

'If she saw me she'd pull in and take me to a gas station.'

'Wouldn't she be enraged that you just walked out on her to see me?'

I pounded the arms of the chair. 'If she tried to kill me, why the hell would she want to marry me now?'

'People change. I certainly do. You did. Sanford did. She could.'

'Look. If she did that it would just make things harder for her. She couldn't leave me behind. She'd have to think about me all the time. It would be on her conscience.'

Lucy shook her head. 'I think it would have made things easier for her. She could leave you behind and marry Sanford without regret. If she ever got hot for you, she would just think of those stumps.'

I said, 'She wouldn't do it. No way.'

'OK. Suppose she was driving that way and saw you at the last second – those curves on Brooklyn Heights Road are bad – and pulled over a little too fast. She skidded on the gravel. You were out in front of the car, or behind it, and you had no time to move.'

That I never thought of. I wouldn't move out of the way if I saw it was Esther. My phantoms were wiggling around since I came in here. Now they were filling out, getting kind of solid. Like I could really feel my legs again. I could see them standing there on Brooklyn Heights Road. Then came the Jaguar. My legs cramped like they were in a vice. I wanted to scream. It was all I could do not to grab my stumps. I didn't want to do that in this place. They'd put me in a straitjacket and I'd never get out.

I made myself calm down, and ran through the scene

once more. I got out of the Camaro. I had the hood up. In came Esther in her Jaguar. I waved. She slid in the gravel . . .

I had it! 'I'll tell you what's wrong with that. If she hit me she would have taken me right to the hospital. And you're the one who took me to the hospital. That's what you said. Unless you're lying about that too.'

Lucy said, 'She wouldn't leave you there? You just walked out on her. She could drive through a carwash and no-one would ever know. Not even you.'

I shook my head. 'You know, Lucy. I listen to you. I always figure you're being fair. But when you say things like this . . . Let's put it this way. I would ask you if you're loco. But then I remember where I'm sitting.'

She went on like I said: nice weather we're having. She was really gone. 'Then suppose you were stopped on the side of the road and I found you there. We were looking at your car. Esther pulled in. I don't trust her so I got out of the way. But you didn't.'

Now I was getting mad. 'Then you lied to the police. You told them you found me lying there.'

'I'm not saying any of this happened. This is all hypothetical. I'm just asking questions.'

'Bullshit. If she did, you would have gone straight to the cops.'

'Why?' Lucy said. 'How would that have changed anything for you?'

'You would have wanted her locked up. You wouldn't let her get away with it.'

'Don't get so excited. I'm not accusing anyone. I'm just trying to set your mind at ease. Suppose Esther was standing with you, then I pulled up, coming in from the other direction. She saw me and jumped out of the way. But you were looking at her car and you never saw me.'

So I still would have seen the Jaguar when I went down. Yes, this was possible. They were all possible.

'What are you trying to do? Drive me crazy?'

She put her finger across my lips. My body was in an uproar. I was feeling that instinct to get up and run.

She said, 'But why would I drive into you?'

'I don't know. Why would you?'

'I might have slid across the shoulder by accident. However, I might have been enraged to see you with her, when you were hours overdue at my place. Or I might have been aiming at her and missed.'

'Stop!' I yelled. A little woman wearing gray glasses peeked around the side of a chair.

'I'm sorry,' she said. She took my hand and stroked it.

'Stop talking like this.'

'I'm sorry. Let's talk about something else. Have you picked out your patterns yet?'

I grabbed her hand. 'I have to know one thing.'

'Anything.'

'You would tell me if Esther did it, wouldn't you?'

'You mean, assuming I knew? No, I wouldn't. Why would I want you thinking about her all the time? I want you thinking about me.'

'But you would tell me if you did it.'

'Of course not. I'm every bit as good as Esther and I deserve the same consideration. To be honest, Marty, I wouldn't even tell you if I knew Sanford missed his flight and it was him in the car. It's a good sign you've decided to leave your tigers behind. All that counts is what happens now, how people treat you now.

'That's where I come in. Even looking and sounding like this, I think you know I love you. It's deep inside, a germ that won't go away, not even here. When I rise from this abyss – sometimes it's hard to believe I ever will, but I always have before – I'll be dancing in your living room and playing Tarzan with you, and looking after you the way I have since your accident. Until then, all I can feel I feel for you.

221

'The rest is up to you. I'm not a Judas. I won't turn Esther over to you. I want you to want me for me. You have to find your truth.'

'Turn me over?' It was Esther. I didn't see her come in. 'What is this, honeymoon hints?'

My phantoms changed again. Now my legs were very long and very strong. Like I could jump over Esther and Lucy with one bound, the way I used to jump the net. Then run out the door. If Lucy was mad she didn't show it. She didn't show anything. She was just as cool as when I came in.

It was all timing. A few months later, in a different mood, anything could have happened. She could have smeared the room with jello and wrestled her.

Lucy said, 'Esther. What a surprise.'

Esther said, 'I hope I didn't interrupt. I just came in to check on our schedule.'

'Marty has been telling me about your plans together. I'm sure you'll be very happy.'

'Thank you. Marty, are we about ready to go?'

I was ready to go before I got here. More ready than I was now.

Lucy said, 'I want you to know how much I appreciate the visit. Some people never get visitors. Their loved ones are so unsettled by their changes that they stay away altogether. Marty and I were discussing that.'

'Were you,' Esther said to me.

I said, 'I was mostly listening.'

'Doctors say that visits are important because love and honesty are the only things that can get people back on course. Does that sound right?' said Lucy.

Esther said, 'Yes. Especially the honesty part.'

'Funny,' said Lucy. 'I thought you'd go for the love part.'

Esther said, 'If someone loves you he tells you the truth. Marty would do anything to keep me on course. If he knew something about my life, even if it was awful, he would tell me. Wouldn't you?'

There was something going on and I wasn't following it. I figured I'd end it faster if I took a guess. 'I think so.'

Lucy said, 'How about if somebody you knew was the cause of her misfortune. Would you finger him?'

Lucy was watching her. She didn't say anything. The quiet made me nervous. The lady with the gray glasses peeked out from behind the chair again. I said, 'Am I supposed to answer this?'

Lucy said, 'Try, Marty.'

I said, 'I'm not sure I know what we're talking about.'

'Somebody you know did something to Mrs Shoreham. Do you tell her?' said Lucy.

I said, 'Are we talking about something bad? Like an attempted rub-out?'

Esther said, 'Yes.'

Lucy said, 'Or it could just be an accident. It comes to the same thing.'

They looked at me. I had to try. 'People forgive you for an accident. If it's a rub-out, no. You can't let anybody get away with that.'

Esther said, 'That's what I said. You have to tell the whole story.'

Lucy said, 'I agree.'

Esther said, 'Do you?'

Lucy said, 'Of course. But say two people are standing on the same spot watching the same thing. They will report it differently, at least in certain details. Who's to say which version is the truth?'

'To me fact is fact. The rest is a lie,' Esther said. 'What do you think about that, Marty. Do you think there is more than one truth?'

I thought about this once. 'For me there are two kinds of truth. One before my accident. The other after. I don't have to tell you that.'

'No, you don't,' said Lucy.

'No, you don't,' said Esther.

Again they stopped talking. They were both looking right at me. Real serious looks. I felt like I was the one people were coming to visit. Hell, I was just a visitor. And I was ready to get the hell out of there.

I wheeled up to Lucy and kissed her on the cheek. 'Take care of yourself. I'll send your underwear and stuff.'

She gave one last little smile. 'Thank you. Esther, I want you to know that I have feelings for you deep in my heart, and I hope as fervently as I can that you get only what you deserve.'

Esther said, 'That's lovely, Lucy. I accept it in the spirit in which it was intended.'

Twenty-six

Esther drove a lot faster on the way out of Cedar Knoll than she drove on the way up. She was making me a little nervous on the curves.

She was thinking about something. I could see it in her face. I figured it was the talk with Lucy. I was sure it was something big when she missed the turn to go back to my place. I told her.

'I know what I'm doing,' she said. She wouldn't look at me.

Before I knew it we were on Brooklyn Heights Road. Then the engine started making a groaning noise, faster and slower. The car lurched forward and back. You expect more from an $80,000 car.

Esther pulled off. The wheels crunched in the gravel. She stopped the engine. She said, 'I don't like the sound of that at all.'

'You gonna call for help?' We had the phone in the car.

'It's not working. Jerold threw it the other day. Why don't you take a look? You used to be very handy in mechanics.'

'I'm a little out of practice. It's been three years.'

'Give it a try. The car is older than that. And it'll take forever until someone sees us here and sends help.'

'How am I going to be able to see over the engine?'

She said, 'Try. If you can't do it, you can't.'

I pulled out my chair and wheeled around to the front. The jaguar was right in front of my face. 'Release the hood!' I called. I heard the pop. I reached under the side of the hood and squeezed the catch. The hood rose. And that damn cat came leaping right at my face.

225

I had seen this before. Exactly this. At this angle. Except that when I was standing here three years ago I was a few feet higher. I felt it like a knife going into my chest. I was never so sure about anything in my life. I did not fall over this jaguar. It had come up at me.

My pulse was beating so hard I could see it pushing out my chest. I rested my forehead on the front of the car to try to calm down. I could feel my pulse against the steel. It took me a minute to get hold of myself. I was glad Esther couldn't see me. The hood was in the way.

Then I wheeled around the side of the car and pulled the hood down. I went back out front. I raised and lowered the hood in my face, making the cat leap at me over and over. This was it. The moment that changed my life.

I noticed my chair was in a rut where the asphalt gave way. What luck. Three feet either way and I would still have knees.

There was no need to look under the hood. There was nothing wrong with the car or the phone. Esther did this on purpose. She was making a very big point.

I heard her steps in the gravel. She appeared next to me. She said, 'How could you live with the uncertainty? How were you going to live with me, not knowing if I did it to you?'

'I don't know. Maybe I just believed in you.' Maybe I just gave up thinking I'd ever know.

'I hope you believe in me as much as you believe in the Cedar Knoll poster girl. The time would have come, some day, when you would have to set your mind at peace. Otherwise it would have followed you the rest of your life.'

I looked at her. I didn't get it. She didn't seem too upset. Maybe this was the kiss-off. She left me here the first time. She was going to leave me here again. I said, 'You seem pretty laid-back about the whole thing. It's not your style.'

'Why shouldn't I be?' Vintage Esther. Who else could say that?

She said, 'Oh, do you think this is a confession? No, no. I'm showing you how you were standing when she hit you.'

'When she hit me? Then why would I have been staring under the hood of your car?'

'I poured water into your gas tank that night.'

'Into my Camaro? You bitch!'

'I knew you were going to see her, and it was the only way I could stop you from getting there. I took Sanford to the airport and then I came after you. You were standing where you are now, completely baffled. I pulled over and offered you a jump start. I had my car facing yours, bumper to bumper. I knew it wasn't going to work, and when it didn't I was going to take you home.'

'You poured water into my Camaro? I can't believe it. That car was sacred.'

'I was more concerned with the sanctity of your body that night. I wasn't going to let her have you.'

'I never even let people open a Perrier inside that car.'

'So you popped open the hood, and that's when it happened.'

'That's when you poured water into my beautiful 427 Hemi with aluminum block?'

'That's when Lucy came in from behind you and hit your car.'

'Lucy respected that car. If she hit it she was trying to get it to puke up the water you gave it.'

She bent over and grabbed my shirt. 'Forget your fucking car. Listen to me. This is where you were standing when that woman came and put you in a wheelchair for the rest of your life.' That brought me around.

She let go of my shirt and spoke softly. 'I never would have believed that those great muscular legs of yours could be shattered so easily. But when she hit the Camaro, your bumper glided into mine as easily as if your legs weren't there at all.'

'Now wait a second. You're telling me that Lucy hit me. Even though I was sitting here in front of your car. With you inside at the wheel.'

'That's right.'

'What if you just turned on the gas?'

'Would I bring you out here if it was me? Would I want to marry you if it was me? I didn't turn the engine on. You hadn't even put the cables on the batteries yet. You were just opening my hood when it happened.'

I was opening this hood. That was for sure. But I didn't know who did the driving. It would have looked the same from where I stood. The result would have been the same too. After all this time, and it was still her word versus Lucy's.

'But why? Why would she do it?' I said.

'Maybe it was an accident.'

'Maybe?'

'I have to tell you the truth, Marty. I don't think it was. It was the only way she could get you away from me.'

'You must be kidding. You think she would cripple me to get me?'

'It's almost too revolting to imagine. But look how it worked out – she did it to you, and she got you. It's hard to argue with results.'

'Nobody in their right mind would cripple somebody to have him. Then he's not worth having.' She didn't say anything. I looked up at her. There was a tight little smile on her face. 'What's so funny?' I asked.

'I think you just hit the nail on the head. Nobody in her right mind . . .'

A car went whizzing by. Some dust from its wake got in my eye. I bent over and turned away from Esther. I had to think. If only Lucy would walk out of that place and get in her car and come after us, I could finally settle this. But she was a flounder, on the bottom. Waiting for both eyes to end up on the same side of her nose. Pretty crazy.

Her other season was pretty crazy too. When she wasn't at the surface, she was skimming above it. The dancing all night, the not showing up for days and then not remembering. She was a loon all right. But could she have done this? Could she have made me into her Tarzan on purpose?

Esther was right about one thing. I couldn't stand the doubt any longer. Maybe I overlooked certain possibilities before. I wanted so bad to put everything behind me. No more. I couldn't see myself in any household until I knew if the woman lying next to me drove a car through my legs.

I turned back to Esther. 'Take me back to Cedar Knoll.'

'Back to the nut house? You must be kidding.'

'I have to talk to Lucy some more.'

'She just gave you her best shot. She has nothing more to say.'

'Take me back. If you're telling the truth, what have you got to lose?'

'I am telling the truth. Going back into the madhouse isn't going to make anything clearer. Probably just the opposite. You'll start feeling sorry for her and feel you're obliged to believe anything she says. She's very persuasive when she's craziest.'

'I'll have to take that chance.'

I put the wheelchair back into the car and got into the seat. She got in next to me. She said, 'Lucy hit you. Nothing she says is going to change that.'

'OK. Then I want to discuss it with her. Wouldn't you if you were me? After all the time I've spent with her?'

'When is it going to end, Marty? It's three years now. When are you going to believe it and forget it?'

'You laid it on me five minutes ago. I need a little more time than that.' She looked straight out the window. I said, 'Let's go.'

'No.'

'No? You're not going to take me?'

'That's right. Someone has to end this, and I guess it's going to be me. Ironic that I turn out to be the heavy in this when I'm the only one of the three of us who never maimed anyone.'

'I'm going. If you don't take me, I'm going by myself.'

I sat there. She didn't answer for a minute. Then she said, 'I'm not taking you back there. I have had enough of Lucy for one lifetime.'

'Well, thanks to you, I haven't. Not just yet.' I got out and left the door open, just in case she was thinking of taking off with my chair. I got the chair out. I wished I had Hell on Wheels. I said, 'I'm going to get there, you know. Even if it takes awhile.'

She said, 'Don't be silly. Get back in the car.'

'Will you take me?'

'Anywhere but Cedar Knoll.'

'Then have a nice ride home.'

'Don't be a fool.'

I wheeled out on to the side of the lane. A car came down the lane from behind me. It was probably doing no more than fifty. But I didn't see it coming. Sitting in a regular straight wheelchair out in the road I felt like a rocket shot past me. The wind spun me around and pushed me hard. I tried to stop, but I was too high in this chair. I was afraid of tipping right over.

I was blown about twenty feet. I smacked into Esther's car. My body fell over the front of the hood. Once again my face met that silver cat.

I slid back into the wheelchair. I wasn't hurt. But this time I knew something and it didn't feel like a knife at all. I felt pain free. Better than pain free. I felt set free. All the tingling in my legs stopped. My phantoms flew away.

230

Now I finally knew that Esther was telling the truth. The push of the wind, the roar of the car behind me, and the scowl of the jaguar told me. And that gouge on the back of my Camaro. I remembered that I saw it at Leon's lot.

Three years ago my car was hit from behind. I was in front of it looking at the Jaguar. I never saw the car, or the face inside. But it had to be Lucy.

I was expecting more shivers and puking, the way I reacted to Avenging Angel. I didn't get anything like that. It was such a damn relief to finally know. I felt happy, really happy. It was over.

I was about to tell Esther. To apologize, to end it, and go with her. Then I saw her angry face through the windshield. What was it? That I hit her precious car? That I defied her? I waited for her to react to what just happened. Was she going to let me go out into traffic again after watching that?

'Well, I'm going,' I said. I was hoping she'd offer to take me over there. Then I wouldn't have to accept. I wouldn't have to go back to Cedar Knoll.

She didn't. I carefully rolled up my sleeves and fixed my hair. I gave her a good five minutes. Still she let me wheel back out into Brooklyn Heights Road. Cars drove circles around me. I was on a straightaway. Soon I would hit the tight curves. Then they would be right on top of me before they saw me. Even here I was catching the wind of every car. It was scary as hell.

I still thought she was bluffing. I still thought she'd come get me at the end of the first bend. She didn't. She was going to let me go all the way like this. She wasn't afraid that I was going to talk to Lucy. After all, Lucy clipped off my legs. Esther knew I was bound to figure it out sooner or later. Once I did, how could I face Lucy, no less be with her.

The problem was that I wasn't doing what Esther wanted. If I didn't, she wasn't going to help. When I lost my legs, I really messed up her plans. That goof

231

cost me three years. She knew I was being taken care of by the woman who crippled me. She knew and she didn't do anything about it. She didn't even warn me. Even though now warning me was so damn important to her.

I was defying Esther again. I wanted to go down the road. She just saw that I could get myself killed. That wasn't enough to make her help me. Esther wanted things done the way she wanted them done. Or else she didn't want any part of them.

Esther started talking about getting back with me some time ago. But as I wheeled up the first hill, I wondered what she really ever expected of me. How would I have fit into the glamorous plan? Maybe I was so caught in her smell that I wasn't really listening.

When did she decide to marry me? Not until Sanford was laid up in the hospital. Until Sanford crossed up her plans even worse than I did. If they were both there the night of the incident, why did Lucy, and not Esther, take my bleeding body to the hospital? Esther had a faster car. Now I was sure I knew: Esther didn't want to stain her seats with me. It would have upset her plans.

I kept wheeling down the road. I looked back every now and then. A few times I saw the front of the Jaguar peeking around the bend. She was following me, at least for a while. Close enough so she could keep an eye on me. Far enough so she couldn't protect me.

The story of the last three years.

232

Twenty-seven

The next day I woke up feeling different. I couldn't stand the mess in my place. Not one more day. I hired a couple of guys to come and take out the tigers, or what was left of them. For garbage. I didn't figure anybody would want them.

They carried out Sidney and Brute. Avenging Angel was much too big. They wanted to leave it. No way, I said. One of the guys went back to the truck for an axe. He thought that was going to change my mind. I loved it. He chopped off the front legs, then the head. Then he broke the torso in two. The clay was dry and it fell in big chunks. It was like flesh falling off a skeleton. The whole place filled with clay dust.

They carried Avenging Angel out in lots of pieces. One of the guys swept up the dust. More kept settling for the next two days. I was coughing up a storm.

I hired the maid who worked in the next apartment, the other side from Mr Casey. She washed the floor for me. She let it sit a night, and washed it again. Then she waxed it. It shined. I never saw it so good. You couldn't tell there was ever a dirty tiger in the place.

Now I had room to stretch out. To breathe.

Finally I had enough extra space on the floor to paint a parking spot for the new Hell on Wheels. I decided it was worth it having a racing chair. I could get around town without anybody's help. I climbed a rope and got in it. I backed it into the new space. This was a little tricky. It was harder to see the lines from the racing chair than from the regular chair. When I stopped the wheels the damn chair skidded. The wheel was on a paper bag. It smeared right over the new line. I picked up the bag. Under it was my broken trophy. My legs statue.

This thing was getting on my nerves. Like a little dog that follows you around and you keep sitting on it. I was glad I found it the first time. It was good thinking back on that day in my old place with my buddies. But that's all the thing was good for.

I tossed it into the garbage.

Esther took the other part with her. Talk about crazy. Why would anyone want half of somebody else's trophy?

Funny what was happening when I thought about Esther. It was only a couple of days since I saw her.

I was thinking about the house we talked about, the one we were going to live in. I pictured it in my mind. Nice cosy place. High ceilings. I saw the garden. The trees. And her and Jerold out front. I tried to see myself in the picture. There was a guy in a wheelchair, but I couldn't put my face on him.

This bothered me. I figured it out in a dream that night. The house looked the same, and Esther and Jerold looked the same. The difference was that the yard was filled with bomb craters. This time I got a good look at the guy in the wheelchair. It was Sanford.

That made me think about Sanford. I called the hospital and got that nurse on the phone. She said his neck was still all swelled up. They didn't know if he was going to recover. It was going to be awhile.

I could see him lying there. Divided down the middle, like Brooklyn Heights Road. He was looking at a grim life. He must have been real depressed.

Then I saw me lying there too. Two doors down. He didn't give two shits. He stabbed me in the back. Took my woman. That pissed me off. I was damned sick of thinking about it.

I turned on the tube and flipped through the channels. Same old garbage. Just before I turned it off I found a Popeye cartoon. An old one, in black and white. When I was a kid I used to love the old sailor man.

I sat down on the couch. The cartoon was in the middle. Popeye was already in bad shape. Bluto was riding a steam roller over him, flattening him like a pizza. Then Bluto picked up Olive Oyl and carried her away. He was laughing real loud. His ugly pinhead sitting on that huge weight lifter body. Olive was screaming at him. Beating on his back with those skinny arms. As if he gave a shit.

This is what always pissed me off about Olive. Five minutes ago she probably dumped Popeye for the guy. Because he was driving a new car, and Popeye was in some old jalopy. Or he was all dressed up and asked her to go dancing, and Popeye was in dirty old clothes because he was fixing her furnace. That's all it took for her. She was one fickle bitch.

Bluto got what he came for. Now he was dragging her off, like a cat drags a mouse into the grass. Olive was surprised. She's the only one in the United States who was surprised. Who did she yell to for help? The guy she just dumped on. The guy who probably just got the shit beat out of him trying to stick up for her.

I'm not into brutalizing women or anything. But Popeye should have let her get what was coming to her. You can't let people think they can treat people like that and they'll stick around. She dumps on him like that every episode. He keeps letting her get away with it.

Sometimes I think Popeye spends too much time at sea with the fellas. It was time for him to get a new girlfriend already. Somebody who would treat him well. Somebody whose voice didn't kill flies. Somebody with tits.

Anyway, Popeye was lying there flat as a map. He couldn't move. You could only tell where his head was because of his sailor's cap. With all his might he flexed one of his flattened pectorals. The end of a can peeked out of his shirt pocket. He turned his pipe over and it turned into a torch. He cut a hole in the can and sucked up the spinach with his pipe. I grabbed my neck. I was thinking the guy just burned the hell out of his throat.

Now came the amazing part. The spinach went into his stomach for just a second. Suddenly these tanks came out and rolled down his legs, from the inside. The legs exploded back to their old shape. His fists turned into anvils. Battleships appeared inside his biceps and said Mighty Mo. They started firing shells.

Popeye punched Bluto so hard with one of the anvils that he flew across the town and into the side of a barn. The barn went up in the air and came down tooth-picks, into the shape of a kid's nursery. This must have been where the guy at the CRP art show got the idea. A sheet off the clothesline became Bluto's diaper. His clothes were gone. He was crying. He was just a big baby.

Bluto had dropped Olive off in a corral with a bull. It was charging at her. Popeye got there just in time. He punched the bull so hard that it came down as hamburgers.

Now Olive really loved him. She covered him with kisses shaped like those big fat lips. Such fat lips on such a skinny broad. She wrapped those arms around him. They could go around three times.

Popeye was real happy to have her back. That's all he cared about. It made me sick. It was all wrong.

This made me think. Not about somebody's legs coming back. I don't think about that. Especially not having them rolled out by a tank. I thought about what I would do if I was Popeye.

I wouldn't want Olive Oyl. It wasn't that she's a skinny ugly bitch with a voice that makes you want to put your head underwater. I could get used to that, I guess. Popeye did.

I couldn't deal with her splitting on me when I was in trouble. If she goes she's gone. I wouldn't want her trying to come back to me when she was in trouble. Bluto and her wanted each other, and they had each other. Just leave me out of it.

I looked down at my hands. They were squeezing so tight that they were trembling. My knuckles were white. It took a few minutes to settle in. I was amazed I didn't see it before.

It was hard to think of Esther as Olive, because Esther made my blood boil and Olive made it run cold. But Esther had me, and she split.

It was kind of funny thinking of Sanford as Bluto. I could see them both behind the wheel of a Jaguar, proud as peacocks. Then I could see Sanford in the hospital, wrapped in his diaper. Another baby, just like Bluto.

Esther didn't want him now. She wanted to come back to me. She would say nice things and leave big lipstick marks on my face and smell great. And try to make me forget everything else.

But this old sailor man wasn't falling for it. He was going to do her a favor. He was going to help her find out about life on the outside.

I grabbed a rope, swung over to the door and locked it. It took some doing because it was a bit rusty. I never locked it before.

It was another magic moment. I felt free all over again. Like I was on Hell on Wheels all alone on the track at Flanders Field, with the wind blowing.

I ape-walked into the kitchen for a beer. When I came out I decided to leave the tube on, to see if the next cartoon was anywhere near as good as the last one.

It may not seem like it to most people, but I have a pretty good life. I can sit here and watch as long as I feel like it. Then I can go to bed and sleep as long as I want. I don't have to take a bath if I don't feel like it. I can make all kinds of body noises and no-one will stop me. I won't even have to go out the door again until my stocks ran out.

I won't have to go out at all if Lucy comes back.

If Lucy comes back. That's the question I guess I've been ducking. What if she does? The lock wouldn't keep her out. She has a key. Would I want her here, after what she did to me?

I wonder how much I have to say about it. It's hard to keep Lucy out, anywhere, anytime. If I'm busy jump-starting a car and Lucy wants in on it, she drives in. I can see her doing it, too. It's dark and frosty outside, and she's in her danskin, windows wide open, blond hair blowing. Rock 'n' roll is blasting. She sees the red Camaro. There aren't many like it. Maybe she calls my name. She's going to rescue me and take me back up the road for an endless night of her special mania. She can't see Esther, because Esther's hood is up. Or maybe she can and just doesn't care.

Lucy pulls over behind my car, probably opening the door and waving at the same time. She isn't careful. What else is new. She nudges my bumper. She's probably nudged a thousand of them.

It's different this time. She knows that quickly. My life is changed forever. She picks me up and rushes me to the hospital. Esther disappears.

Esther wants me to think Lucy did it on purpose so she can own me. Esther doesn't understand Lucy and her moods. Lucy was flying that night, in high season. If she was gunning for me she would have crushed the back of my car, not nudged it. Or she would have smashed into the Jaguar.

I have to respect Esther's intelligence. She graduated from law school. But sometimes I think she should have spent more time out in life and less time in school. Some things happened that aren't supposed to. Esther thinks Lucy hurt me on purpose, and she thinks I hurt Sanford on purpose. That's a legal mind at work. But it wasn't so, either time. Things just worked out that way. Now we have to live with it.

Lucy and I used to watch some tube together, when she was up for it. I can't wait to tell her about this last cartoon. She'll get a big charge out of it. She'll tell me that's what she's been saying all along, about Olive and Esther.

You can never tell how long they'll hold somebody in the nut factory. It could be hours or months. I want her to stay as long as she has to. Some day they'll let her out. Then she'll come back and everything will be back to normal. I wish I knew when that was going to be. I'd go buy her some peonies.

But I don't want them to turn brown before she gets here. So I'll wait.

THE END

Also by Daniel Evan Weiss

THE ROACHES HAVE NO KING

When Ira Fishblatt's girlfriend, Ruth Grubstein, moves into his apartment, he has his kitchen renovated to make her feel at home. She is tickled pink, but hundreds of other houseguests aren't – the cockroaches who'd been living high on the hog before they were Sheetrocked in and starved out. Famine slowly drives them into a frenzy until one, named Numbers, comes up with a diabolical plan: with the unwitting help of Rufus, the local cocaine dealer, they'll encourage a romance between Ira and that pretty neighbor, Elizabeth, and rid themselves forever of Ruth and her damnable tidiness. And there's always Ira's hot-blooded ex-girlfriend, the Gypsy, who loved to throw tantrums and food around the apartment. . . .

'Shades of Kafka, Swift, and Don Marquis. Daniel Evan Weiss has written an appealing, often mordant satire about the urban condition as seen from the point of view of a roach . . . dark and erotic in addition to being clever and charming.'
New York Times Book Review

THE SWINE'S WEDDING

Daniel Evan Weiss took on the fierce conflict between humans and insects in his last book, *The Roaches Have No King*. Here he turns to the struggle between Jews and Christians joining together in holy matrimony. When Allison Pennybaker and Solomon Beneviste announce their engagement, the trouble begins: the Pennybakers plan a church wedding they can't afford, while Solomon's mother traces the bizarre Beneviste genealogy all the way back to the Spanish Inquisition as a nuptial present to the couple. This comic tragedy chronicles the ill-fated engagement as it slides into the chasm between the faiths, then crashes and burns.

'I think *The Swine's Wedding* is brilliant, important, and telling. It is compulsively readable. It is beautifully constructed.' **Fay Weldon**